WHY YOU SHOULD NEVER KISS YOUR EX

WHY YOU SHOULD NEVER...

ERIN NICHOLAS

THE SERIES

Why You Should Never…

Kiss Your Boss (Ben & Jessica)
Kiss Your Blind Date (Sam & Dani)
Kiss A Grump (Mac & Sara)
Kiss Your Fake Boyfriend (Dooley & Morgan)
Kiss Your Ex-Husband (Kevin & Eve)
Kiss Your Brother's Best Friend (Ryan & Amanda)
Kiss Your Ex (Shane & Isabelle)
Kiss Your Enemy (Nate & Emma)
Kiss Your Best Friend (Cody & Olivia)
Kiss Your Roommate (Conner & Gabby)

ABOUT THE BOOK...

She never should have said yes to that first date, but she couldn't resist his larger-than-life personality.

Now that Isabelle Dixon has been given a chronic pain diagnosis and she has to make some major lifestyle changes, she realizes that means she'll lose the life-of-the-party, fun guy she's fallen for.

Except now Shane seems determined to make their no-strings fling into something more. The longer it takes to convince him this can't work, the bigger the heartbreak in the end.

Breaking up should really be easier than this.

Shane Kelley has always prided himself on being the good-time guy. Exactly her type...or so he thought. Yet ever since he suggested her moving in, she's been pulling back. Well, he's not about to let her get away that easily. He does everything with passion—especially falling in love.

CHAPTER
ONE

BEING in love with Shane Kelley was a lot of work.

Isabelle Dixon groaned as she stepped through the door to Trudy's Tavern and looked around. Trudy's was the usual hangout for everyone who worked across the street at St. Anthony's Hospital. Her sisters had started hanging out here with their brother's football team after games. All of the guys on the team worked at St. A's or were buddies with the guys from St. A's.

Shane was one of the buddies. He was a cop, so had plenty of opportunity to work with and get to know the paramedics, ER docs, firemen and others that made Trudy's a regular spot.

Though tonight it was a little hard to recognize it as the bar they all knew and loved.

Shane had the place looking like a carnival to remind her of one of their first dates. He always went all out—with everything—so the place was decorated extravagantly, including balloons, a cotton candy machine and six tabletop games that the patrons thought were a hoot. Probably even more so as the alcohol flowed.

Last week he'd decorated Trudy's to look like a casino.

She'd hate to see how he was going to make the place look like the demo derby they'd gone to.

"Shane Kelley has balls. Huge balls. Balls to be envied by all men and admired by women everywhere." Emma, one of Isabelle's sisters, appeared at her side and tugged her through the crowd to an empty booth.

Isabelle tossed back the shot of schnapps that Emma handed her and took a moment to be grateful that her sister knew her so well before saying, "You need to shut up about Shane's balls."

"Shane's attempts to get you to move in with him have turned into the topic of *all* conversation at the hospital, I guess," Emma went on anyway. "There are betting pools all over the place about if you'll say yes or no this time, how he's decorated, how many times he's going to say 'never-ending love and devotion', even what you'll both be wearing tonight."

Oh, god. Isabelle signaled the waitress for another shot. Tonight would be the fifth time Shane had gotten up on that stage and declared his never-ending love and devotion to her and asked her to move in with him. She'd said no four times now.

"Next week he said he's making this place up to look like a rodeo."

Actually, being in love with him was easy, Isabelle conceded. Too easy.

It was the breaking up with him that was proving to be difficult. Impossible even.

"I'd say yes to anything if a guy got me a cotton candy machine." Their younger sister, Olivia, slid into the booth.

"He rented the machine," Isabelle said, grumpily. "It's not like he bought it for me or anything."

Olivia smiled. "I'll go tell him that you'll move in with him if he *buys* you the machine. I'll bet you have it in your kitchen by midnight."

"He'd put it in the bedroom."

Too late she realized that she'd said it out loud. Both of her sisters turned to look at her.

"What's that?" Emma said. "Cotton candy in the bedroom?"

Isabelle felt her cheeks get hot. It was so stupid. These women knew her better than anyone. Emma not only knew her, but had been present for most if not all of her most embarrassing moments. In fact, Emma was very often the *cause* of those embarrassing moments. Blushing around Emma was silly. Especially when Emma had twice the number of risqué experiences in her past.

But when it came to talking about Shane, Isabelle often blushed. There was no doubt that Shane had pushed her boundaries and made her do—and importantly, *want* to do—a number of things that were blush-worthy.

"That's why he got the stupid machine tonight," she said. "When we went to the carnival we took cotton candy home and…"

"Used it in ways it was never intended?" Emma filled in with a huge grin.

"Something like that."

"Was it Shane's idea?" Olivia asked.

Isabelle shook her head. "It was all me." Shane also had a strange way of making her very creative. And daring. And completely wanton.

"How many times are you going to make the poor guy ask you to move in with him?" Olivia asked.

"I'm not *making* him get up on that stage," Isabelle said. "I'd love if he'd stop." What more could she do than say no?

Shane had started all of this the first Friday night Isabelle and her sisters were back at Trudy's after their car accident. She had only been a little bruised, but Emma had sustained a bad pelvic fracture that required surgery and rehab, and Olivia had been in a coma for several hours. They'd both bounced back, but it had been a few weeks before they'd felt like partying at Trudy's again. Their first night back, Shane had gotten up in front of the crowd on the stage they used for live bands and karaoke and told her that he loved her and asked her to move in with him. He'd made her get up on stage—and use the mic—to give him her answer.

Because Shane didn't do things small or quiet or conventionally.

There was always a twist. Or two.

He'd proceeded to repeat the declaration and question each Friday night with elaborate decorations and a crowd that grew every week.

The second time he'd done a medley of love songs with the help of Ryan Kaye, who was dating Isabelle's sister Amanda, and Cody Madsen, the fire chief. They'd strategically changed some of the lyrics to fit Isabelle and Shane's relationship and he'd ended by presenting her with a set of keys on a sparkly pink keychain.

When she'd said no *again* he'd simply grinned, tipped her back, kissed her soundly, then whispered in her ear, "This ain't over, honey", before letting her go, buying a round for the bar and going on to enjoy a Friday night with his friends as usual.

News of those two spectacles had quickly spread at St. Anthony's and the third Friday night had seen double the usual crowd at Trudy's. Never one to shy away from an audience, Shane had covered one wall of the bar with a huge piece of paper and had passed out markers, asking everyone to add their names and messages to Isabelle to the paper. It had ended up covered with things like *Do it!* and *Take him back!* and *If you don't say yes, I WILL!*

He'd pointed to it as a kind of petition when he'd asked her to move in again. When she'd said no, he laughed and said to the crowd, "I guess we're gonna have to go even bigger, folks."

He'd gotten a rousing cheer at that. Which only encouraged a guy like Shane. There was no such thing as a spectacle too big.

She hadn't known *exactly* what to expect the next Friday night, but she hadn't been surprised to walk into Trudy's to find the place done up like a casino, a nod to the date where Shane had won almost two grand at craps with her by his side.

And now tonight's carnival had drawn the biggest crowd yet.

He hadn't gotten up on stage tonight. Yet. She knew he was waiting, letting the anticipation build. For her…and for the crowd.

"You really want him to stop?" Emma asked. "I mean *really*? You want him to leave you alone?"

Isabelle shifted on the seat. "It's for the best." She'd actually tried to break up with him before the accident. He'd first asked her to move in with him a week before that. That was when reality smacked her in the face—the hot little fling she'd intended to have had blown up into much, much more.

She'd fallen for him. And vice versa. But there was a tiny problem—if she lived with him, shared a space and her life twenty-four-seven, she couldn't keep her secret from him any longer.

So she'd told him they were over.

She'd even had a very convenient excuse. He'd jetted off to Vegas to help an ex-girlfriend out with a not-quite-ex-boyfriend issue. Isabelle didn't think for a second that Shane would cheat. He did everything one hundred and ten percent and that included relationships. If Shane was with someone, there was no room for anyone else. But she'd made a good show of being upset and wanting to end things. Or she thought she had.

Shane, however, was having nothing to do with any of that.

And here she was, more than two months later, still telling him no. It was going to drive her insane.

People who gave up smoking, addicts who kicked their habits, and food lovers who lost a hundred pounds all had her sympathy and admiration.

Repeatedly saying no to something she wanted so much was killing her.

She totally understood falling off the wagon. In fact, she'd done it a week ago. For the fourth time. She'd shown up at his place at two a.m. for a booty call—complete with chocolate body pens.

But now she was firmly back on the wagon, or the horse, or however the sayings went. It was going to stick this time. It had to.

Emma leaned in, pinning her with a serious, direct look. "You're in love with him."

Isabelle focused on Emma's left earring instead of her eyes. The left earring that was actually Isabelle's. "Yeah. In case you haven't noticed, I have an unhealthy attraction to big, loud, enthusiastically fun people who instigate trouble."

Of course Emma had noticed that. Emma was one of those loud, enthusiastically fun people who instigated trouble and who always talked Isabelle into going along with her.

In fact, it didn't take a psychiatrist to figure out that Shane reminded Isabelle a lot of her favorite sister. Emma and Shane were, plain and simple, a hell of a lot of fun. Everyone thought so. It was impossible not to like them and Isabelle had a special weakness for getting caught up in the waves people like Emma and Shane created.

She was hooked on it, in fact.

Ever since Emma had shown her how to unlock their back patio door when Isabelle was four so they could look up at the moon while they swung on their swing set in the middle of the night, Isabelle had been addicted to the rush of breaking the rules.

But she wanted to be in cahoots with someone while doing it.

She'd snuck out once by herself to swing on the swing set in the night. It had been scary in the dark, there had been creepy noises in the bushes and she'd accidentally locked herself out.

From that moment on, she'd vowed not to venture out on her own. She was firmly and forever Emma's shadow. Emma's daring and confidence gave Isabelle the ability to be daring too. Isabelle wasn't the wild, daring, fun type on her own. But she was a fantastic sidekick.

Being with Shane gave her that same rush—times a hundred —with the same built-in sense of security.

That was why she'd finally said yes to dating him. He'd asked her repeatedly—and she'd turned him down repeatedly— for three days. He was loud and boisterous and loved crowds and going out and did everything with passion and gusto.

He was the epitome of everything that she should be trying to avoid.

He'd shown up right when she was trying to make some positive, healthy changes that did *not* involve staying out all night, Jell-O shots and a punch card at *Tease*, the lingerie and sex- toy shop downtown.

He was…too much.

But even as she'd tried to stay away from him, she was drawn to his larger-than-life style and the way he pursued her with such energy. He was the life of the party and she wanted to be beside him at the party in spite of herself.

And then there was the sex. There was definite chemistry between them from the very beginning, but when she'd finally agreed to go out with him, *she* ended up being the one to initiate things physically. The first night.

Not that he'd fought her on it.

He'd tempted her to do things she'd only read about, and he enthusiastically supported her trying new things. And, with him, she loved every crazy minute of it.

But those minutes were supposed to have literally been *minutes*. Okay, maybe days. A few weeks at most. It was not supposed to be six months' worth of crazy minutes.

It was supposed to have been a fling. One last hit, one final binge, before changing her life.

"First of all," Emma said. "The word *trouble* all depends on your perspective. And second, what's wrong with being attracted to enthusiastically fun people? We're awesome."

Isabelle smiled at her. "Yes, you are." They were. They totally were. But there was an important difference between Emma and

Shane. Emma had to love her—she was her sister. Emma couldn't break up with her. She was stuck.

Shane wasn't.

"Listen, if I can't keep up with him, or I start telling him no now, he's going to get bored and frustrated. He's not going to hang in there for long. And that would…" She stopped and cleared her throat before she said *devastate me*. "Better I be the one to call it quits."

Olivia sighed. "Iz, he's madly in love with you. He's been telling you that since you broke up."

Isabelle pressed her lips together and looked around the table. These women were more than her sisters—they were her best friends and the people she trusted more than anyone. She took a deep breath.

"He's in love with the woman he *thinks* I am."

"But that is you," Olivia insisted. "You're fun and sexy and creative and daring and…"

"I can't keep doing that," Isabelle interrupted. "We weren't supposed to last this long. I really thought it would be super hot, but burn out fast. I can't keep going like this, ignoring all the things I *should be* doing." Isabelle took a deep breath. "I've decided that I have to take control of my…knitting."

She'd only said *fibromyalgia* out loud three times since she'd been officially diagnosed a little over nine months ago. She knew she wasn't handling it well. She'd tried a few positive changes in the first month after the rheumatologist confirmed that her pains and fatigue and upset stomachs and mood swings were legit. But then she'd met Shane and she'd thought, *What the hell?* One more fun fling wouldn't hurt. Like one last piece of cheesecake before going dairy-free. A great big, best-she'd-ever-had piece of cheesecake.

She had planned to only indulge with Shane for a few weeks. Not six months. And she certainly hadn't meant to fall in love with him.

A few weeks had turned into months of trying to keep up,

trying to keep him from knowing that she was struggling, so she could have one more night, one more kiss, one more good time.

It hadn't been that hard to keep him believing she was all he wanted and more. Isabelle was a fantastic actress. It made her a successful pharmaceutical sales rep. She put on a great façade and could convince anyone of anything. That they told the funniest jokes, that they were her favorite clients, that they absolutely needed to try the new drug her company was carrying.

For eight months now—the six months they'd been together and the two months she'd been trying to break up with him—Shane had believed that she was the perfect woman for him and that he wanted her more than anything.

And now she was going to have to convince him of the exact opposite of all of that.

"You're going to start *knitting* again?" Emma asked.

Isabelle met her sister's gaze. She wasn't sure which made Emma more uncomfortable—the fibromyalgia that had led to her learning to knit or the actual knitting. Both were equally foreign to Emma.

"Yes, it's definitely time to start again. I've been ignoring it for too long."

When she'd first told her sisters what was going on with her, Amanda and Olivia had been sympathetic and supportive. Emma had been shaken. She'd realized instantly that Isabelle's crazy lifestyle was going to have to drastically change. And that was going to impact Emma directly.

Emma was the one who loved to stay out until the wee hours of the morning, but she didn't like staying out alone. Which was exactly what a trusty sidekick was for. However, staying out until the wee hours made Isabelle's disrupted sleep patterns even worse. Which made her fatigue and muscle pain even worse the next day. Which made her stress levels go up, which made her irritability worse.

Emma had felt guilty for her part in making Isabelle's symptoms worse and she'd been uncomfortable and unsure about asking Isabelle to go out and do things with her, not knowing what was good and bad for Isabelle's condition. She'd also started making adjustments in her own routines—coming home earlier, buying protein bars instead of her favorite chocolate brownies, and trying to act interested in the book that Isabelle had brought home about fibromyalgia.

It had been painfully clear that Isabelle's condition was changing their relationship.

When Isabelle had started knitting and doing other craft projects in an attempt to keep busy on the quiet nights when she stayed home, Emma had actually tried a few with her.

It had bored and frustrated her within an hour.

Isabelle had finally sat Emma down and told her that she needed to keep doing things for *herself*. Emma needed to live her life the way she wanted to. Isabelle gave her permission to go on without her.

And the relief had been immediate and obvious.

After that, they'd started referring to the fibromyalgia as "knitting". It was less uncomfortable, for some reason, for Emma to ask, "Are you staying home to knit tonight?" rather than ask if Isabelle was missing a party because she didn't feel up to it physically.

That had gone on for only two weeks and was, she knew, a big part of why she'd finally said yes to Shane. Dating and going out with Shane was proof that things hadn't changed that much, that Isabelle could still do all the things she and Emma had always done and, most of all, that Emma didn't have to worry.

Emma's reaction was also why Isabelle hadn't told Shane about her diagnosis.

For one, why would she tell a guy she intended to have a short but steamy affair with something so personal? It was a… fluke…that they were still together months later. For another, if her sister, her best friend, reacted with discomfort and awkwardness, she could only imagine how Shane would react.

"Are you going to tell Shane about the knitting?" Olivia asked.

"The actual knitting or the figurative knitting?" Isabelle asked.

Olivia looked confused for a moment. "Yes."

"Wait, you're going to tell him about the knitting?" Emma asked.

"I think I have to," Isabelle said. Breaking up with a guy like Shane Kelley wasn't any easier than getting a full night's sleep with him next to her. For one, she'd missed him within six hours of telling him they were done.

For another, he didn't give up.

"He thinks he wants me to move in. We either break up or I tell him all about the knitting. It's not like I can hide it from him if we're living together." Figuratively or literally.

Shane needed excitement, spontaneity, the unpredictable, anything but routine. As a cop, he had that rush of adrenaline every day. His free time was spent on a four-wheeler or playing football or driving in demo derbies. And he liked just as much thrill in his sex life.

Their first time had been on the hood of his car in the rain.

And that had been the first time of three in that same night. The first night they'd gone out.

Then they fell in love—something Shane also did with gusto. He was romantic and sexy and sweet and amazing. She got lots of surprise flower and gift deliveries at work, sexy text messages during the day and even love notes tucked in her briefcase and purse at random times.

But living apart, she at least had a break once in a while. They didn't see each other every single day. If it was going to be twenty-four-seven there was no way she was going to be able to constantly deliver the spontaneous fun Shane had come to expect. And there was no way she could hide her need for downtime. At least, not without lying. Which she had stooped to already more than once since she'd known him.

"Do you think he's going to be okay with the knitting?" Emma asked. "Either kind?"

"Well, he wouldn't *break up* with you because you...knit," Olivia protested. "Would he?"

Isabelle signaled the waitress for a mojito. "It doesn't matter. I'm breaking up with him."

"Yeah, that hasn't really been working for you, sis," Emma pointed out.

Isabelle hated that she didn't feel she could talk to Emma like she used to. She hadn't confided any of her fears about what was going to happen with Shane, she hadn't told Emma any of her plans, she hadn't told Emma any of the ways that she needed her relationship with Shane to change. Because there were many parallels to how she needed her relationship with Emma to change and Emma would know that. It was easier to avoid it and keep things status quo than to potentially hurt her sister or ruin their relationship.

Emma was the woman all women secretly—or not so secretly—wanted to be. Even her sisters. She was fun and sexy and unapologetic. She was no angel, so a lot of women might not *admit* to wanting to spend time in her shoes, but deep down they did. Especially her four-inch Gucci leopard-print heels.

Isabelle knew that a lot of people assumed she and Em were two peas in a pod. But the truth was Emma was her role model. Em was fearless, sure of herself and had never met a man she couldn't win over.

Except for Nate Sullivan. But that was another story.

Bottom line, Isabelle wanted to be like Emma.

Over and over Emma charmed people into letting her do exactly what she wanted and she always brought Isabelle along for the fun. Riding on amusement park rides before they were old enough, summer cheerleading camp when they were in junior high, tattoos on their spring break trip. Going on their spring break trip in the first place.

All of the fun stuff she'd done had been because of Emma.

Even as an adult, when it came to being daring and exciting, Isabelle relied on Emma's example.

Emma *was* sexy and fun.

Isabelle was a good actress.

She cleared her throat and started to explain. "That's because I haven't told him *why*. He's not buying the whole thing about me being upset about his impromptu trip to Vegas because I'm *not* upset about it. He's not buying that I don't want to be with him because I *do* want to be with him. I have to be honest with him so he'll end these ridiculous stunts and we can both move on."

She looked around the bar wistfully as she said it. She kind of liked these ridiculous stunts. And moving on was not something she was great at.

"But what if he still wants to be with you after he knows about the…knitting?" As Olivia asked the question it was clear that she wasn't absolutely sure which knitting she was referring to at this point.

Not that it mattered. Isabelle's answer to the question was the same. "Shane does not want to be with me if I'm going to knit… in any way. Jumping on a plane in the middle of the night to jet off to Vegas is something he does without blinking. It's normal. Excitement and fun and crazy is normal for Shane. Asking him to curl up and cuddle and watch TV or get a massage or do yoga or take a cooking class or…"

"Knit," Emma supplied.

Isabelle sighed and nodded. "Or decoupage or sit and read or play checkers…all that nice quiet, normal stuff that I should be doing instead of going out, is not Shane's kind of thing. It would drive him crazy. Even faster than it drove Emma crazy."

"Hey, I—" Emma broke off as Isabelle gave her a look. "Yeah, okay, it wasn't my thing either."

She glanced over to the pool table where Shane was laughing with a bunch of guys. She didn't even have to be over there to know that he'd told some hilarious story, that someone was offering to buy him a beer and he'd thrown the game to let someone else win. He won about thirty percent of the time. He *could* win one hundred percent of the time. But he knew that no one liked the guy who won all the time and took all their money, but they also didn't like to play the guy who sucked. "He's just so…"

"Shane," Olivia and Emma said at the same time.

Isabelle nodded. "Exactly. He's *Shane*. He's loud and crazy and fun and everyone loves him."

"And?" Olivia asked.

"I want to be with him," she admitted. "And he knows it. I can't keep playing this game with him. He's going to keep asking because he knows deep down I want to say yes. If I can explain why I can't say yes, he'll stop."

Which sucked.

She wanted to be the woman Shane thought she was. She *had been* that woman for a long time, in fact. She liked tequila shots and a good deep bass beat and sexy heels. Isabelle had been right beside Emma when they'd splashed around in the public fountain in only their bra and panties. She'd been the instigator behind more than one scheme to get a guy's phone number and more than one road trip and more than one all-nighter.

But she'd also discovered the beauty of time alone, how productive she could be when she woke up and didn't need a caffeine IV to make it through blow drying her hair and how wonderful fuzzy socks felt compared to three-inch black leather boots. She liked a cup of gourmet hot chocolate as much as a great mixed drink. She liked her soft flannel pajama pants as much as she liked pretty lingerie. She liked sitting at home knitting as much as she liked getting sweaty on the dance floor at the clubs.

She felt like Jekyll and Hyde. One minute she was the wild, sexy, naughty girl Shane loved and the next she was content with her latest knitting project and reruns of *Firefly*.

That would, understandably, drive Shane nuts and make

their relationship tense when they both wanted different things. Like how things had been with Emma and Isabelle before she'd started dating Shane.

"That makes me sad," Olivia said.

"Me too." If she let herself think about it. Which she made a point of not doing.

"How are you going to tell him?" Olivia asked.

"I have to do it kind of publicly. I can't seem to get it done in private."

She barely managed to keep her clothes on for ten minutes when she and Shane were alone, not to mention having any kind of serious conversation. And it wasn't him initiating it most of the time. She couldn't resist. Like a perfect, rich, decadent cheesecake sitting there and tempting her. *Just one piece won't hurt* was like a mantra in her head. And then, inevitably, like every great addiction, it was never just one piece.

The two a.m. booty calls were all she was allowing herself at this point. She showed up, stripped, rocked his world, then got back in her car and got the hell out of there before he had a chance to ask her to move in without the big crowd and the stage and the ridiculous theme decorations. He was doing her a favor by asking her in public. In person, she would have never been able to say no.

"You're not going to tell him up on stage or something are you?" Olivia asked.

"I'll probably pull him over to the side in here," Isabelle said. "Or maybe we can go outside for a little bit." Though they'd certainly done plenty of hot making out in parking lots.

"You can't dump it on him in here," Emma said, wide-eyed. "He's going to be…"

Isabelle waited, very interested. "He's going to be what?"

Emma looked a little regretful as she said, "Shocked that you're so good at covering up what's going on with you. Mad at himself for thinking that he knew you when obviously he didn't pay close enough attention. Worried that he's going to do something to make things worse without realizing it and afraid that he's never ever going to know how you are unless you flat out tell him."

Isabelle felt her heart clench at Emma's not-so-subtle confession of her own feelings.

"I'm sorry," she said softly. "I hate that this has to affect you too."

Emma seemed to shake herself out of the melancholy. "It's what happens when you love someone," she said. "What affects them, affects you. Just…ease him into it. It'll be easier on him if he has a chance to get used to a few things at a time."

Yeah, maybe working up to it would have been easier on Emma too. But Isabelle had needed to dump it all on her sisters at once, like it had been dumped on her. She'd needed someone else to know. To know that her body was not letting her live the life she wanted to live, that it wasn't a choice. To know that she *wanted* to keep up, but couldn't.

For a little over a year before the diagnosis, from time to time, when the symptoms got the best of her, she'd say she had to work late or that she was taking a late spinning class. Then she'd go home and take a warm bath and slip into bed while Emma was out, so that she could get more sleep. She had faked a sprained ankle for a couple of weeks to avoid dancing and the club scene when she was going through what she now knew was a flare-up. Another time she'd pretended she'd gotten food poisoning. It wasn't all the time, but it had become more and more common and had finally bothered her enough to go to the doctor about the muscle aches and the fatigue that never seemed to go away no matter how much she slept.

"I should suggest a *Firefly* marathon or something and see if he runs screaming?" Isabelle asked lightly.

"Work up to the space cowboys, too," Emma advised with an eye roll.

A couple of friends stopped by the table then and the girls

moved on to other topics, but Isabelle couldn't keep her mind on anything but Shane. As usual.

As if he felt her gaze, he glanced over and gave her a wink. She smiled and turned away.

He'd repeatedly asked her to move in with him, she'd said no and he was still winking at her.

He really did think he wanted her.

And that made her feel warm and tingly.

She wanted that feeling for the rest of her life.

Tears stung her eyes. Dammit.

Isabelle took a deep breath. Okay, she was going to do this. It was time.

A woman could not live on booty calls and chocolate body pens alone.

CHAPTER
TWO

SHANE KELLEY WAS a great pool player.

At least he had been at one time. Before he'd started hanging out at Trudy's. Before he'd met Isabelle Dixon.

That woman had been distracting him since they'd first said hello.

Of course, he told her that he threw games on occasion to keep the other guys happy.

Truth was, he hadn't had a solid game in almost a year.

Isabelle slid out of the booth where she and her sisters had been drinking and gabbing for the past thirty minutes and he completely missed his shot.

Ryan Kaye laughed. "I love taking your money, Kelley."

Shane handed over the twenty they'd put down on the game. "You know it's because I'm not playing up to par, not because you're actually good, right?"

Ryan pocketed the money. "All spends the same."

Uh-huh. Shane propped his cue against the table and reached for his beer, keeping Isabelle in sight. She had headed in the direction of the restrooms, but she had her phone out, her thumbs moving over the screen.

He gripped his bottle tighter and took a drink. She distracted him and made him crazy. He should just let her go. He should find someone else. He should see a psychiatrist before he turned into an insane stalker.

Or he should marry her.

That was his favorite idea. And the one he'd been thinking about more and more since she and her sisters had been in a car accident two months ago. Isabelle had only been banged up a little, but he'd never forget the feeling of sheer terror at the idea that he could have lost her.

Getting over her wasn't going to happen.

So marrying her seemed like the only thing that made sense.

Convincing her of that was turning out to be the hardest thing he'd ever done. He couldn't even get her to move in. How was he going to get her to say *I do*?

He knew that their romance had been whirlwind, that it didn't make sense to be talking this seriously this soon. He wanted to live with her before they even knew what kind of toothpaste they each preferred or if either of them sang in the shower. Whenever Isabelle was in the shower and he was around, he was in the shower with her. And she didn't have any breath left to sing.

But it hadn't worried him. He'd *felt* it—she was the one. They had a lifetime to learn about each other, and what better way than to live together?

He felt his phone vibrate in his pocket and reached for it, realizing that Isabelle must have slipped into the bathroom while he was lost in thought.

I need you.

Shane felt his heart kick in his chest.

Isabelle had that effect on him no matter where they were or what they were doing. Three little words via text and his reaction was simply *yes*.

It was a little pathetic. Or maybe a lot pathetic.

But whatever Isabelle needed from him, he was all hers.

He tipped his beer back, finishing it off. "Gotta go, guys," he said.

Ryan raised an eyebrow, glanced toward the table where the Dixon girls had been seated, noticed that Isabelle was missing from the group and looked back to Shane. "Everything okay?"

Shane nodded. "I'll make sure of it."

"Good thing Mac has Conner occupied," Ryan said, nodding to a table behind Shane.

He glanced over to where Isabelle's brother, Conner, was sitting with Mac Gordon, one of the best—and cockiest—paramedics in the city.

Mac loved to give Conner shit and it had very little to do with Conner being a fellow paramedic. It mostly had to do with Conner's blatant crush on Mac's wife. Mac wasn't at all worried about losing Sara to Conner—which was exactly what he gave Conner shit about.

That most definitely worked in the favor of all the guys who liked to get the Dixon Divas' attention. Even Ryan, who was openly dating Isabelle's oldest sister, Amanda, appreciated when their brother was distracted. Conner frowned on too many public displays of affection.

Shane shot Ryan a grin and took the opportunity to head after Conner's third sister.

There were moments when he almost felt sorry for the guy. He had four younger, beautiful, outgoing sisters.

But then Conner opened his mouth and said something cocky and Shane figured he deserved those four sisters and all the trouble they brought with them.

He stepped into the back hallway. There was only one stall in the bathroom and the door locked, so he was fine meeting up in there. It wouldn't be the first time. But before he got to the bathroom door, a hand came out from the storage room and pulled him in amongst the brooms and cleaning supplies.

Even without the light, he instantly knew from her body spray that it was Isabelle. He gladly pressed in close so she could shut the door behind him. Once the latch clicked she flipped on the light and pushed him up against the door.

"We need to talk," she said simply.

Her long blond hair was pulled back into one of the complicated twists that she often wore for work and his hands itched to unfasten the pins and let it loose.

"Damn right we do. When are you moving in?" He lifted a hand and ran his thumb along her jaw instead of messing up her hair. For now.

"Shane, I'm serious."

Her hands were pressed flat against his chest and he couldn't help but flash back to the week before when they'd last had sex. On his kitchen table. She'd pulled out chocolate body pens and had drawn on him—all over—before licking it off.

"Shane?"

He focused on her. "Sorry."

"We need to talk about something serious."

"Sweetheart, I know there's cotton candy out there, but this is serious. I've got the moving truck waiting."

"I can't move in with you."

"See, honey, that's just not true." He settled his hands on her hips and moved her closer. "It's easy. You throw your stuff in a box, you let the big strong moving guys throw it on the truck and it's done."

Isabelle gripped the front of his shirt in her hands. "Shane. I. Am. Not. Moving. In. With. You."

He stared into her green eyes. Why did he put up with all of this? She was *a lot* of work.

Most of the guys he knew would instantly assume it was about the sex. Isabelle was always up for it, anytime, anywhere, and it was exciting and fun and spicy every time.

But it wasn't that. Well, it wasn't *just* that.

He couldn't exactly explain what it was, but it wasn't only about the sex.

"This isn't about Vegas," he said, confident that Isabelle knew nothing had happened between him and his ex.

"No," she admitted, letting go of his shirt. "It's not."

He pulled her close again when she tried to step back. "And this isn't because you're not in love with me. You are."

She nodded. "Yes, I think I am."

Relief rushed through him. He knew it, on some level, but damn, hearing it was really, really good. "Then help me out here, darlin'. Because this doesn't make any fucking sense." He ran one big hand up and down her back, loving the feel of her in his arms.

She bit her bottom lip and stared up at him. Finally she said, "You're right. You deserve an explanation as to why I keep saying no."

Well, the relief had certainly been short lived.

Shane worked on not tensing. He knew he came on strong. He knew that he'd blown into her life—and her family's lives— like a hurricane mated with a twister. Her brother definitely was having trouble adjusting. Shane was the newest addition to the Omaha Hawks and Conner Dixon's inner circle. He knew he was there more because Conner quickly decided he liked Shane and Shane was the best at protecting the quarterback from the guys on the other side of the line of scrimmage who wanted to take his head off.

But Conner had liked him *before* Shane had laid his eyes on Isabelle. Because the minute that happened, Shane had fallen hard and fast. And, like everything in his life, he jumped right in.

He knew asking her to move in was a major change in her life. She and Emma were tight and this would mean leaving her sister and best friend. Not that anyone was really worried about Emma. Emma Dixon would always land on her feet. In fact, of all Isabelle's siblings, he and Emma got along best. They were kindred spirits. They believed that life was made to be lived.

He knew Isabelle loved him. He knew she wanted to be with him. But was it possible that he'd intimidated her? Flustered her? Pushed too hard, too fast?

Yeah, six months of a relationship and two months of fighting a break-up wasn't very much time. But he had this driving feeling in his gut that if he didn't make her fully his, he was going to lose her. He couldn't pinpoint it, but sometimes it felt like Isabelle was holding back. And he wanted everything. Having her under his roof, in his bed, sharing everything from cereal to car payments, seemed like one way of getting her close and keeping her there.

He would make this okay. Whatever she thought was keeping them apart, he'd fix. He'd been fixing other people's angst and worries since he was a kid.

"Isabelle, there's nothing you can tell me that will change how I feel." He ran a hand over the top of her head, freed the clips holding it up and let her hair fall. He smoothed his hand over it, loving the warm silkiness. "We'll figure it out, whatever it is."

She shivered under his touch and he smiled. He knew this woman, knew her body, knew her buttons. That was a shiver of pleasure. And he knew how to do a lot more of that.

"Living together is very different from dating. You might not like some of the…stuff I bring with me."

He wanted to keep this light, show her that she was worrying over nothing.

"If you're asking if I can live with a giant stuffed gorilla, the answer is yes. Do I have room for a massive collection of souvenir thimbles? As a matter of fact, I do. Do you buy ketchup in those fifty-five-gallon drums? I think that could save me a lot of time and money over the long haul."

Isabelle narrowed her eyes, obviously not amused. "What if I have some really bad habits?"

Shane ran his hand up under her hair, sliding his fingers onto her scalp, massaging lightly and relishing her little sigh of pleasure. "I knew it—you buy avocados, forget to use them and they go bad in the vegetable drawer, right?"

She closed her eyes, but there was still a little crease between her eyebrows. "Maybe I'm talking about *actual* annoying stuff."

"Oh, you're one of *those*."

She tipped her head back slightly, pressing closer to his massaging fingers. "One of those?"

"You take your socks off in the living room and leave them lying in the middle of the floor for days."

She sighed, opened her eyes and lifted her head. "Shane. I'm talking about stuff that will affect you. Actual things that could drive you crazy."

He still managed not to smile. It was fun, and sexy, riling her up. "Give me an example." He ran his hand down to her ass and brought her closer to him, sure that she could feel the hard rock behind his zipper.

She gave a little groan. A very quiet little groan that made him feel confident that everything would be fine. They affected each other, in ways no one else did. That was worth fighting for. Even if he was fighting her.

"Vanilla sex."

He tuned back in and blinked at her. "What?"

"That's one of the things that's going to happen if we live together," she said. She arched closer to him, pressing against his fly. "And I don't think you're going to go for that."

He was having a hard time keeping his hands resting on—okay, gripping—her hips and butt instead of pressing her up against the wall. Vanilla sex from Isabelle Dixon? The woman who had introduced him to the Position of the Day blog and insisted they try each one? He paused for a moment. God, he loved that blog. "Define vanilla," he finally said. Maybe it wasn't what he thought it was.

"In bed. No...paraphernalia. No pulling from the Position of the Day blog."

He grinned. They were meant to be. But damn. Vanilla sex *was* what he thought it was. "Paraphernalia?" he asked. "You're the one with the toy box, Iz."

He didn't need 'em, but when she brought them along he never said no. Sex with Isabelle was like knowing your friends were planning a surprise party for you—you knew it was coming, you knew it was going to be a lot of fun, but you weren't sure *exactly* what was going to happen.

"Well, the toy box is staying at my condo," she said firmly. "If we're living together, we're going to have only good old-fashioned, in the bed, lights-off sex."

He shook his head. "Lights on."

She sighed. "Fine. Lights on. But nothing…funny."

Shane leaned in close, his lips nearly on hers. "Iz, sex with you is a lot of things. Like the hottest fucking thing I've ever experienced. But it's not funny."

She sucked in a quick breath. Then said, "And no dirty talk."

He chuckled. "What the hell are you talking about? You're hot and sexy and creative now but if we live together I'm going to find out that you're secretly boring deep down?"

She scowled. "Yes."

"Uh-huh." Okay, she was testing him. He didn't know why or what she was trying to accomplish, but she was evidently trying to warn him, or push him, or something.

"And we're going to watch *Animal Planet* together," she said. "Every night."

"I love animals."

"And we're going to…play checkers. At least three times a week."

That tripped him up a little. "Checkers."

"Yes. I'm…addicted to checkers."

"No you're not." That was ridiculous. No one was addicted to checkers.

"What if I am? What if I've been hiding it from you? What if

I've been afraid to tell you because I thought you would think I was weird or boring?"

Okay, he saw what was going on here.

"I get it, Iz. You're nervous about living together. You're afraid I'll be turned off by your morning breath."

She raised an eyebrow. "Morning breath," she repeated. "Uh, yeah. That's what I was thinking about."

"And you're probably worried that *I* might have some weird habits."

"Bad habits," she corrected. "The term is *bad* habits. And I think I'm aware of a few. Being a know-it-all is a bad habit, don't you think?"

He grinned. This was fun. He needed her to see that this was something worth joking about, that they could smile even through morning breath. They were going to be fine. "Don't worry. I don't collect anything and the only thing I buy in bulk is snack-sized chips."

She stared at him.

He shrugged. "I like having the variety. Some days you're in the mood for sour cream and onion and then the next day you might need barbecue, you know?"

Isabelle shook her head. "Wow. Well, hey, good. It's all cleared up then and there's absolutely nothing to worry about."

Isabelle knew she should be annoyed. Part of her was, of course, because he wasn't taking this seriously at all. But he was effectively making his point.

From where he was standing, they didn't have any insurmountable obstacles.

Even as they talked about buying chips and ketchup in bulk, she was thinking about how great it would be to open the cupboard and see those little bags of chips and think of him.

And the fact that snack bags of barbecue potato chips were

suddenly a little romantic only proved how far gone she was over him.

She'd *almost* told him that her stuff didn't include stuffed animals or strange collections. It was a lot bigger than that. It was going to make a mess of a lot more than his living space.

She'd tried to work up to it, mentioning the vanilla sex, alluding to the fact that there was even more to it. But, then, instead of anything about her fibromyalgia, she'd said *checkers.* Yeah, she was really worried about him not liking checkers. That was hardly a deal-breaker.

Why couldn't she tell him? Why couldn't she say the damned word? Fibromyalgia. It wasn't even all that long or technical. But she simply could not get the word out of her mouth.

Because Emma's words had hit her hard. Clearly there were a lot of emotions there for her sister—guilt, anger, confusion, fear, worry.

All of that would happen to Shane too.

When she thought of Shane, she thought of his easy grin, his big laugh, his inappropriate sense of humor, the way he made everyone around him feel accepted and happy. The way he made her feel like the sexiest, most beautiful woman in the world.

That was the Shane she loved. The Shane everyone loved. And she knew he loved being that guy. Being the good-time guy with the jokes and the sucky pool game and the cotton candy machine was who he wanted to be. And she wanted that Shane. Not a worried, guilty, angry Shane that would act awkward and *careful* around her.

That's what she hated most about how Emma sometimes treated her. Like she couldn't go on a shopping marathon or do Monday mango margaritas at their house or take a road trip to see the Goo Goo Dolls.

She loved that Shane would throw her over his shoulder, or push her up against the wall, or get creative on the living room floor. That was where the damned Position of the Day thing came from. She'd wanted to prove to herself that she *wasn't* delicate or breakable. Sure, she felt some of it the next day, but she was *not* going to let her condition keep her from asking Shane to bend her over the back of the couch.

And speaking of some of her favorite positions…

Yeah, she was going to ease him in, all right. She wasn't going to say one damned thing about fibromyalgia tonight. Screw it. One more night of denial wouldn't hurt.

"You know…" Her gaze went to his lips and that damned beard that she loved and could practically feel against her inner thighs right now. She felt the very familiar hot flush of desire. The things he could do with those lips should come with a warning label. "I had specifically planned on *not* kissing you in here tonight."

"Is that right?" His hands curled into her hips and his attention focused on her mouth as well. "Why is that?"

"Because it never ends with kissing."

Even the kissing was enough to make her willing and able to keep the part of her life away from him that she was afraid would turn him off. And the other stuff that the kissing led to… Well, she had no problem understanding why she'd kept up the act.

And if the sex was enough to inspire her façade, then everything else he was and did was enough to convince her she could keep it up long term.

Until she was away from him again.

He was like a drug. When they were together it all felt good and right and doable. When they were apart, she'd remember that this was never going to work long term.

"Do you want it to?"

Her gaze flickered back to his. What were they talking about? Oh, yeah, the kissing thing. "We never just kiss," she said. "The first night we went out we had sex."

His voice was a little gruff when he said, "I remember." He pulled her even closer. "I also remember that *you* initiated the entire thing."

She couldn't deny it. The entire night had felt like foreplay. Which was a little crazy and a lot dangerous. They'd been at Trudy's. Like they had been dozens of times before. They hadn't even been there together. He'd asked her, for the third time, if she'd go out with him. She'd said no. Then he'd gotten up on the karaoke stage with Ryan and Cody and sung "Just a Gigolo" by David Lee Roth. There was something about him—the confidence, the big grin, the way he not only had a great time wherever he was but made sure everyone around him had a great time, something—that drew her in. She'd fought it to that point but after he left the stage, she'd asked him to dance. From there she was a goner.

"I remember too," she admitted.

Shane lifted a hand and traced the neckline of her top, his finger sliding along the top swells of her breasts. "When you pushed me up against the side of my car in the parking lot and laid that first sexy kiss on me I was willing to beg for more on hands and knees. But I wasn't about to suggest sex on the first date with a classy woman like Isabelle Dixon," he said.

Classy. She'd quickly shown him her opposite side to that persona. "You didn't have to suggest it, did you?" she asked, memories shifting through her mind like a kaleidoscope.

He chuckled. "No, I certainly didn't. And trust me, I was very pleasantly surprised by the dirty mind and mouth behind the polished, sophisticated front you put on."

Yep, she'd already shown him a little of her talent for switching personalities. And he'd been pleasantly surprised because it had gotten him laid. Well. Three times that night.

He lifted his hand to cup the back of her head and pulled her closer until their lips were a mere millimeter apart. She was a good six inches shorter than him, but she usually wore heels that put her at exactly the right height for things like dancing and kissing and for him to put her up against the wall, hike up her skirt and drive deep.

She wore skirts and thongs a lot when she was with Shane. For those very reasons.

"You want me to just kiss you, Iz? I can be happy with that."

"You sure?" Her hand slid up the back of his neck and into his dark hair. He wore it a little longer than most of the cops, and she loved the way it would flop over his forehead in the front. She loved the way she could thread her fingers through it and grip it when he kissed her—wherever he was kissing her.

"Very sure," he said softly. Then his mouth met hers.

They'd kissed in every way there was to kiss. Soft and sweet, hot and heavy, long and delicious, all over each other's body. This was a combination of all of those and then some.

His mouth moved against hers, lip to lip, for a long time. He'd press, then retreat, change angles, open slightly, lick along her bottom lip, then back off and softly kiss the corners of her mouth.

Shane lifted his hands to her cheeks, cupping her face, holding her still. Then he kissed her forehead, her nose, her chin, the side of her neck, then returned to her lips.

Isabelle sighed against his mouth.

"I could do this all night," he muttered against her lips. "So many places to put my mouth."

"Thought we were *kissing* only," she managed breathlessly.

"Well, French kissing is kissing. And trust me, honey, I can French kiss you in lots and lots of places."

She started to respond, but then he turned up the heat. He moved one hand to the back of her head, the other to her thigh, lifting it, pulling her close and holding her there, then he opened his mouth on hers, stroking his tongue in possessively.

This time she moaned.

The deep, hot kiss went on and on. Isabelle felt her whole body respond. Wet and hot and tingly. All over. Her scalp prickled, her nipples tightened, her stomach felt warm and everything below that was...all of the above.

She gripped the front of his shirt and arched harder against him, wishing they were naked, wishing she had worn her four-inch heels instead of the two-inch tonight.

God, she needed him.

She slipped a hand between them, running her hand over the hard bulge behind his zipper.

He released her so suddenly she stepped back.

"Whoa girl. I'm tryin' to be good here. Show you I can do some vanilla kissing."

That was vanilla kissing? Yeah, right. "I changed my mind," she said, reaching for him.

He held his hands up and shook his head. "No way, babe. You wanted just kissing. I'm just kissing."

"I want more than just kissing. Come on, Shane." She stepped close and grabbed him by the shirt again. "You never say no to me."

"Until now." He gripped her wrist gently, but she knew she wouldn't get her hand free until he let her go. "I'm gonna pass this test, Iz. I'm gonna pass *all* your tests." He leaned closer until they were nose to nose. "I want you to move in with me. I want to be with you. I'll have vanilla sex and play checkers. I'll keep my hands completely to myself and make dinner for you every night. Or—" he leaned in close again, "—I'll rock your frickin' world as often, as hard and as loudly as you'll let me." He settled back on his heels. "It's up to you."

Isabelle stared at him, her heart pounding, heat swirling through her body. "Yes," she finally said. "Yes. That last one. Right now."

He touched his finger to her nose. "I'm gonna do this, Iz. Pretty soon you'll be moving your panties into the top drawer of my dresser and wondering why you ever even thought to resist."

Then he reached behind him, found the doorknob and pushed the door open.

But before he stepped through he said, "I'll make room for

your stuffed gorilla and I'll be sure to buy extra mouthwash for that nasty morning breath you apparently have."

As the door bumped shut behind him, Isabelle couldn't help but think that maybe a stuffed gorilla was a better analogy than the knitting. It was big, kind of ugly, and definitely took up space in her life she wished she could use for something else.

And Shane had no idea what making room for it would entail.

It was two-fourteen in the morning. Shane knew who was ringing his doorbell and he couldn't help but grin as he made his way through his dark condo to the front door. It had been five days, but he'd known she couldn't stay away for good.

"Good mor—" Shane stopped mid-word as he took in the sight before him.

Isabelle wore one of his dress shirts, buttoned up nearly to the top, the sleeves rolled up, the hem hitting her mid-thigh. Her hair was down and loose. And she held a bottle of Kahlua.

"Hi." She gave him a little smile that said she'd had exactly the effect she'd been going for.

"You drove over here wearing only that?" he asked, swinging the door shut behind her. Not that he was protesting. Exactly.

"Yep."

"I'd be willing to put money down on the fact that you're not wearing underwear."

"You know me so well."

"What if you'd gotten picked up?"

"I obeyed every speed limit, came to a full and complete stop at every stop sign and made sure I had my seatbelt on and my phone put away," she said with a shrug that pulled the shirt up a few centimeters on her thigh.

"You're here for a bedtime story?"

"I'm here to drink Kahlua," she said, spinning away from

him and heading for the den, where his bar was.

Okay. Well, he liked Kahlua.

"This is your Kahlua-drinking outfit, then?" he asked, following her.

"I don't have a Kahlua-drinking outfit," she said. She uncapped the bottle then lifted it to her lips and took a long drink.

"You want to drink Kahlua naked? I'm fine with that." He stopped in front of her and reached for the bottle.

She held it up away from him. As if she could actually hold it high enough that he couldn't reach it. But he let his hand fall back to his side.

"The shirt's only here to keep the Kahlua from getting all over your bar," she said.

"What do you—" But what she meant became crystal clear as she unbuttoned the shirt with one hand, took another drink from the bottle in her other hand, and backed up to the bar. The shirt parted as she boosted herself up onto the closest bar stool, then scooted up onto the bar.

And she hadn't been lying about not wearing anything underneath. The front panels of the shirt fell open to show her firm breasts with the hard nipples, her flat tummy with the little purple gem in her belly button, the beautiful bare mound at the apex of her thighs, and the smooth tanned lengths of her legs.

Then she lay back on the bar, her hair spilling around her, the shirt falling away from her body as her breasts thrust into the air. He watched, stunned and incredibly turned on as she raised the bottle and tipped the sweet brown liquid out onto her breasts, drizzling it over her stomach and letting it run down between her legs.

The Kahlua painted her skin and soaked into the shirt that lay around her.

And Shane was hit by a sudden, intense thirst. They hadn't been together in almost two weeks. If Isabelle had her way, they wouldn't have slept together even then. She'd been trying to break up with him for two months now. She was fine, able to keep him at arm's length when other people were around, but thankfully he'd gotten her alone in the parking lot at Trudy's one night and had gotten his lips on hers. That night she'd shown up much like she had tonight.

"I brought enough Kahlua to share," she said huskily. "Don't you want some?"

The leg farthest from him was bent at the knee, but the closest hung partially off the edge of the bar, showing him all the delicious rivulets of liquor.

"Maybe a little taste," he said, moving toward her, his gaze unable to leave hers in spite of the glorious bare body she had laid out on his bar for him.

These were the moments when Isabelle was the most beautiful. Not because she was naked, not because she was turned on, but because there was a confidence in her eyes that he didn't see often enough.

She came across as confident, there was no doubt, but people didn't look deep. If they did, like he did, they would have seen that she was acting a good part of the time. She was a notorious flirt, sexy and sweet at the same time, a combination most men found irresistible. But even when she was in the midst of a flirtation, it was superficial and not quite real. She didn't get the look on her face that she had now with anyone but him. The look that was a combination of mischief and power and I'm-having-a-hell-of-a-good-time.

"Trudy would make a killing if she served her Kahlua like this," he said, reaching out and running the pad of his finger through the liquor above her belly button and lifting it to his lips.

Isabelle's stomach jumped at his touch and she squirmed restlessly. "There's no way in hell I would ever do this with anyone else."

"I know." And not just because he'd tear the heart out of anyone who ever got close to her like this. He swirled his finger through the brown liquid between her breasts. God, he loved her breasts and her nipples. He couldn't wait to pull one into his mouth. Even without the Kahlua it was sweet and made him feel a little dizzy in the head.

"You do?"

He glanced up and saw that she was honestly surprised. He gave her a little grin. "Well, yeah. What did you think? That I was only looking at your ass the whole time I've known you?"

"Well no. My breasts too."

He grinned, tracing his finger up past those beautiful mounds to her mouth. He ran his finger over her bottom lip. "Here's the thing, babe. You're never more beautiful than you are when you're with me. And that's not conceit that makes me say that, but gratitude. Whatever it is that makes you feel the way you do and act the way you do and look the way you do when I'm around, I just pray every day I can keep it up for the next eighty years or so."

Her lips parted and her eyes suddenly sparkled with moisture.

He'd stunned her. And he loved it. "Iz? You okay?"

"You keep talking like that and I might want to cuddle all night."

He bent his head to one nipple. He brushed his beard over the tip making her moan. "How 'bout I stop talking all together for a while?"

He sucked the hardened tip into his mouth, swirling his tongue over the stiff point and relishing her gasp, then groan. Her fingers tangled in his hair as she said breathlessly, "That's fine. I can do the talking. I want you, Shane. Take me hard right here on the bar."

Absolutely no argument from him.

He suckled one breast while plucking at the other nipple with his opposite hand. She was squirming against him, moaning his name, when his hand slid from her breast to find the wet heat he craved. But he bumped into her hand.

Lifting his head he looked down her body to find her fingers doing some of the work for him.

She started to move her hand when she realized she was in his way.

"Oh, no, don't stop on account of me," he said gruffly.

She paused, but then her hand drifted back, her middle finger stroking over her clit.

"Fuck, that's pretty," he said sincerely, glancing up at her face.

Her cheeks were flushed, her breasts moving up and down with her ragged breathing.

"Help me," she said.

His eyes still on hers, Shane moved his hand past hers to her hot entrance. He knew she'd be wet enough that he could slide right in without hesitation but he wanted to build her up. He ran his finger over the hot folds, then eased the tip of one finger in, stroking shallowly a few times before adding a second finger.

Isabelle's finger moved faster over her clit and he felt a beckoning pulse in her inner muscles. He pressed deeper with both fingers, stretching her slowly and loving the feel of her body trying to pull him in.

"Like this?" he teased. "Is this what you want?"

"For now," she said. "But I want you inside me. Soon."

He pressed his fingers in fully and she gasped.

"What were you saying?" he asked, stroking back out and in with a long stroke that went deep. "This isn't enough?"

Her eyes were shut and her back arched off the bar. He grinned. Uh-huh. He knew this woman's body as well as he knew his own. He knew her nipples were the key to getting her hot and wet, he knew that two fingers curled just right would hit a spot that would take her almost to the edge with only a few strokes, and that talking to her while he played with her made her willing to beg.

"Shane—"

He slid his fingers free, her disappointed gasp music to his ears. He waited until her eyes flew open to lift his hand to his mouth and lick his fingers.

"I do love Kahlua," he told her.

"You—"

"Come on, Iz. A girl doesn't pour Kahlua in places she *doesn't* want a guy to taste." He moved to the end of the bar, leaned to grasp her hips and pulled her down where he could get at her. "After all, everyone knows that Kahlua goes best with cream."

She barely had time to gasp over his dirty insinuation before he put his mouth between her legs and took a nice, long, hard lick from bottom to top.

He looked up and licked his lips. "Yep. I'm feeling a little intoxicated already."

She watched his tongue, her hands curling around the edges of the bar on either side of her. Yeah, she better hang on.

He lowered his head again, not intending to lift it for a while. He licked, plunged, sucked and then started over again until she was babbling a bunch of words like "Shane", "yes", "more", and "please" over and over. Finally he returned his fingers to the play, stroking two in deep with the little twist that would take her to the pinnacle. Then he sucked hard on her clit along with the twist and she came apart, crying out, arching up off the bar, her knuckles turning white where she gripped the wood.

Finally she slumped back onto the surface and Shane moved back enough to push his sweatpants to the floor. He hadn't bothered with underwear when he heard the knock on his door. Having Isabelle show up on his porch in the night wasn't new.

Covering herself in liquor on top of his bar was.

He really loved that spontaneous, naughty, creative side of her.

He climbed up onto the stool at the end of the bar and pulled Isabelle around, sliding her from the bar onto his lap.

They were both clean and monogamous and Isabelle had been on the pill for a couple of years now, so they didn't need to worry about condoms. She straddled his lap and immediately sank down on his aching cock.

"Fuck, yes," he hissed as he buried himself to the hilt. "I've missed you so damned bad, Iz."

One hand rested on her hip and he threaded the other into her hair, cupping the back of her head in his palm. He brought her in for a hot kiss as she wiggled her feet up onto the top rung of the stool. Breaking the kiss, she leaned back, putting her elbows on the edge of the bar.

"How about this?" she asked, using her legs and arms to raise and then lower herself on him.

"Holy shit," he breathed, gripping her hips. "Damn, Iz. Yes."

The view was spectacular, the sensations indescribable. Watching her body take him over and over while he felt the tight hot sheath milking him had him racing toward his climax far too soon.

Reaching between them, his thumb found her clit as he reached up to roll a nipple between his thumb and finger.

Isabelle's head fell back, her hair falling to the bar behind her as she picked up the pace.

Then Shane really had to hold on to avoid getting to the end without her. She looked gorgeous, completely open and free, taking what she wanted and reveling in it even as she offered her body up to him for his pleasure.

"Isabelle, come for me, baby," he urged as his body tightened. "You're driving me crazy. I want you there with me." He grabbed both her hips, bringing her down harder each time, his hips lifting to thrust deep and firm and fast.

Her hands went to his shoulders, her fingers digging into his muscles as she gasped. "Yes, God, Shane, yes."

Moments later her muscles clenched hard and she cried out, her orgasm crashing over her and pulling Shane's from him. He pressed her hips down tightly, holding her against him, wanting her to feel the hot wave and throbbing of his climax. It was all about her. He wanted her to feel every bit of it while he celebrated what he could do to her body. What they could do to each other.

It had never been like this with anyone else and it was like this with Isabelle every time.

She finally slumped forward, wrapping her arms around his neck and pressing her breasts into his chest. "Wow. I can't believe I went two weeks without that."

He cupped her butt in his hands and buried his nose in her hair. "Babe, if that is vanilla sex, I've been eating all the wrong flavors up 'til now."

She pulled back to look at him. And she wasn't smiling.

Well, that wasn't a good sign.

She chewed on her lips for a moment, watching him. Then she pushed her hair back from her face with both hands, and extricated herself from his lap, sliding to the floor and reaching for the shirt that was still spread out on the bar.

It was wet and sticky but she shrugged into it and buttoned it up as she turned to face him.

"I need to tell you something."

Oh, boy. He did *not* like the feeling of trepidation her words brought on.

He slid off the stool. "I think I might need pants for this conversation."

She bent to snag his sweats off the floor and tossed them to him.

Once he was covered, he propped his hands on his hips. "What do you need to tell me?"

She wet her bottom lip and his nerves kicked up another notch as she acted nervous.

"Iz," he prompted.

She took a deep breath and he worked on breathing and *not* grabbing her and shaking it out of her.

Finally she looked up at the ceiling and blew out the breath, then she met his gaze directly, spread her arms wide and said, "Shane, I...knit."

CHAPTER
THREE

ISABELLE WATCHED Shane's expression change from one of unease to confusion.

"I don't know what that means," he finally said.

She sighed and pushed a hand through her hair. This wasn't how she should have done this whole thing. This wasn't how she'd *planned* to do this whole thing.

She'd been fine. She'd been down to one booty call a week. Then she'd snuck into that closet with him and he'd gotten his hands on her and they'd talked about sex. Sure, they'd talked about vanilla sex, but still…she'd been tingling ever since.

Even alone time in a broom closet was too much alone time to keep her head on straight. Dammit.

On her way home from Trudy's, she'd decided she needed to get away. She was too befuddled here, surrounded by bad choices that were *so* tempting. She needed some peace and quiet far from Shane's influence. Somewhere he couldn't find her and make her forget all her good intentions. She'd decided to take her boss up on his standing offer for her to use his cabin in the Black Hills. It was eight hours away from Shane and Omaha.

There was a hot tub and a workout room and a wine cellar. All she needed.

And she was taking all of the books about fibromyalgia that she'd bought right after that first doctor's appointment with her. It was time to get a handle on this thing. She was done with the denial. She was done with the lying.

Right after she had one more taste of him. One more bite of the most amazingly rich and sinful cheesecake she'd ever had. Of course, what they'd just done was kind of like eating half the cheesecake without even coming up for a breath.

Still, the plan had been to climb right back in her car and go home afterward.

Not to confess everything. Not tonight.

But now the words were out there. Well, some of the words anyway. She wasn't ready—*he* wasn't ready—for her to tell him *everything*. The knitting would be enough to start with, like an appetizer to the whole seven-course what-the-hell-have-I-gotten-into-here meal she was going to eventually serve him.

"It means that I like to sit at home on the couch and knit."

"Knit?" he repeated. "Like with yarn?"

She found herself actually smiling. Was he trying to rack his brain for a sex act that was referred to as knitting? "Yes, with yarn."

"And this is important somehow," he said, more as a statement than a question.

She stared at him. "Well…yeah."

He shrugged. "I don't think I get it."

"I also bake. From scratch. And I decoupage and scrapbook and I'm in love with the show *Firefly* and I…knit." She ended with a shrug. That was a pretty good list to start with.

He blinked at her.

"Did you hear me?" she asked.

"Yeah. I'm thinking about how much I like brownies from scratch."

"No you're not."

"Okay, I'm thinking I have no idea what decofage is."

"Decoupage."

"Still have no idea."

"It's taking pictures and applying them to—" She shook her head. "Never mind. That's not the point."

"Okay," Shane said, relaxing his stance. "You have some hobbies."

"Yeah. *Boring* hobbies. Really boring."

"Hey, I love brownies."

She took a step toward him, needing him to honestly hear her. In her mind, she'd planned to have a few relaxing days at the cabin away from Shane and his influence over her, to learn what she needed to know and put a plan into place about the changes she was going to make. She was going to be strong and sure and fully knowledgeable by the time she came back and sat down to have a mature, serious conversation about what they both wanted and needed from life and this relationship.

But if he was going to freak out about the knitting—the *actual* knitting—right now, then she could use the time at the cabin to nurse her broken heart. And drink a boatload of wine.

Maybe scaring him off now was the easiest thing.

"My hobbies are solitary hobbies, Shane. And quiet. *Really* quiet hobbies." She watched him carefully. He hadn't flinched. Yet.

"Okay."

"Hobbies where I actually sit still for long periods of time."

He swallowed hard.

"Without talking. I don't even turn on music a lot of the time. I often like to sit with no noise at all."

She could tell he was biting the inside of his cheek.

Sitting still and quietly was *not* Shane's style.

"And I like to be alone."

And there was the flinch she'd been waiting for.

She spun away and started for the door. "It's not going to

work with us, Shane. And it's time you knew that. I'm sorry I've been leading you on—"

Her words were interrupted by him grabbing her arm and spinning her back to face him. "Just wait a fucking minute," he said, clearly annoyed. "Give me a fucking minute to process stuff, Iz."

She pulled her arm from his grasp. "You're not exactly the decoupage kind of guy."

He rubbed his hand over his face. "Yeah. Not even knowing what it is, I'm guessing you're right."

"You're not the peaceful, quiet, still type at all."

He nodded. "Right. But if you want to do something new together, we could go to the shooting range or to that new bar with the dueling pianos or…" His eyes lit up and he reached for her again. "Let's take a trip. How about Disney World? I'd *love* to go to Disney World."

She stared up at him torn between laughing at his clear excitement over the idea and growling in frustration. "I know you would." She shrugged away from his touch again. "That's the point."

"You wouldn't like Disney?" he asked. "Seriously? Who wouldn't want to go to Disney World?"

Disney World was *exactly* the kind of place Shane would love. Constant noise and action and people everywhere.

"I would like it because I would be with you and *you* would like it," she said. "But I think maybe we need to find something you'll love to do with me that *I* like."

He opened his mouth to reply and she said quickly, "Besides sex."

His mouth closed and he frowned. "With you? Like you're on the couch doing…whatever…and I'm…"

"On the couch beside me," she filled in for him, working on not smiling. This was not funny. But watching him try not to squirm kind of was. "Maybe model airplanes would be fun."

He didn't react but she could tell he was fighting the urge to grimace. "I've never done model planes."

Wow, what a shocker. "Or jigsaw puzzles," she suggested brightly. "You could start small with like a thousand pieces."

"A *thousand*-piece *puzzle*?" he repeated.

"Sure. You can work up to the five-thousand-piece ones."

She could see his mind spinning, imagining sitting still long enough to put one thousand tiny shapes together to make a picture of a mountain scene or a field of flowers. She bit her lip to keep from laughing. She couldn't imagine it either.

But his panic over doing something quiet and still wasn't funny. It was the reason that he wouldn't last twenty-four hours with her in her real world.

"Um, I was thinking—"

"Crosswords?" she asked. "Yeah, that might be better. Or Sudoku."

"No." Finally, he breathed. "Iz, none of those things are me."

And reality crashed in—for both of them.

"Babe, I'm—"

"I know," she snapped. "I *know* those aren't you. That's the point. They are me, though. You'd rather be yelling at a game or rodeo or tractor pull." She crossed her arms. "And I don't even understand that last one. No one can hear you over the stupid tractors anyway and it's not like it matters who wins. I mean it's not like there's a Great Tractor Pull Off and—"

She realized she was ranting about tractors and stopped.

Shane was looking at her with one eyebrow up.

She took a deep breath. "I bet you wouldn't last even three days at the cabin."

"Cabin?"

Ah, crap. She hadn't meant to say that. She grimaced. "A cabin. You wouldn't last three days at *a* cabin."

He wasn't buying that. "Why are we talking about random cabins?"

"It was an example of a quiet, peaceful place that you would hate."

"Isabelle," he said, watching her closely. "What cabin are you talking about?"

She sighed. "The cabin I'm going to the day after tomorrow."

"Why are you going to a cabin?"

"For…a retreat." Kind of. "It's my boss's cabin."

"Where's the cabin?"

"The Black Hills."

"You're flying out to Rapid City?" he asked.

"Driving." She knew immediately that she'd messed up. But she did try to keep the lying to the bare minimum necessary.

"With a bunch of people from work?"

She should just say yes. She knew where this was going. But she couldn't. "No, alone."

He looked at her for several heartbeats. Enough time to clearly communicate that he didn't think that was okay. "What time are you leaving?"

She knew *exactly* where this was going. "Not sure. But early. Or whenever I get around to it. But probably *really* early." Shane didn't do early mornings. Mostly because he did late nights so well.

Shane moved in close, not touching her, but looking down at her with a combination of exasperation and affection. "Good try. What time are you leaving?"

She crossed her arms. "Whenever I want to. This is *my* trip and it doesn't matter to *anyone* else what time I leave."

"You're not driving clear across the state of South Dakota by yourself and you're certainly not spending the night in some remote cabin you've never been to by yourself."

"Oh, really?" She hated being told what to do. Shane did it all the time anyway.

"Yes. Really."

"I'm not sure what you're going to do about me leaving whenever I want to."

Of course, when she said stuff like that Shane took it as a challenge.

"I'll camp out on your porch if I need to so you don't leave without me knowing about it."

"You can't go. You're not invited."

"Why not?"

"Because I'll be...*working*." He couldn't come to the cabin with her. She was trying to get *away* from him so she could think. And relax. She hadn't felt relaxed since he'd first asked her to move in with him over two months ago.

She also couldn't have him around while she was trying to do homework on the fibromyalgia. If he was there she'd be distracted and very likely tuck the books under the bed and forget about them. Like she'd done eight months ago when she'd first started dating him.

Of course, that wasn't entirely accurate. She'd started with the books on her bedside table. She hadn't moved them to the floor and pushed them under the bed until the first time Shane spent the night.

"You can work if I'm there."

She raised an eyebrow and waited. Finally he sighed.

"If I was into puzzles and stuff you could work while I was there."

"Exactly."

"How long will you be gone?"

"A week. Maybe two."

His jaw dropped. *"Two weeks?"*

She shrugged. "However long it takes to get my work done."

"Fine. I'll follow you up there on my bike. Then I can go and sightsee or something while you work." He dropped his voice. "Right on your ass is one of my favorite places to be anyway."

She pushed him back. "No. You're not invited."

He lifted an eyebrow. "You're not driving that far alone and you're not spending two weeks away from me."

"Wow, you been taking stalker classes?"

He sighed. "I know. It sounds creepy. But I don't like this."

She smiled in spite of agreeing that he was overreacting. "I've been away from home, away from you, before."

"But you've flown. And stayed in nice hotels. And had work functions where there were other people around who knew you. This whole cabin thing doesn't sit right."

Why hadn't she told him she was going to Boston to stay in the Four Seasons for a work conference? Dammit.

She tried to appeal to his practical side. "You're going to take off work and drive over five hundred miles to babysit me?"

Of course, this was the man who'd brought a helium tank, a ring toss and a cotton candy machine into a bar to show her how he felt. *Practical* wasn't the perfect word for Shane.

"Yes," he said. "Besides, I love Mount Rushmore."

There was no way she was going to win this argument. "You want to sleep outside on the porch? Fine. Whatever. I'm not telling you when I'm leaving."

He grinned. "God, you're a lot of work."

She rolled her eyes. She'd heard that a time or two from him as well. "Look who's talking." She headed for the door before anything stupider happened. "You better bring the Kahlua too."

"Love the sound of that."

"Yeah, it'll help you keep warm. It's only March. It's gonna get chilly outside at night."

Shane could honestly say that a yoga studio was in the top three on the list of places he never thought he'd go. Yet here he was. Because Emma Dixon was a pain in the ass.

He needed to talk to her and since she lived with Isabelle, he'd suggested the bar or a coffee shop. She'd said he'd have to come to her studio because she had a late class.

He knew it was actually because she wanted to see him totally uncomfortable in her girly shop.

He loved girly stuff. On girls. Around girls. Because of girls.

But he didn't do pink, he didn't do instrumental music, he didn't care about smelling things that would relax him and he didn't do workouts that included sitting with his eyes closed. He wasn't completely convinced he could sit on the floor with his legs crossed like that anyway.

"You're just in time," Emma said with a huge grin as he stepped through the front door.

"I need to know how serious this knitting thing is with Isabelle," he said without preamble. He didn't want to start breathing in too much of the aromatherapy fumes. He might get mellow or something.

Emma's eyes widened. "She told you about the knitting?"

"Yeah." Knitting. Wow, he hadn't been expecting that.

Then Emma's eyes narrowed. "You mean about the *knitting*? Like with yarn and needles and stuff?"

He frowned. "Yeah. Is there another kind of knitting?" Oh great. There was more than one kind? He had no idea what to think about the first kind.

Emma shook her head. "No. Never mind."

"But she's serious about it?" he asked. "Like she means it? This is a real thing to her? Sitting at home on the couch and *knitting* for hours?"

"Yes," Emma said. "It's very serious. But I can't get into all that right now. Class is starting."

"Class? I thought you were done."

She brightened. "Oh, just one more. This is a special session."

The look on her face—mischief, pure and simple—made Shane sigh.

"You're thinking I'm joining this special session?"

"You can watch if you want," Emma moved to lock the front door. "But it might be good for you."

"Yoga's a little—calm—for me," Shane said.

"Yeah. No kidding. Exactly what this session is about."

She opened the tall white French doors at the end of the room. "Come on."

"Maybe I don't want to talk to you this bad," Shane said, starting after her anyway.

"But you do," she said confidently. "Quit being a baby."

Being a part of Isabelle's life meant putting up with Emma on a regular basis. While they had a lot in common, Emma Dixon could wear even him down.

Shane followed her through the doors that opened into a huge inner room with twenty-foot ceilings, a light-colored wood floor and a mirror that took up an entire wall.

The most interesting thing in the room, however, was the collection of people gathered for the "special session". That they were all men was note-worthy. More so was the fact that Shane knew them all.

"Hey, buddy!" Ryan called in greeting. "Emma said you were coming but I didn't believe her."

More specifically, Shane was shocked to realize that all the class participants were paramedics at St. Anthony's who worked with Ryan and Conner. They were all members of Sam Bradford's crew—including Sam.

Ryan was positioned up in front of the group, sitting on a thin purple foam mat, seemingly in charge.

"Yeah, well, Em left out a few important details," Shane said. "What the hell are you guys doing here?"

"Yoga," Dooley Miller said with a shrug. "We have very high-pressure jobs, you know."

Emma handed Shane a rolled-up mat. "They're learning stress reduction, how to quiet their minds, how to focus their positive energies."

Shane looked down at the mat. "Uh, no."

"Kelley, get your ass over here," Kevin Campbell called. "You need to relax as much as any of us."

Shane shook his head. "Being wound up keeps me sharp."

Emma shrugged and moved into a spot between Mac Gordon and Sam Bradford. "No yoga, no advice," she said simply.

Shane gripped the soft foam in his hand.

Dammit.

He didn't want to breathe deep and stretch and he definitely didn't want this to be a group therapy session. "We can do the advice another time," he said, tossing the mat aside.

"Kelley." Mac stretched to his feet.

The guy was as big as Shane, even wider through the shoulders.

"You're staying."

Shane lifted an eyebrow. "Oh?"

Mac was big but he was also more than a decade older than Shane. If nothing else, Shane could outrun him. He was pretty sure.

"You've now seen all of us here, getting ready for yoga," Mac said. "I can't let you leave until I'm sure that you won't tell anyone."

Shane snorted. "No one would believe me anyway."

At least they were all dressed in shorts and T-shirts. The only leotard in sight was the one on Emma. And she wore it well.

Mac put his hands on his hips. "Get your mat. If you're doing it too, you won't be blabbing about it."

"But—"

Kevin got to his feet too. He was leaner than Mac but he'd played football in the NFL. He was younger too. "Get your mat," he said.

Shane started to reply, then looked at Em.

Fuck.

Shane dropped his head. It wasn't their physical threats—that he didn't take seriously anyway—it was that Emma was a pain in the ass and would definitely withhold information about Isabelle if he disparaged her beloved yoga by not participating.

He was stuck.

With a heavy sigh, he retrieved the mat and unrolled it next to Dooley.

"Why are you all here anyway? Seriously?"

"Look at 'em," Dooley said, gesturing to Mac and Sam. "They look like shit."

Shane had to admit that Sam and Mac had both looked better.

"Sam's got twin baby girls at home and is up all night and worried all the time," Dooley said. "Which, by the way, is hilarious considering how many times in the past he was up all night and making other people worry."

Sam flipped him off.

"What's wrong with you?" Shane asked Mac, settling down onto his mat.

"Sara's pregnant," the big guy said of his wife.

"Yeah." Shane knew that. Everyone knew that.

It was hard to miss Sara Bradford Gordon even if she weren't hugely pregnant, looking like she'd stuck a beach ball under her shirt. "Congrats," Shane said to Mac.

"Thanks."

Shane looked at Dooley for further clarification but it was Kevin who answered with a chuckle, "Turns out Mac's a worry-wart too. Who would have guessed? He needs to learn to chill out before she goes into labor or *he's* going to be the one they have to sedate."

"They're not sleeping well and the worry is a little out of control," Ryan said from the front of the room. "They're concerned that all of this is going to affect how they do their jobs, so I suggested some meditation and yoga."

Thanks to his mom, Ryan knew all about herbs and acupuncture and all kinds of other stuff that sounded really strange to Shane. Shane had never met an illness that didn't respond to rest, orange juice and ibuprofen. But Ryan wasn't weird about it. In fact, he had a sense of humor about all of it, so on occasion Shane would say yes to one of the healing creams

Ryan's mom made for bumps and bruises or would actually drink some of the strange-tasting tea she made to help with inflammation and circulation.

So far he'd never felt *worse* for using the stuff, so he went along with it when Ryan brought it up.

"And what are *you* doing here?" Shane asked Kevin and Dooley.

"We're here for moral support," Kevin said.

"And entertainment," Dooley added, trying to touch the toes on his outstretched leg. He was several inches short of his goal. "I've seen beautiful women get into amazing poses doing yoga. I can't wait to see these guys try."

"We're not going to be the only ones falling on our asses," Mac told him. "I'll make sure of that," he added.

"And you're the fearless leader?" Shane asked Ryan.

"Em thought the guys would be less intimidated having me here."

"Is *intimidated* really the word you want to use?" Mac asked.

Ryan chuckled. "They'd be more *comfortable* with me leading."

"Now see, if I have to watch someone bending and stretching in front of me, I'd rather it be Emma," Dooley commented.

She blew him a kiss. "Thanks. But I think I need to hang out over here by Officer Kelley."

"You are going to help me?" Shane asked.

"With yoga *and* with Isabelle."

"Okay. *Why* does she knit?"

Emma grinned. "Shh…Ryan's starting the class."

"Tonight we're going to introduce you to the basics. Deep breathing, focus and a few beginning poses," Ryan said.

He was seated at the front facing the group, his knees bent and the soles of his feet together in what Shane thought of as a traditional meditation pose. Shane was impressed that he was flexible enough to not only get his feet together like that, but that his knees fell out and nearly touched the floor.

Shane was still struggling to get his left knee bent far enough to even start.

But Mac and Kevin were having just as much trouble. Mac swore when his knees only went a third of the way out. Kevin grunted as he tried to sit tall while having his legs pulled up.

"Yoga has many health benefits," Ryan went on. "But most important to all of you is relaxation, getting in touch with your body and working to reduce your stress." He gave Mac and Kevin pointed looks. "It's not about being perfect. It will all get easier with time as your strength and flexibility improve. Follow along as best you can but don't stress out."

"Ten bucks says Kevin's the first one to fall over from the Triangle Pose," Dooley said to Sam.

"What's the Triangle Pose?" Sam asked.

"You bend and touch one foot and put your hand up toward the ceiling," Dooley told him. He stood and started to move into the position. He was okay until he reached up. Then he lost his balance and fell, bracing himself with his hand before he hit the floor.

"Nice," Sam said with a grin.

"We'll start slow," Ryan said from the front. "But it does require quiet concentration. So if everyone can kind of chill and listen, that'd be great. We're going to hold each pose for five to ten seconds, depending on how you're doing. Remember, nice deep breaths, in and out."

Yeah, quiet concentration and deep breathing was so not Shane's thing.

"How do you even know that pose?" Sam whispered to Dooley as Ryan led them into the first pose.

"Morgan's sister got her into it," Dooley told him. "I highly encourage endurance and flexibility."

"*Why* does she knit?" Shane whispered to Emma now that everyone was engaged in activity.

"Downward-Facing Dog, big guy," she told him.

"I don't even know where to begin."

"Get on your hands and knees," Emma instructed. "Then push back, raising your hips and straightening your legs." She demonstrated, making it seem easy. Of course.

Shane looked over to Ryan who was on his feet, his hands on the floor in front of him, ass in the air.

It looked ridiculous, but not difficult. Shane sighed and moved into position.

Once he was set, Emma said, "She decided that she needed more downtime in her life. She figured she could knit or watch TV and eat ice cream to unwind. With the knitting, she ends up with scarves. With TV and ice cream she ends up with bigger hips. The knitting won. She does other crafty stuff too."

They all breathed and Shane noticed the soft instrumental music drifting around them for the first time since he'd stepped into the room. He knew it. He knew there would be relaxing music.

He tried to get some Green Day or even Train playing in his head, but it was strange—every time he thought of a song, the harp from the stereo system would distract him again.

Dammit.

Ryan moved them into the next pose, the extended side something. They had to step out toward one hand, then turn and extend their other arm.

He looked over at Emma. She was totally cheating. "You too, chick."

She shook her head. "Can't quite get there with my hip. Getting close though."

Emma had been in the car accident with Isabelle and had come out in much worse shape. Iz had been bumped and bruised, but Emma had suffered a broken pelvis.

He knew from Nate that she'd worked hard in rehab. And Emma was her usual spunky self, back to flirting and teasing. It was hard to believe she wasn't one hundred percent physically.

"I guess I haven't seen you dancing in high heels lately, have I?" he said, realizing it just now.

"I'll be back at it—and everything else—soon," she said with a little wink.

"You haven't been able to do 'everything else'?" he asked, moving into the next pose as Ryan demonstrated how to squat to the floor, elbows between the knees.

He hadn't been paying attention to the other guys, but this one had Sam swearing and Mac stood frowning, not even trying it. Ryan opened his mouth to say something to Mac, but then apparently thought better of it and moved them back into the Downward-Facing Dog.

"A sore hip that has reduced range of motion makes it hard to do 'everything else'," Emma said, posing.

"Ah. Sorry to hear that," Shane said.

She laughed. "I'm surviving. I'm missing the advanced yoga poses the most."

"But you're getting better."

"Definitely. I'll be damned if I'm going to show up in Nate's office without making progress. He'll assume it's because I'm lazy or don't understand how important it is." She was frowning intensely now.

Nate Sullivan seemed to have that effect on her.

"Hey, I thought this was supposed to be relaxing," he teased.

The frown eased as she looked at him sheepishly. "Yeah. It is. As long as I don't think about Nate, my blood pressure stays fine."

"Okay, then let's go back to talking about Isabelle."

Ryan moved them into the Warrior Pose, one foot forward and both arms extended to the ceiling.

"Fine. What do you want to know?"

"Isabelle is making a big deal out of nothing, right? I mean, so she likes to knit. That isn't a commentary on our relationship or anything."

Emma looked over. "It isn't?"

"Is it?" he asked. Shit. Maybe it was. It was certainly a commentary on the fact that Isabelle didn't tell him everything.

They moved into the Warrior Two Pose. "It's a big deal to her," Emma said.

Shane liked these standing positions. He extended his right arm in front of him, his left behind him. He straightened his back leg, keeping his front knee bent. Then he sucked in his stomach and focused on breathing. This wasn't so bad.

Until Ryan showed them the Tree Pose. Ryan easily stood on his right leg, his left leg bent and supported with that foot against his right knee. He put his palms together, fingers up, elbows out. Mac again stood, hands on hips, scowling at Ryan. Sam and Kevin both got into position but could only hold for a few seconds. Dooley stood perfectly balanced, grinning at them all like a dumbass.

Shane got there and balanced long enough to say, "I don't think the knitting matters."

Ryan sighed. "Okay, let's try something else. Everyone on hands and knees."

"Lots of good things happen on hands and knees," Dooley said to Mac. "Lighten up."

"I don't feel more relaxed," Mac said. "I feel annoyed."

"Okay, lift one arm, fully extended. Then straighten the opposite leg back behind you," Ryan said.

Mac growled.

"Get your leg up," Emma coached Shane.

He lifted it higher and wobbled a bit.

"That's all you've got?" Em asked him, critiquing his form.

"I'm on a purple foam mat in a room that smells like…"

"Lavender," she supplied.

"It's giving me a headache," Mac groused.

Emma rolled her eyes.

"Yeah, I'm trying here," Shane said.

Emma acknowledged that with a nod. "At least you're not whining and bitching like *some* people," she said.

"You haven't even begun to see me get grouchy," Mac told her.

"What's your question?" Emma asked Shane, ignoring Mac.

"How big is the knitting?"

"She has an entire plastic tub full of yarn and other craft stuff. One of the big tubs. And it's at least three nights a week."

He groaned.

Emma nodded. "I know."

"How could I not know about that?" he asked, honestly confused.

"Well, since she's been dating you, there's a considerable lack of glue and yarn at my house," Emma said. "But she was recently saying that she needs to get back to the…knitting."

Shane wondered briefly about the way Emma always hesitated before saying the word *knitting*. But she went on before he could comment.

"She's been putting it off since she met you," Emma said. "But you have to understand, it's not really the knitting or crafts. It's the downtime. She likes the quiet, likes doing something all by herself, likes just zoning out."

Yeah, *that* could be a problem. Where glue and yarn might be something he could get used to, the quiet alone-time thing was going to be a much bigger challenge. Shane was nearly phobic about quiet and downtime. He was aware of it, he had good reason for it, but he couldn't get over it. If he was completely honest, he didn't want to get over it. The people-party-public thing worked for him. He liked it, craved it even.

He lived alone, but didn't spend any more time in his condo than he needed to. Otherwise, he liked to work out at the gym with other people around, he liked to be out with friends, he liked to be at big public events where even if the other people were strangers, there were a lot of them.

"Why hasn't she ever told me about all of this before?" More precisely, why did she put on the act of loving the same stuff he did?

They moved into the Plank Pose. All the guys did fine with it since it was essentially the top of a push-up.

"Because she didn't think you'd want her if you knew she was…into knitting."

Emma effortlessly moved into the Side Plank as Ryan did it. Dooley was right there with them. Once Mac got balanced on one arm, with one leg bent, one extended and his opposite arm up toward the ceiling he crowed, "Ha!"

"Well, this is a *variation* of the Side Plank," Dooley said smugly. "Right, Ryan?"

"I think this is enough for tonight," Ryan said.

Sam frowned. "Come on. Mac sucks but the rest of us are doing okay for our first time."

Mac clearly didn't care about their opinions on his yoga technique.

"I think the full Side Plank is a bit much for tonight," Ryan said again, moving into hands and knees again.

"Dammit, I want to be as relaxed as possible," Sam said. "Show us."

Ryan sighed. "I think that maybe the relaxation thing is going to take a few more sessions."

"Show us."

Ryan moved into the position, balancing on one hand and one foot only with the other leg and arm both extended up to the ceiling.

Sam fell to the mat without even trying. Mac growled again. Kevin laughed. Even Dooley couldn't get it. "I did it the other night at home," Dooley told them.

"Don't even think I'm not asking Morgan about that," Mac said.

"You want to try another position?" Ryan asked.

"No," they all said in unison.

"You guys are pathetic." But Ryan slumped onto the mat, then lay back flat on the mat, arms and legs extended. "In case any of you care, this is the Resting Pose."

"This I can totally do." Mac rolled to his back.

"Love this," Kevin agreed.

They all assumed the position and were, miraculously, quiet for thirty seconds.

Until Dooley said, "And I guess we can move onto the part of the night where we all give Shane relationship advice."

"Flavored body powder," Sam said.

"You finally tried the powder?" Mac asked.

"Yeah, it's awesome."

"Told you."

"What's flavored body powder the answer for, exactly?" Emma asked. "And where do I get some?"

"I'll have Sara text you," Mac said. "And it's the answer for how to get on a woman's good side. Works like a charm."

Emma nodded. "Sure, relationships are just that easy."

"That's it?" Ryan sat up and looked around. "The sum of all of your advice is flavored body powder?"

Dooley nodded. "Yep. Women are like…" He trailed off and frowned, as if thinking hard. Then he shrugged. "I got nothing. I'm too mellow after all the yoga."

Ryan flopped back onto his mat. "Okay, how about everyone just breathe," he said. "Quietly."

Shane stared up at the wooden beams that crossed the ceiling for a few minutes.

Finally he said, "I love her, Em."

Emma lay beside him and turned her head to look at him. "But?"

"I don't love jigsaw puzzles."

"Jigsaw puzzles?"

"I'm not a sit-around guy," he said. "Isabelle's not wrong about me liking the action and fun."

Emma pushed up to sitting, stretching her legs out in front of her and leaning back on her hands. "She made me try decoupage. I decorated this cute little jewelry box that my mother absolutely loved and now cherishes."

Shane sat up and faced her, mimicking her sitting position.

"You're telling me there are good things about living with Isabelle. That I should give it a try?"

Emma frowned and swatted him on the arm. "No. I'm telling you that living with Isabelle led to me learning to *decoupage*. You know that's gluing little pictures on stuff, right?"

"What kind of stuff?"

"Frames, jewelry boxes—" She shook her head. "It doesn't matter. The point is, I did that because she's my sister and I love her. We have to compromise because we don't have the option of ending our relationship." She paused and looked at him meaningfully.

He did have that option. "You're telling me to walk away?" Dammit. That was *not* the answer he wanted.

"That's *not* what I'm telling you," Emma said. "I'm saying that you can*not* let yourself think that all you have to do is decoupage a jewelry box and everything will be fine. But," she added, "don't let her convince you that if you don't make a jewelry box, your relationship is doomed."

Shane frowned. This seemed complicated. "So are you telling me I should decoupage or I should *not* decoupage?"

Emma pinned him with a direct stare. "Iz and I have a long history of her being awesome in spite of the arts and crafts. She was there every day when I was in the hospital. She was there when I changed majors five times in college. She loved me even when I broke the vase that she'd had since my dad gave her flowers on her eighth birthday."

"And you don't think she and I have enough history," Shane said, feeling a huge knot form in his stomach.

Emma didn't have to confirm that. He'd known Isabelle for eight months—six of crazy passionate love and two of...whatever they'd been doing since she tried to break up with him.

"Go to the cabin with her and learn all about decoupage and...the knitting," Emma said. "Spend twenty-four-seven together. See how it goes for real. She's going to try to scare you off. With decoupage. And maybe with stuff that's even worse."

Emma's expression made it clear that she was having a hard time imaging something worse.

She went on. "Even though she wants to be with you, she's going to try to push you away. Show her that you can still be together even if you never glue a stupid tiny picture of a flower onto a stupid wooden box."

The knot in his stomach pulled tighter. Emma was suggesting they test their relationship. A week ago he would have said *hell yeah* because he would have been confident that he'd come through with flying colors. Now, though…well, the thing about a test was that there was always the chance that you wouldn't have all the answers. Without all the answers, you failed. "Yeah, okay," he finally said.

He wanted this woman more than he'd ever wanted anything. And he knew about wanting. And working to make it happen. He'd spent his whole childhood that way.

"Repeat after me." Emma leaned in closer. "Decoupage sucks, but being without Isabelle sucks more."

"Decoupage sucks, but being without Isabelle sucks more."

Emma pointed a finger at his nose. "And when she pulls the glue and the glitter out, you keep telling yourself that."

He gave her a short nod. "Got it."

"Do you know the difference between a scalloped edge and a deckle edge?" Emma asked.

"Of course not."

"You will," she told him. "But it doesn't matter. It's just fancy cutting. Remember that."

"Got it."

"Good. Oh, and boxes and vases and jars are the same. You just take one piece of paper at a time and you stick it on the same way no matter what shape you're dealing with. Do not let her intimidate you with this stuff. At the end of the day, it's just paper and glue."

Shane appreciated Emma's sort-of pep talk after all. She seemed very determined to keep him in the game, prepping him for the opponent's strategy and helping him keep perspective.

He and Isabelle needed to take one piece of this at a time and approach this newly shaped relationship the same way they had approached their relationship when it had been working.

He had no idea how Emma Dixon, the woman who was allergic to monogamy and commitment, had gotten so insightful about relationships, but she was right.

"You been dating a psychiatrist or something?" he asked Emma.

She shrugged. "I'm just that good."

Dooley gave a low whistle. "Damn, I am a sucker for gorgeous, smart women. You still being single means there are a lot of dumb guys in this town."

She winked and stretched to her feet. "A lady never kisses and tells how many guys have been…smart."

The guys all chuckled, but Shane sighed and slumped back onto the mat, throwing his forearm over his eyes.

Mellow. Relaxed. Calm.

He wasn't any of those things.

Scalloped edges versus deckle edges? Seriously?

He squeezed his eyes shut.

Just as he'd suspected, yoga kind of sucked.

CHAPTER
FOUR

THE MISSION BEGINS AT NOON. *Code word: Emma.*

Isabelle frowned at her new text message. "Emma!" she called from the kitchen.

She heard Emma's footsteps on the stairs. "Yeah?"

Emma had gotten up to say goodbye, but she was still dressed in the short shorts and tank top she'd worn to bed.

Isabelle turned her phone so Emma could see the screen. "Do you know what this is?"

Emma looked at it and nodded. "Yeah."

Isabelle waited. When Emma crossed to the coffee pot instead of answering, Iz asked, "What does it mean?"

Emma took a sip from her cup. "I'm helping you."

Oh, boy. "Helping me what?"

"Keep Shane interested."

"Keep him interested?" Isabelle said, surprised. "In me?" What had they talked about at the yoga studio last night?

"In the trip," Emma said. "The way you have it set up, he's sure to bail early. You're going to make it all serious and complicated and dump all this downer stuff on him at once. But I think he needs to see that you can still do a lot, that you can still have fun too."

Isabelle watched Emma retrieve the cream from the fridge and add it to her cup. People who only knew Emma socially might not believe that she had a serious side, but when Emma got serious—mad, frustrated, worried, whatever—she did it with the same zeal she did everything else.

"As a matter of fact," Isabelle told her. "I have a bunch of fun tourist stops mapped out."

"I know. I saw the list by the computer," Emma said. "The Corn Palace? Seriously? If he's not on his way back to Omaha after the stop at the Lewis and Clark Interpretive Center in Sioux City, then the Corn Palace will definitely do it."

Isabelle frowned at her. She wanted to argue but…Emma had a point. Museums weren't exactly Shane's speed—even if they were interactive.

"Did Shane say something last night? About thinking he'll be bored?" Isabelle knew she should think that was a good thing. If he was already worried about the trip, maybe he'd stay home. That was what she wanted anyway. So the stab of disappointment didn't make any sense.

Emma put the cream back, shut the door, stirred her coffee and sipped again before saying, "Just because Shane doesn't know what a deckle edge is, doesn't mean he can't be your boyfriend."

Isabelle shook her head. "What are you talking about?" Emma remembered what a deckle edge was?

"Start with something easier to understand, something less daunting."

Deckle edges were *not* daunting. Isabelle crossed her arms. "We're not really talking about crafting, are we?"

Emma took a seat at the breakfast bar and met Isabelle's gaze directly. "I know that you're going to give him the worst-case scenario." Emma paused, then said, "Like you did with me."

Isabelle distinctly remembered the day deckle edges came

into Emma's life. The various crafting scissors had driven her crazy. But they weren't talking about scissors right now. Not really.

"I was telling you about my flare-ups," Isabelle said. They'd talked about her fibromyalgia flares that day as they'd decorated jewelry boxes. Isabelle had been grateful for something to concentrate on besides Emma's reactions...and her attempts to cover up her reactions.

"And they're bad, I get it," Em said. "But they're not all the time. A lot of the time, most of the time, you do fine. And it's not fair to make Shane believe that he has to do things differently or he's going to break you or something."

Emma had preferred to stay with the regular scissors, making plain, straight cuts. And she preferred to believe that everything with Isabelle was still regular and straightforward as well.

Isabelle looked at her sister, recognizing the emotion in Emma's eyes—a combination of sadness, frustration and purpose. She knew that Emma was constantly looking for proof that Isabelle was okay, that she was the same person she'd always been.

The last few months of dating Shane had only perpetuated Emma's belief that the fibromyalgia was more like an occasional headache versus a chronic condition. Which was probably why Emma was so determined to keep Isabelle and Shane together.

"Em, I have to make some changes," she said.

"But you've already given up a lot," Emma said. "I don't want you to have to give up this guy who makes you so happy."

Well, that was sweet. "Thanks, hon, but he needs to know the truth."

"I know, but you can do it gently and not focus only on the bad stuff."

Emma definitely needed her to not focus only on the bad stuff.

"Okay," Isabelle said, giving in. "What is this code-name-Emma thing?"

Emma's frown quickly turned into a smile. "It's a spy game."

"A what?"

"A spy game. The company is called Big Time." Like a light switch Emma's gloominess changed to enthusiasm. "They do parties for adults, like murder mysteries and treasure hunts and spy adventures. One of my friends did it for her husband's birthday last year. I decided it's perfect for this road trip you're doing."

Isabelle fought the urge to say *no way*. Emma had a way of jumping in before she had all the details or had thought things through.

But she glanced back at the text and felt a little flip of excitement in her stomach. "A spy game? Really?"

Emma grinned. "Really."

Okay, Emma had her attention. "This will keep Shane from getting bored and leaving?"

Emma nodded. "I was afraid you'd push him away and not let him in on all the stuff you *can* do. You need to be sure he knows all the things that *haven't* changed too."

"And you think playing spy will show him that I can still have fun even when I tell him about the…knitting."

Emma nodded. "And it will show *you* that you can still have fun."

And it would prove to Emma that Isabelle was still adventurous and willing to go along with Emma's crazy plans.

Isabelle sighed. "I *have* to tell him everything."

"Yes. And you also have to help find the magical dragon pendant and deliver it to the drop site in the Black Hills."

A magical dragon pendant? How could she say no to that?

Emma grinned knowingly and Isabelle felt the tension leave her body.

"What does this entail, exactly?" Isabelle asked, trying not to let on how intrigued she really was.

"I don't know." Emma's grin grew. "From here it's up to Big Time. They'll send you messages and missions and stuff, I guess…and you do them. And enjoy. Oh, and Shane doesn't know about it. He won't be getting messages—only you. It'll be more fun that way, don't you think?"

Isabelle wasn't sure what Shane would think about this, but she was in. How could it not be a good time? Besides, it was clearly making Emma happy. She thought she was helping.

If nothing else, Isabelle could—and would—play along for those reasons.

"A magical dragon pendant, huh?"

Isabelle almost tripped over Shane when she stepped out of her front door ten minutes later. He hadn't been there when she'd been loading the car, so he'd obviously just arrived.

He hadn't called, texted or come over since their Wednesday night hook-up, but she wasn't at all surprised to see him.

"Emma told you what time I was leaving?"

"Yep."

Shane stretched to his feet from his seat on the top step. "I threw my bag in the backseat of your car so I don't have to strap it on my bike."

She glanced at her car. "What if you need to bring it back with you on the bike?"

"You mean if the trip sucks and we break up?"

She flinched slightly at the words. It was what she was thinking, but hearing him put it like that—and in that pissed-off tone of voice—made it hard to swallow.

"Yeah, I guess," she said quietly.

"How about we not start all of that first thing in the morning?" he asked.

She didn't especially want to get into all of it *ever*. She wanted it to all be fine and turn out that they were madly in love when it was all over.

"Fine. You want coffee?"

"No."

Okay. Shane was crabby about something. Which for anyone else would be fine. It was early and there was some definite tension in them both about this trip. But this was worse. Shane was never annoyed with *her*. The last time he'd been frustrated was when she'd gotten mad about the Vegas trip and he thought she wasn't listening to his explanation.

Until Vegas, they hadn't fought at all.

Well, they had a nice long drive ahead of them for him to cool off.

"Then I guess we should go," she said.

"Guess so."

She didn't want to go. Suddenly in that moment she was seized with the desire to grab him, hold on and take him to bed.

But they had to do this. They couldn't stay in bed forever.

The trip would be fine. Great even. If nothing else, she was going to be in the car by herself for hours. She could listen to whatever she wanted on the radio. Or nothing at all. She could listen to a new audiobook. She could sing to herself. The options were endless.

She started to move past Shane and was surprised when he grabbed her arm and pulled her around to face him.

"Just—" he started. Then rather than finishing the sentence, he cupped the back of her head and brought her in for a kiss.

It was one of those kisses like the one in the supply closet at Trudy's—soft, sweet and sexy all at the same time. It was a lot shorter though.

He lifted his head and looked down at her with an expression she could only label as sad. "Just tell me that won't be the last one."

"Why—"

But then it hit her. Everything had sunk in for him finally.

He had truly realized that this trip could end with them going in opposite directions.

Emma had told her that she'd been completely honest with

Shane. She hadn't spilled anything more specific than that, but clearly that had been enough. Emma knew all about living with Isabelle. But again, Emma *had* to keep loving her.

Shane didn't.

"I don't want it to be the last," she said sincerely.

He looked at her for several seconds. Then he brought her mouth to his again. This kiss was much less sweet, but was fully hot. He urged her lips open and stroked his tongue along hers as he walked her backward and pressed her into the side of the car.

He tangled both hands in her hair, holding her still for his possession.

Like she was going anywhere.

She loved Shane's size. She wasn't tiny, but Shane could make her feel dainty in the way he touched her and held her. He often let her be the aggressor, but when he wanted to put her somewhere or do something to her, he could and did. And she loved it every time.

Now he had her effectively trapped against the car and his body—just like she liked it.

He lifted his head, changed angles and kissed her again, drawing her up onto her tiptoes and pressing close so that they were against one another from belly to toes. Her body heated and softened, welcoming him, wanting more.

Isabelle gripped his biceps, giving as good as she got, rubbing against him, exploring his mouth, eliciting a groan from him that made her tingle. She loved getting him going, knowing that she could do that to him, knowing that he needed her as much as she needed him. It was definitely addictive.

She started to move her hands to his back. She loved feeling his muscles bunching and moving when he touched her. But he lifted his head.

He stood looking down at her, breathing hard.

"Iz."

"I love you, you know." She wasn't sure why those were the first words to come out of her mouth. But they were right.

They'd said those three magic words to one another crazy early in their relationship. But it had been true after about two weeks and it had felt natural to tell him.

Like now.

Something flared in his eyes at her words and she felt his fingers flex in her hair.

Somehow she knew she'd been right to say it just then. He'd needed to hear it. How she knew, she wasn't sure, but hearing it had mattered.

This trip was scary. It wasn't about her not feeling those things for him. It was about the future and if it could be what they both wanted and deserved.

It wasn't like she thought she'd ever *not* love him.

"When I was six, my mom brought me home after school, gave me a snack and then put me down for a nap."

Isabelle frowned. What was he talking about? The intensity in his eyes was enough to keep her quiet, though.

He still held her head in his hands, their faces only inches apart, but she settled back on her feet and put her hands back on his arms, holding onto him too.

"She told me that I needed to sleep for a while and not to come out of my room. When I woke up later and went looking for her—I don't even remember how long it was—I couldn't find her. I looked all over the house, outside in the yard, everywhere. I called and called for her but...she wasn't there. It took me a while to notice that the car was gone. And her purse."

Isabelle gasped, but couldn't speak. Her fingers curled into his arms, holding on tighter. She'd known he'd been in foster care, but that he'd been happy. He'd had a loving family—a huge, loving family—and he'd been well cared for. He'd only ever been in the one home and had eventually been adopted by the family. He talked to them all regularly and told funny, crazy stories about them with an affectionate grin.

She'd never known what put him in foster care or how old

he'd been. She'd assumed he had been tiny and didn't remember his life before the Kelleys took him in.

Clearly she'd been wrong.

He pulled in a long breath, then went on. "I don't know how long I was alone. She'd apparently decided to go to a friend's house. She had been upset about something at work and a guy she'd been dating. She was very drunk and was driving too fast and rolled her car. She was thrown free and died instantly."

Isabelle's whole body ached. She wanted to make it all better. She wanted to comfort him. To love him so much that none of that mattered. But she stood completely still, not moving, barely breathing, sensing he needed to keep going.

"The thing was, she was out on a country road that didn't have a lot of traffic, the ditch she rolled into was deep—hard to see into from the road—and her friend didn't know she was coming over so no one knew she hadn't made it. It was hours before anyone found her."

"You were alone that whole time?" Isabelle's voice was scratchy from the tears that she was holding back with all she had.

He gave one quick nod. "I remember getting hungry at dinner time and eating leftovers from the fridge. Then I went to bed. I got under the covers and didn't move until the next morning."

"Someone finally came?"

"They had her I.D. They came to the house, I'm guessing to try to find family. I remember someone knocking on the door, but there was no way I was answering that. I was convinced that bad guys had taken her away and were coming back for me."

Isabelle felt cold all over and she put a hand over his heart, wanting to feel his heat, wanting to feel his heart beating. "God, Shane."

"The next day I didn't show up at school. The school called mom's work and were told about the accident. Anyway, it finally came up that I was missing. They knew I hadn't been in the accident, so the cops came back and broke the door down. Scared the shit out of me."

"When?" she asked. "How long had it been?"

"It was the next day. Almost lunch time."

"Jesus," she whispered.

"But I remember seeing those men in those uniforms, looking so strong and determined and *there*. To this day I've never been happier to see someone than I was to see them."

Her heart was breaking. This man, this wonderful, strong, amazing man who made her laugh and feel things she'd never felt before, had been an abandoned, scared little boy at one time. He could have become hard and bitter. He could have crawled inside himself. But instead he was outgoing and fun and charming and everyone loved him.

A bright light bulb went off in her head. "That's why you became a cop."

"Yes."

"And why you're the life of the party."

"I *hate* being alone. I *hate* the quiet. It feels...wrong to me. It always has."

She felt some of the tension in his body release and she stroked her hands over his arms.

"I went from that—and it had always just been me and my mom anyway—to a house full of kids. There were twelve of us and there wasn't a prayer for quiet or alone. And I loved it. I stirred most of it up. Not that it was hard to do."

Isabelle felt a smile pull at her lips. "I don't have a bit of trouble picturing you as the instigator."

"Then one of my foster brothers got sick. Well, he was sick to start with. His mom had used drugs and his heart was bad. He got sick and I remember them telling us all that we had to be quiet and couldn't play hard and to not mess around because Paul didn't feel good and needed to rest. Then he passed away and our dad kept telling us we had to be quiet and play nicely because Mom was so sad and she needed time to be by herself and rest."

He drew in a deep breath, then let it out in a quick huff.

"I fucking *hate* quiet and peaceful, Iz. It reminds me of being sad and scared. I like the laughter. I like music and friends and having a good time."

She stared into those big brown eyes, not sure what to do, if there was anything she could do. "Let's stay here," she finally blurted.

He sighed, then dropped his hands. "No. That's not why I told you."

She didn't let go of him when he tried to step back. "I know. You told me so I would understand. And I do. I can deal with all of that, Shane. I can do that for you. Let's stay here. Forget all this crazy talk about my…knitting." She could so ignore all of her issues if it brought back the happy, fun Shane. She hated seeing him sad or stressed.

He stepped back in spite of her hold. "You know what? I might go for that if I hadn't talked to Emma last night."

Isabelle scowled at that. "Emma's a big talker. But her longest meaningful relationship has been about three months."

"Wrong. Her longest meaningful relationship has been twenty-six years. With you."

Dammit.

"You haven't been *really* truly you with me, Iz," he went on. "And I've made a lot of assumptions about our relationship based on what I thought I knew."

"But this all sounds so stupid," she said. "We're talking about possibly breaking up because I like to knit and you don't know how to sit still." People didn't break up because of knitting. But they did break up because their lives didn't fit together.

He gave her a grim smile. "I know. It does sound stupid. But it's not. Not really. Because of what's behind all of that. You like to knit—but it's actually because you can only take so much stimulation and need something to help you chill out. I don't know how to sit still because I don't *want* to sit still."

"Not even with me?"

"Well, there's the thing we need to find out. We need to find out if we can do this."

They did. He was completely, absolutely right. And she needed to tell him her whole story, tell him what the chilling-out anti-stimulation-thing was all about. She intended to help him know her, understand, and then let him make the decision about what was next for them.

But right now she felt the need to…heal him. Or something. Somehow. She didn't fully understand it, but she wanted to make him feel better. Yes, it had all happened when he was six, and when he was six she was four, but still…it really, really, really sucked that she hadn't been around then to hug him, or give him cookies, or tell him it would be okay, or *something*.

It was stupid to think that way, but she ached with the inability to help him. So *now* she needed to do something to make him feel good. And that definitely didn't include telling him about her pain and getting into all the things that would mean.

Not right now. There was time for that later.

"Let's go." Shane gave her a quick kiss on the mouth and then turned toward his bike.

She didn't have a better idea—yet—but she would, so for now, they could drive. Because yeah, the vacation-alone-at-the-cabin thing had to happen too.

Dammit. If only her body would let her reach out and grab the life that Shane had and wanted. Tears pricked her eyes as she watched him swing his leg over the motorcycle and settle onto the seat as he pulled his helmet on. She was so often frustrated with her condition and the fricking limitations it put on her. But falling in love with Shane was by far the most unfair of all the things that had happened.

This was the craziest fucking thing he'd ever done.

He was going on a trip with a woman he had a fifty-fifty chance of breaking up with after about twenty-four hours.

He knew it. She knew it. And yet, here they were, driving north on I-29 anyway.

Well, why not? He liked things unconventional. He was definitely not a fan of predictable and lackluster. If he was going to break up with the only woman he'd ever really loved, why not drive over five hundred miles to do it? And why not take ten hours to get there instead of the seven and a half it should have taken?

In fact, the way Isabelle was going right now, it might take them double the time to get there.

Isabelle's brake lights lit up just then and she signaled to exit. In Vermillion, South Dakota.

They were never going to get to the cabin.

Vermillion was only two hours from Omaha, yet they'd left three hours ago. They'd already stopped in Sioux City to visit the Lewis and Clark Interpretive Center.

Considering they were going there to potentially break up, Shane realized he shouldn't be so anxious to get there. He should also probably appreciate that Isabelle seemed to be drawing the trip out for the same reason.

They exited, but just as he expected her to pull into one of the gas stations, she kept going. For several more miles. Finally she turned and pulled into the parking lot of a long brick building.

It was a museum.

At least the Lewis and Clark place had been right off the interstate.

Shane sighed and pulled in to park beside her. She got out of the car as he pulled his helmet off.

"You've always wanted to visit the W.H. Over Museum?" he asked dryly.

"I saw this online."

"You planned all of this? A thousand stops on the way to the Black Hills?" he asked, swinging his leg over the bike.

She smiled and nodded. "Yeah."

He paused. "You did?"

"Well, yeah. That's what road trips are all about, right? Seeing things along the way."

"I thought this trip was about going to the cabin to see if we can spend the rest of our lives together."

Her smile died. She nodded. "Yeah. It's that too."

He stepped close and took her hand. "I'm anxious about it too. But dragging it out like this won't make it any easier, will it?"

She opened her mouth to say something, then stopped and pressed her lips together. Finally she took a breath and said, "I planned to stop along the way because it's hard to sit and drive that long. I want to break the trip up. And," she added, narrowing her eyes slightly. "I thought I was going to be doing the drive alone. You weren't invited, remember?"

"Now knowing that you're going to stop every hour along the way, I'll never let you do a drive alone again. You don't know who you're going to meet out here alone. You need to be more careful. I need to know you're safe and—"

She cut his lecture off with a kiss.

When she pulled back, she smiled up at him. "Let's go in and see Hero the elephant."

Shane sighed and let her take his hand and pull him along the sidewalk leading into the museum.

It was a typical museum in every way. Glass displays, small and large, including butterflies and a stuffed bison, a one-room schoolhouse, clothes and tools from long ago, stuffed native animals, displays of local plants. And then they arrived at the display for Hero the elephant.

It was a huge elephant skull mounted above a collection of bones.

Holding hands with Isabelle, Shane found himself drawn in to the story of the circus elephant and his demise. When he finished reading he looked at Isabelle. She had tears in her eyes.

"You're *crying*?"

"Well, it's sad," she exclaimed. "He was a poor, defenseless animal that they shot. Repeatedly."

"He trampled two horses to death and tried to kill his trainer."

"His trainer who was being mean to him." She sniffed and swung her big-ass purse from one shoulder to the other.

Shane reacted on instinct, grabbing the strap just in time to keep her from knocking over a display of rocks. "Watch it, girl."

She sniffed again, unconcerned with the rocks.

Moving her purse where she couldn't do any damage, he said, "Hey, he was a hell of a fighter. They shot him repeatedly and chased him for twelve hours before he went down."

Isabelle swatted his arm. "If they'd treated him well, he wouldn't have gotten mean. And then they killed him because he didn't like being *flogged*."

"He weighed five tons. He would have taken them all out."

"Whatever." She wiped at one of her eyes and turned away from the exhibit. "Let's go."

Shane blocked her purse from knocking over a box of fossilized animal teeth and followed, glancing back at Hero as they left the room.

Okay, so out-of-the-way pit stops weren't all bad. That was kind of interesting.

Back at the curb he asked, "Now where?"

She lifted a shoulder. "You'll see. Or feel free to keep driving when I exit. I didn't realize you were so cold hearted."

He chuckled and grabbed her. Even as she stiffened and tried to push away, he hugged her against his chest. "Okay, I'm sorry. It is sad that they didn't treat Hero better. I feel bad for those two ponies that got in the way of his temper tantrum too."

She relaxed a little, but didn't hug him back. "Yeah, me too."

He kissed the top of her head and let her go. "And remind me to never take you to the circus."

They were finally back on the interstate, headed for Sioux Falls. Shane breathed a sigh of relief when they made it through Sioux Falls without a stop and were finally on I-90. His relief lasted another hour. When they reached Mitchell, South Dakota.

The home of the Corn Palace.

He wasn't even the slightest bit surprised when she signaled to turn into Mitchell and a few minutes later parked in front of the unique tourist attraction.

"I should have known," he said as she joined him beside his bike.

"Oh, come on. You can't see something like this just anywhere."

He looked at the gaudy building and had to agree with that statement. He also had to be grateful for that. "A building covered in corn? Yeah, that's true."

"They use corn and other grains to make the murals," she said, starting across the street. "And they change the murals every year according to a theme and they use local artists. They use different colors of corn and all of it is grown by a local farmer." She looked back at him. "You have to admit that's a little cool."

It was still a building covered in corn. He almost dreaded seeing what was inside.

The building was huge. Could they actually fill it with corn-related displays? And if they could, did he really want to see what those displays consisted of?

"This is a lot of time and space to spend on corn," he commented as Isabelle again took his hand and they stepped through the doors.

She laughed lightly. "This is a multi-purpose building for the city. They play basketball here, have shows and festivals. It's not floor-to-ceiling corn, don't worry."

Well, that was something.

They wandered through the building to the inner arena area where the walls were, again, covered in artwork made of corn. There was a huge stage, stadium seating and on the floor of the arena was a collection of booths that sold everything from hand-made jewelry to snacks.

"They hold the local high school's graduation here," Isabelle told him, reading from a brochure she'd picked up as they came in.

"This is…unique," Shane agreed, checking out the gigantic murals on the walls around them.

She giggled. "It is." She started weaving through the racks and displays of crafts and goodies, stopping here and there to study something that caught her eye.

Twice, Shane caught her purse from knocking over a display until finally, he was too slow.

A stand of decorative corncobs tumbled to the floor as her purse smacked it directly. She swung around at the sound and knocked over a small rack of postcards. She started to turn again, when Shane grabbed her.

"You can dance in four-inch heels but you can't walk through a souvenir shop without creating a disaster?" he teased.

Her cheeks were bright red. "I don't usually carry this huge thing."

They both knelt to the floor to begin picking things up as a sales person hurried over and several other tourists turned to look. Her purse kept swinging and banging into the counter next to her and her leg, until she finally sighed, slid it off her shoulder and tossed it to the side.

"Here, let me help." A man in typical tourist attire knelt beside her and began gathering the postcards that had fallen and slid in all directions.

Isabelle gave him a smile. "Thanks."

"Is anything broken?" Shane asked the woman who was carefully inspecting the corncobs.

"A few," she said, giving Isabelle an irritated look.

"We'll pay for anything damaged," Shane said calmly.

"It was an accident, I'm very sorry," Isabelle said quickly, handing a corncob to the woman.

"You should watch where you're going," she snapped.

"Yes, I should," Isabelle agreed.

The lady was right, but that didn't stop Shane from giving her a frown. She didn't have to be bitchy about it. They were corncobs. There had to be hundreds, even thousands, where these came from.

"The postcards are all intact," the man next to Isabelle said. He smiled at the sales woman as he handed her the neat stack. "Not a broken one in the bunch."

The woman didn't say anything, but she took the postcards from him with another frown.

"I'm so embarrassed," Isabelle said, getting to her feet.

"It could have happened to anyone. It's pretty tight quarters through here," the man said, bending to pick up her purse and hand it back to her. Clearly surprised by how heavy it was, he grinned. "Of course, I think you're supposed to have a license to carry a weapon like this."

Isabelle reached out to take it with a smile. "Well, I'd hate to be caught without…practically everything I own."

He laughed as he let go of the strap. But Isabelle didn't quite have a grip yet and the heavy bag hit the floor, contents scattering.

"Good lord," Isabelle sighed, again kneeling to gather her items.

Shane got down next to her, but the first thing he reached for made him pause. As did the second and third thing.

They were medicine bottles. Pills.

He looked at the label. Yes, they were prescribed medications. Prescribed to Isabelle.

He didn't know what any of them were, but he hadn't been aware she was on anything at all.

Just more proof that they hadn't known each other that long

and not that well in that time, in spite of how intimate they had been.

Knitting and medication. What else did he not know about her?

How sick was she? Was it allergy medicine or something more serious?

"Shane?" Isabelle turned and saw him with the bottles.

He watched her.

She looked like a kid who had been caught hiding beer in her closet. Without a word, she reached out her hand.

He gave her the bottles and watched her tuck them into her purse.

"Let's try that again," the man said, stretching to his feet and handing her the purse again.

This time Isabelle firmly grasped the straps before he let go with a smile.

"Thanks," Isabelle said.

"Sure thing." The man moved off, perusing a collection of photographs of the area.

"We should go before I break anything else," Isabelle said to Shane, holding her purse against her stomach.

Shane hoped it was to keep it from knocking anything else over, but it looked like she was using it as a barrier between them.

"We owe the lady for the corncobs," Shane said, staring into her eyes, willing her to talk to him.

"Oh, right. I'll go pay her."

So she wasn't going to say anything. Okay. Fine. She knew better than to think that he was going to let it go for long. "I've got it," he said, reaching for his wallet.

He tracked the woman down and settled the bill—which was outrageous for four painted corncobs—and then headed back to where Isabelle was leafing through the postcards she'd dumped on the floor.

"You ready?" she asked, her smile a little too bright.

But he didn't want to get into this here.

"Yeah, let's go. You want to eat something?"

"Oh, I'm okay—" she started, then she saw his expression.

He was quite sure it said, *We're going to eat* now.

"Sure," she said.

He grabbed her hand and headed for the parking lot. They'd take her car and find somewhere close to eat, then come back for his bike.

Shane opened the passenger door for Isabelle. She looked from the door to him. "You're driving?"

"Yep."

"I think—" She stopped when she saw the look on his face.

Yeah, he wasn't happy. She had a secret. Maybe more than one. And that wasn't okay with him.

"—that's a great idea," Isabelle finished.

"Me too." He put her in the passenger seat, then headed around the front of the car.

He could tell that she was nervous as he started the car and pulled out onto the street. He didn't like that either but damned if he could *not* be visibly tense about this. He needed to know if she was okay. He needed to know why she hadn't told him about whatever it was. And he needed to know what this meant for the future. Was this why she was pushing him away?

He drove to the first place with food. It was a Mexican restaurant somewhere between fast food and fine dining. Mariachi music played from the speakers and the aroma of garlic, cilantro and other spices flavored the air. They were seated in a booth by a hostess and handed trifold menus. The chips came in a wicker basket and the salsa in a deep ceramic bowl, but there were definitely no cloth tablecloths or candles, and the napkins were paper.

Once they both had waters, the hostess left them alone to peruse the menus.

Shane laid his to one side and leaned his forearms on the tabletop. "Talk," he said simply.

Isabelle leaned back in the booth, her menu still open. "I was going to tell you all about it after I got back from the cabin."

"We've been dating for eight months," he pointed out.

"Yes."

"How long have you had the pills?"

"Ten months."

His gut clenched. She'd known about whatever this was for ten months and hadn't said a word?

"So this conversation is eight months overdue," he said, working on calm.

"Eight months ago I was just beginning to get a handle on things. Then I met you. Eight months ago you were the guy I drank margaritas with and had hot sex everywhere but a bed with. Not the man I shared every detail of my life with."

Okay. She had a point.

"Then it's seven months overdue."

She leaned in. "I spent the first month of our relationship caught up in this whirlwind of fun and the best sex of my life. I was sure it wasn't going to last, but I decided to enjoy it while it did. The next two to three months of our relationship I spent thinking that it was still a lot of fun—too much fun. I was starting to realize I was a little in over my head with you, but couldn't quite break it off because it was so great. The next two months I spent trying to figure out how to keep up with you, reading books about sex, buying toys and whipped cream and lingerie. Now I've spent the past two months trying to stay away from you."

He'd spent the first month trying to convince himself that he was really with her, the next couple enjoying the hell out of every minute convinced it was going to last forever, the next three making plans for the future, and the last two trying to convince her to move in with him.

"Do the pills have something to do with you wanting to stay away?"

She nodded. "Yeah."

He took one of her hands on the tabletop. "I *knew* it was never about my ex."

She let him hold her hand. "No." She sighed. "I mean, Candy is the kind of girl I wish I could be for you. Spontaneous, stay-out-all-night, adventurous."

"But you—"

She stopped him with a squeeze. He clenched his jaw. He'd let her go on, but if she thought there were things that he wanted that she hadn't given him already…

"I do some of those things, yes. Way more with you than usual. But I pay for it later."

He frowned. "Pay for it?"

The waitress arrived, interrupting.

They each placed an order. Having not looked at the menu—and not caring about the food anyway—Shane ordered a number three combo. Every Mexican restaurant had a number three combo.

When she left, he turned his focus back on Isabelle. "What do you mean?"

She took a deep breath and squeezed his hand a little tighter. "Okay, do you remember the business trip I took to Denver right after Emma and I went to that outdoor music festival last October?"

He did. Isabelle traveled a lot for her work. It was usually only a day or two at a time and it was often last minute. "Sure."

"I didn't go to Denver."

He frowned. "I don't understand."

"I didn't go to Denver. There was no business trip. I went to a hotel downtown, got a room and climbed into bed for two days."

"I don't understand." But the knot in his gut pulled tighter.

"I haven't traveled for work in all the time I've known you, Shane."

"You've been on four trips."

She shook her head. "No. I told you I was on four trips. What

I really do is go somewhere no one can find me, turn off my phone, order room service and get in bed."

His throat and chest were now as tight as his gut. "Why?"

"Because I go and go and push and try to keep up with you and Emma until my body says 'enough' and I shut down. It's been happening for a while—over a year—and getting worse. I thought at first I'd gotten a bad virus or something, but the doctor couldn't find anything. Then I thought maybe I wasn't sleeping enough or had too much stress. But I worked on both of those things and, while they helped, it wasn't enough."

She focused on the tabletop instead of him, but kept her hand in his.

Shane stroked his thumb over her knuckles, consciously keeping his grip from getting too tight.

"The first time I pulled away from everything was after a ski weekend with Emma. I was so much sorer than I ever had been before and was so tired that the idea of going to work on Monday made me cry. I thought, 'If I could just be *alone* for twenty-four hours, I know I can get over this'. So I told Em I had to go out of town for work, I called in sick and went to a hotel and climbed into bed. It was awesome. I did it the next time I felt like that too. And the next. It became my coping mechanism. I had to do it about once a month."

She took a deep breath and blew it out slowly before going on. "But it kept happening. I'd have great days where I'd feel fine and want to go and do anything and everything. But then, inevitably, I'd go through another bad time. I'd hurt, I'd feel depressed, I'd get so tired I couldn't focus. I was convinced I was bipolar. But the doctor ruled that out. Then I thought I might have MS or cancer or a thousand other things that scared the crap out of me. But the doctor did all the tests and everything was fine. Finally she told me that she thought I had fibromyalgia."

Isabelle looked up at him. "That was right before I met you.

And the reason I said no the first several times you asked me out. I knew immediately that you'd run me ragged."

She gave him a little smile, but his whole body was so tight there was no way he could even pretend to return it. He pulled his hand from hers, afraid he'd crush her fingers.

"And I did."

She wet her lips and shook her head. "Do you know what fibromyalgia is?"

He shrugged. "I've heard of it."

"It's a chronic pain disorder. They're not exactly sure what causes it. The counselor that I've talked to thinks it's stress related for a lot of people and thinks maybe my dad's death was the trigger for me." She sighed. "Then the car accident made everything so much worse. I didn't think I was ever going to get out of bed. I don't know. I just know that my body doesn't want to let me do all the things I want to do. If I stay out too late or have too much stress or drink too much or don't eat right, I pay for it."

"So things like spontaneous trips to Vegas and wild party weekends are the last thing you need."

She gave him a sad smile and nodded. "Exactly."

It was a lot to wrap his mind around. She looked fine. She didn't seem sick. But he knew that there were a lot of conditions like that. And if she'd been putting on a good front for him, then it would be even harder for him to tell if she wasn't feeling well.

Her trying to pull back from him made sense though. And really sucked.

"I need to learn more about it," he said. "I'd like to understand it."

She looked touched by that. "Thanks. I appreciate that."

He took her hand again. "I *hate* that I made things worse for you."

She pressed her lips together and looked at him for a moment. Then she said, "You didn't do it on purpose. And I could have said no."

"But," he said, confessing it to himself as he said it to her, "enough no's and it would have eventually split us up."

When she'd said no to meeting him in Vegas, all expenses paid, the weekend he'd hung out with Candy, he'd been mad. He could admit that. There hadn't been a good reason—or at least, it had *seemed* that there wasn't a good reason—for her to turn that trip down. If she would have turned him down repeatedly for the things he wanted to do, like the demo derbies or the rodeos or the carnivals or the parties, he would have figured she didn't want to be with him and their relationship would have ended shortly after beginning.

She nodded. "Yeah, it would have. And I kept thinking that's what I should do before we got more serious. But I couldn't resist. I kept thinking, 'just one more weekend'…but every weekend we spent together I fell harder and harder."

Shane took a deep breath, processing everything. He was in love with a knitter who not only preferred to stay home at night, but *needed* to in order to function and feel good.

Their waitress approached with their food and Shane bit into his supreme burrito without really tasting it. They ate for a few minutes in silence.

"So staying out late, drinking too much, too much stress are all bad for you. What else?" he finally asked.

She chewed and swallowed, then said, "Well, everything has to be balanced. Everything in moderation, as they say. I can drink, I can go out, but I have to not overdo. Too much noise, too much heat, trying to stay upbeat and not let on that I don't feel well, pushing past the point when my symptoms start and I could nip them in the bud, the stress of making sure I'm not the party pooper, all of that can play into it."

"The stress of dating a guy who overdoes it on a regular basis but not wanting him to know that you're not up for it?" he asked, knowing he sounded irritated, but unable to dial it down.

Isabelle frowned at him and laid her fork down. "Yes."

"The stress of hiding this from me, of making me think you're fine, made things worse."

"Yes."

He chewed angrily for a moment, aware of her eyes on him.

"Telling me never crossed your mind?" he finally asked. "Letting me know what was going on? Going home early once in a while, going out one night but not three, telling me to just chill the fuck out once in a while—none of that occurred to you as a solution?"

Isabelle sat back in the booth and crossed her arms. "Of course it occurred to me, Shane. It also occurred to me that you could have closed your eyes and pointed in any direction in Trudy's and found ten girls who not only would be happy to party all night with you, but who could have easily kept up and maybe worn *you* out once in a while. Why would you want to be with the girl who needs ten hours of sleep at night, gets a migraine if the jukebox is turned up a little too loud and has a meltdown if her massage therapist has to reschedule?"

He had no idea what to say to that.

She was right. There were lots of other girls out there. Girls like Candy, his stripper ex-girlfriend. And a month or two into their relationship, finding another girl might have been his solution if he'd known about this. Not that he wasn't sympathetic to her condition, but the idea of them making this work long term when comparing their lifestyles seemed ridiculous.

But by month three he'd been in love.

He'd never been in love before.

Candy had been a lot of fun. So had Tracie and Steph and Lila. Tracie had never met a dare she wouldn't take, Steph had never met a situation that could intimidate her and Lila had never met a rule she wasn't willing to break.

But he hadn't fallen for any of them.

He'd fallen for Isabelle.

And the things he liked to do, the way he liked to live with the noise and the people and the constant activity were the things that triggered her symptoms.

Of course, he wasn't always going to be the guy closing down the bar. He didn't *want* to always be the guy closing down the bar. He knew that someday the parties at the bar would transition to barbecues at home and he was fine with that. While Conner and Cody manned the grill, Shane would be on the Slip 'N Slide with the kids.

But even when he settled down, there wouldn't be much settling. He wanted a ton of kids. He fully intended to adopt a bunch. He intended to learn to skydive and to own a jet ski. He knew he would always want a high-energy, active, crazy, loud, full life.

But he wanted it with a woman who needed a lot less of…all of that.

Fuck.

"I'll be back in a minute," Shane said, sliding out of the booth. He started toward the restrooms, then turned back, leaned in and kissed her. "Thank you for telling me."

CHAPTER
FIVE

ISABELLE SIGHED as he walked away. It felt good that he knew. Right that he knew, somehow. They'd known each other for eight months. She'd been in love with him for almost four of those. She'd known pretty early on that he was exactly the kind of guy she should avoid. She needed someone more laid back, someone who didn't go full steam ahead twenty-four-seven. But she hadn't been able to resist. And then it was too late—she'd fallen for him. It had felt like it was overnight. One day she was thinking that he was fun and funny and a ball of energy that she enjoyed being around and the next she'd realized she was in love with who he was and the things he did and how he made her feel.

She'd cried that day.

Not the reaction a woman was supposed to have to falling in love, for sure. But she'd known she wasn't the girl Shane needed long term.

Her family doctor had confirmed that she wasn't bipolar. It wasn't a psychological condition. It was physical. The doctor had suspected fibromyalgia, but had recommended she talk to a rheumatologist about how to best manage it. When she'd finally gotten to the day of her appointment with the specialist, she'd almost called to cancel. After months of frustration with the highs and lows of her condition and the limitations she was starting to feel more and more, she'd sat in the parking lot to Dr. Raymond's office, scared to go in. Because once he confirmed that she had *something* that was causing her to feel like this she was going to have to admit to herself that the limitations were real and chronic.

After he'd told her that yes, it was fibromyalgia, she'd cried again. Not so much about the pain. That she was going to do everything she could to manage. But because it meant she'd never be able to completely keep up with Emma or Shane. She'd hold them back from their fun, she'd have to bow out of trips at times, she'd have to call it an early night more often than not.

They'd either cut back with her or they'd go on without her.

Both options sucked.

Isabelle trailed her fork through the now-cold enchilada sauce on her plate.

"Harris is in the maroon SUV over your left shoulder."

Her head came up, her thoughts about her fibro and all the things it had ruined fled as she realized that a strange man sat across from her in the booth.

"Excuse me?" she asked.

He was dressed in a light blue button-up shirt, the sleeves rolled up to his elbows. He was blond and looked to be in his mid-forties. He had kind eyes.

"Harris is here, but he's following me. He doesn't know I'm handing the pendant off to you."

He handed her a small package wrapped in white tissue paper.

"The pendant?" The *pendant*? Now? The spy adventure was going to start now? How did they know she and Shane were at this restaurant? She looked around but didn't recognize anyone else in the place.

Of course... The realization came to her and she groaned inwardly. She'd left a list of the stops next to her computer at home. Where Emma could easily find it. And give it to some strange people who ran a spy adventure company. If she and Shane were going to be given missions along the way, surely the people orchestrating the adventure had to know where they were going to be and when. The people from Big Time must have followed her and Shane from the Corn Palace.

That wasn't creepy at all.

"What do I do now?" she asked.

The man looked around then leaned in. "You're Isabelle Dixon, right?"

"Yes."

"Did you get the text?"

"The..." She pulled her phone out of the outside pocket on her purse. "I had the sound turned down." She touched the message icon. Sure enough, she had another mission message. *You'll receive the package from a man in blue. He'll give you further instructions.*

She looked up at him. "Guess I did. Sorry."

The guy smiled. "I was supposed to give it to you at the Corn Palace, but then you made that big mess and I didn't have a chance to pull you aside."

Isabelle grimaced. "Sorry. So now what?"

"We have to deliver that to the drop site by midnight." He pointed to the package she held. "And keep it away from Harris."

Isabelle leaned in closer and whispered, "Are you a player in the spy game too or do you work for the company?" Maybe he'd signed up for an adventure too and they were somehow teamed up.

He grinned and shook his head. "I can't tell you that," he whispered.

She sat back and regarded him. "All right. I'm in. Where's the drop site?"

"You'll get directions later. But remember, Harris's objective is to take it from you. If he gets to the drop site with it first, you lose."

Isabelle couldn't help her grin. This sounded like more fun than spending the drive listening to audiobooks.

"Who's Harris?"

"That guy." He pointed out the window. "The woman is his handler."

Isabelle turned to look. There was a maroon SUV parked at the curb across the street from the restaurant. The people inside were barely visible, but it looked like a man behind the wheel and a woman in the passenger seat.

"What's a handler?"

He grinned again. "It's what I am for you. I've got your back if anything happens."

She smiled back. "And who are you?"

He winked. "Call me Bradley."

Before she could ask him anything further, he slid out of the booth and headed for the front door.

Shane appeared back at the table as Bradley pushed the front glass door open.

All right, she'd told Shane about the fibro. They'd started that conversation. And he was clearly as shaken by it as Emma had been. Isabelle realized that she should take Emma's advice here —she and Shane were a lot alike. If Emma thought this spy game would make this trip easier on Shane, Isabelle would sell it. Her acting job over the past few months had been harder than acting like she believed this whole pendant thing.

"Oh my God!" she told Shane. "You just missed it."

"What?" he asked as he slid into the booth.

"This guy was just here," she said, not needing to try to infuse her voice with enthusiasm. The excitement was real. "His name is Bradley and he gave me this package." She held up the tissue-wrapped pendant. "He said I'm supposed to take it to a drop site by midnight. Then he got up and ran out."

Shane just stared at her.

"Shane?"

"What the hell are you talking about?"

She shook the package. "This. He just gave it to me, told me. He's going to send further instructions later. And we have to keep it away from that guy." She pointed out the window at the SUV.

"That makes no sense," Shane said with a frown.

Bradley appeared at the street corner. "There!" Isabelle exclaimed. "That's him."

"Maybe I'll go—"

But before Shane could complete his sentence, the man in the SUV got out and started toward Bradley. Bradley turned and started running down the sidewalk that ran beside the restaurant. The man, dressed in blue jeans, a T-shirt and a cap—like every other citizen and tourist in Mitchell, South Dakota—ran after him.

They thundered past the window and Isabelle turned to Shane. "We should get out of here. We have to get it to the drop site by midnight."

"No!" He was looking at her like she was nuts. "Absolutely not."

"But—" She thought fast. He was right, it was nuts. "I have it now. What am I going to do with it?"

"The guy's a complete stranger, Isabelle. We're not going to do anything with it." Shane shook his head, clearly baffled. "Why would this guy give it to *you*? He must have mistaken you for someone else."

That was a good question for him to ask. Dammit. "To throw the guys chasing him off?" she suggested.

"That doesn't make any sense. These guys could be dangerous."

Isabelle thought fast. "Maybe he knows you're a cop."

Shane frowned, obviously not convinced. "Let's see this thing."

She unwrapped the tissue paper and held up the necklace.

The silver dragon swung from a silver chain. It was about two inches tall and an inch wide with glittering jewels for eyes and a trail of gems running from the top of its head to the tip of the tail that curled up next to its back haunch.

Shane reached out and took the pendant from her fingers. He snapped two photos with his phone, then handed it back to her. "I'm going to send this to Michael. See if he can find anything about it being stolen or how much it's worth or even where it belongs."

She watched him type in a message. "Michael works for the Omaha PD?" That could ruin the whole thing. The police would figure out this was an adventure game and fill Shane in before they really had any fun with it.

He shook his head as he hit send. "Michael Sullivan."

"Nate's son?" Oh, that was different. Maybe.

Shane nodded. "Yeah. He helps me out with research once in a while."

"No kidding." Michael was seventeen and a great kid. Nate had raised him as a single father and they were very close. But Nate was pretty protective. "Does Nate know?"

Shane shrugged. "It's all online research and it's always unofficial. He finds stuff for me that helps fill in holes or that gives me some needed knowledge when I'm going after something. He's a computer and research whiz. He loves it."

Isabelle tipped her head to the side. "That doesn't answer my question. Does Nate know?"

Shane smiled. "Well, *I* haven't told him. I don't know if Michael's shared anything with his dad or not. Not my business."

"It's nothing that could get traced back to him or get him into trouble?"

Shane sighed. "Iz, he plugs stuff into the internet. Period. He's not hacking high-level government sites." Shane frowned slightly. "I don't think."

"Shane," Isabelle started.

He chuckled. "Geez, give me some credit. I wouldn't use the kid if it was somehow going to be bad for him."

"Yeah, okay, I know."

Shane glanced at his phone. "Michael says it's going to take him a little time."

"Okay, well, let's head out. We have to keep this away from Harris until we know more." She started to slide out of the booth.

Shane clamped a hand on her wrist. "Are you crazy?"

"What?"

"We don't know this Bradley guy. He probably stole that thing. If you carry it for him, that makes you an accomplice. We're taking this to the police."

Okay, well that wasn't exactly according to plan.

Their attention was pulled to the window as a figure walked by. It was the man from the SUV. Harris. He stopped just past the window, then turned to look more fully at them. And right at the dragon pendant Isabelle still held in her hand.

The guy was big. And…brawny. That was the best word. He reminded her of a lumberjack in his blue jeans and plaid shirt. He was hairy, wide through the chest, as tall as Shane and only a few pounds lighter. It wasn't all muscle in Harris's case, but there was definitely something intimidating about him. Especially when he frowned, pointed a thick finger at her and mouthed *Don't move.*

Harris started for the front of the restaurant.

"Shit," Shane muttered before he sprang to his feet, tossed money onto the table and yanked on Isabelle's arm. "I'm not in the mood to make a new friend. Let's go."

"Maybe he's…a cop," Isabelle said trying to defuse Shane's panic but not give anything away. She tucked the dragon pendant into her purse as she jogged to keep up with Shane. He dodged around tables, heading for the kitchen and, she assumed, the back door.

"And maybe he's not. I prefer to be the one going to the cops instead of the other way around. If he is, then us showing up at the precinct will be in our favor," Shane said.

Yeah, until they blew the whole thing by telling Shane what was actually going on before the adventure had even gotten started. She wanted this game to happen. This was much better than talking about her fibromyalgia for three hundred more miles. They stepped out of the back door of the restaurant and Shane quickly looked both ways, then headed to the right. The alley was shorter to the left, but that also led in the direction where the SUV was parked.

It also led to where their car was parked.

"Do you know where the station is?" Isabelle asked, wishing she could kick her sandals off. It would make keeping up with Shane easier. He had longer legs and he was in better shape, no doubt about it, and the small, one-inch heel on her shoes wasn't helping her out at all.

"No." They got to the end of the alley and he looked around. "Can you search for directions on your phone while you run?"

"I bought a new lamp the other day while I was on the elliptical." She pulled her phone out with one hand, but had to pull out of Shane's hold so she had both thumbs to hit the buttons. She continued to jog, trusting Shane to keep her from smacking into a tree or lamppost, but typed a response to the last text she'd gotten from Big Time about the mission instead.

We're headed to the police station with the pendant.

She had no idea if they would relay the message to Bradley or if her text would go straight to him or if anything would happen at all, but the typical participant probably didn't call the cops in.

Suddenly Shane grabbed her arm and pulled her through a doorway.

"Hey," she grumbled.

"Let's give him a few minutes to lose track of us," Shane said.

She looked around. They were in a little book and gift shop.

"You don't think he saw us?" She infused her voice with a bit of concern. She wasn't truly worried. Though if Harris was also playing this game and wanting the end prize—and Isabelle wondered what the prize for getting to the drop site first was—he was going to truly be trying to get the necklace from her. She wasn't worried that things would get violent, Surely Big Time wouldn't allow that. But Harris wouldn't let them get away easily.

"Don't know. I guess we'll find out if he comes in here," Shane said dryly, peering through the window.

"Well, even if he does, he wouldn't do something in a public place, would he?" Though she had to admit that there weren't a whole lot of people inside the shop at the moment.

"You never know," Shane said. "I don't like to gamble on stuff like that. This will give us a few minutes to figure out where we're going and maybe throw him off a little. But he's going to know we went inside somewhere when he drives the street and doesn't see us. He'll come looking." Shane ran a hand over the back of his neck. "We need to get rid of that necklace."

She quickly Googled the information he'd asked for before. "Here we go," she said, handing her phone over to him. "The police station is on First and Cherry."

"Okay." Shane looked around. "Now if I knew where we were right now, that might actually be helpful."

Isabelle moved farther into the store. Pretending to be browsing through the display of bookmarks near the front counter, then picking up a miniature porcelain unicorn, she made eye contact with the woman dusting the shelves a few feet away.

"Hello," the woman greeted with a smile. "Anything I can help you with?"

It would seem pretty suspicious to ask her to point them to the police station. "I was wondering if you have a book club of any kind that meets here?" Isabelle asked instead.

The woman's smile brightened. "We do. Our romance book

club meets the second Tuesday and our mystery club meets the third Wednesday of every month." Predictably, she bustled toward the front counter and produced a flyer, handing it to Isabelle.

"Are you interested in the romance or the mystery group, dear?" the woman asked.

Isabelle glanced at Shane who was still standing near the front door, pretending to read the backs of the books on display on the first table, while actually watching the street.

It gave her a thrill to watch him in police-mode. *Thank you, Emma.* Seeing Shane get all official and determined was sexy.

"Romance," she answered. "Definitely romance."

She thanked the woman for the information and headed back for Shane, typing the bookstore's address from the flyer into her phone and calling up a map of Mitchell.

"We're about twelve blocks from the station," she told him, handing him the phone.

He glanced at the flyer in her hand and grinned. "Nicely done."

She shrugged, pleased that she'd been resourceful.

He studied the map. "We'll have to get back to the car. I haven't seen him drive by, so we might be able to sneak back the way we came."

Another little shiver went through her and she admitted that it was adrenaline.

She looked up at Shane. He didn't seem entertained exactly, but he didn't seem overly concerned either. So far so good.

But she did wonder if Emma had considered the fact that Shane was a cop. He wasn't going to be okay with guys chasing them for long.

All they had to do was get the pendant to the cops twelve blocks away. That would make Shane feel better. Maybe it wasn't according to the game plan, but the Big Time guys were going to have to get more creative in that case. Or call Emma with a refund.

"Okay, let's go," she said.

"Let's see if there's a back entrance." Shane took her hand again and they wandered farther into the store, pretending to browse as they went.

They stopped at the taller bookshelves, looking over the selection while moving surreptitiously toward the rear of the store.

Isabelle found herself in a book section she was fairly familiar with. Books on spicing up a couple's sex life. She'd read a few of the ones on display, but one caught her interest and she pulled it from the shelf, flipping to the table of contents, then paging through to chapter four.

"Hey, is it true that your sleep is often disturbed?" Shane asked, coming around the corner from the next aisle over.

She looked up from the chapter on various sexual positions for the couch. "What are you talking about?"

Shane's eyes were on the book he held as he came toward her. "It says here that sleep is often disturbed in people with fibromyalgia. Did you know that chocolate and bananas can both help with mood and sleep?"

She stared at him. "What are you reading?"

He held the book up. "*Living and Loving with Fibromyalgia.*"

"You're reading about fibro?"

"Well..." He looked back down at the book then up at her. "Yeah."

She felt tears sting her eyes. When he'd left the table at the restaurant, he hadn't been happy. Then everything with the necklace had happened and they hadn't picked that conversation back up.

"Is that okay?" he asked, looking concerned.

"Well, yeah," she said, echoing his words to her. Then she sniffed.

She'd hidden it from him for so long and had worried about how he'd react and now that he knew and he was trying to learn about it and what it really meant in her life—it made her feel...

She stepped close, sandwiching the two books they held between them. "Thank you," she whispered, then kissed him.

Shane's hand came up to cup the back of her head and she gripped the sleeve of his shirt, but the books kept them from getting too close. That didn't seem to bother Shane though. He kissed her like only he could. When he kissed her, it was like everything else he did—he put everything into it. He didn't need his whole body. His mouth was enough to make her feel protected and cherished and hot and needy all at the same time.

They broke apart several moments later.

"Thank you," she said again softly, coming down off her tiptoes.

His hand lingered against her hair, stroking over the back of her head. "We have a lot more talking to do."

For some reason, that made her stomach flip with nerves. She managed to nod. Because yes, of course, they needed to talk more.

She'd wanted him to say he loved her. Or that it would all be okay. Or that he was glad he knew, but that it didn't change anything.

But it did change things.

She hadn't been managing her symptoms as strictly as she should be. She needed to take care of herself now that she knew what was going on. She couldn't keep up the pace she'd been trying for and still be a good employee, sister, daughter and girlfriend. They were both going to have to make some changes if this was going to work.

She didn't know if Shane was willing. She didn't know if Shane knew if he was willing. He didn't have all the information he needed to make that decision.

She forced a smile and tapped her finger against the book he still held. "This is sweet of you."

He didn't reply to that. Instead, he moved past her, pulling his wallet from his back pocket. She re-shelved the book about sex positions for various rooms of the house. Vanilla. That was what they needed to try for a while.

She watched him pay the woman for the book, then come back to her.

"We better see if we can get out of here," he said, taking her hand again.

"I'm right with you," she said, pressing against his side.

She needed to feel him right now. She wanted his heat and strength against her, not because of the guy who was outside looking for them, but because of the silent enemy trying to pull them apart from within.

She could outrun the guy. She couldn't outrun the fibro.

The feeling of frustration and injustice that she'd only recently acknowledged started to well up, but she squelched it as they got to the back door without being noticed.

"Okay, we're going through the door, to the left, to the end of the block. Stick with me," Shane instructed.

"Definitely."

Shane took a deep breath, then twisted the doorknob and pushed the door open.

Shane stepped out first, dropped her hand, and immediately swung left and started jogging. Isabelle was right behind him but had taken only two steps when she felt a hard yank and was swung around by the hand on her purse handle. It was Harris.

"I want the pendant."

Damn. He'd found them.

"Shane!" she yelled.

Harris yanked again on her purse. She felt it slip off her arm, and made a grab for it a second too late. When he tucked it against his stomach and spun away from her, she felt her mouth drop open. Wait a second—he was really stealing her purse? Taken off guard by the unexpected move, Isabelle was slow to respond when he took off down the alley.

She heard the pounding of Shane's feet as he came up behind her.

"Dammit!" he swore. He spun her to face him. "Are you okay?"

She nodded. "Yeah."

"Fuck." Shane looked down the alley. "I'm going after him. Stay here. Go back inside. Wait for me."

She nodded and he wrenched the door to the bookstore open and pushed her inside.

"I'll be right back."

The door shut between them before Isabelle thought to say anything. Like, *Don't hurt him.* Shane was a cop. Who knew what he might do if he thought he was in pursuit of a true criminal?

She also hoped they didn't scuff up her new purse.

She wasn't sure how long she stood there wondering if she should be doing something else—and wondering what else that might be—but she was startled when the door suddenly opened again.

Shane was talking to her, handing her purse to her, and then pulling her up against his chest.

Hey, if this was real, she would have most definitely launched herself at him, relieved he was back in one piece. And damn, having Shane kick into protective-cop-mode was hot. Besides, the whole idea here was to make sure Shane had fun on this trip too, right? She knew a few things he thought were a lot of fun.

She put her arms around his neck and he caught her with his hands under her butt as she wrapped her legs around him.

They kissed hot and hungry. She didn't need much of an excuse to kiss him like she'd thought she'd never see him again. She ran both hands up into his hair and his fingers gripped her butt as he turned and pressed her against the door.

She felt the buttons on the front of her shirt give, then he filled his hand with her right breast.

She bucked against him, pressing closer, her heels digging into his ass.

"Ahem."

Isabelle heard the store owner clear her throat but she couldn't quite bring herself to let go of Shane. He, on the other hand, pulled back slightly, searching her eyes.

"Wow," he said simply.

"And then some." Their chemistry was wow-worthy even on a typical day. This was *not* a typical day.

"Sorry," Isabelle said to the shop owner, who was hovering near the doorway leading to the rest of the shop. She looked like she was half fascinated by their display and considering calling their romance book club down here for an impromptu meeting, and half concerned they were going to ramp the meeting up from romance to erotica and shock the little ladies of Mitchell, South Dakota. "We were looking for the way out."

The woman's eyes widened.

"Oh, here it is," Shane said, knocking on the door he had Isabelle pressed against. "Don't know how I missed that."

The woman opened her mouth, then shut it again quickly, turned and left them alone.

Isabelle giggled as Shane loosened his grip and let her slide to the floor.

"So what was this about?" he asked.

"Adrenaline, I guess," Isabelle said. And a great excuse to get his big, strong body against hers. It was kind of dumb and very simple. She lifted a shoulder. "The hero thing does it for me. Even more when I'm the one you're jumping in to save."

He grinned. "I chase bad guys every day. Maybe I need to take you to work with me once in a while." He leaned in. "'Cause the damsel in distress thing does it for *me*."

She lifted an eyebrow as she adjusted her bra and re-buttoned. "Yeah, I noticed what it was doing to you."

Shane pulled in a deep breath and stepped back from her. "Yeah." He cleared his throat. "When I turned back to see that he had a hold of you I swear to God my blood froze…" He trailed off, seeming at a loss for words. Then he reached out, cupped the back of her neck, pulled her close and kissed her again.

This time, though, it was sweet. So sweet.

Shane Kelley didn't do sweet very often, but when he did it was…devastating.

When he lifted his head a few moments later, Isabelle blinked against the sudden, unexpected moisture in her eyes. She should tell him the truth. It was a game, he had nothing to worry about, there was no danger. But damn, the fact that she might get a few more of *those* kisses made her hesitate.

He just watched her, breathing a little harder than he had been before, even after the hot and heavy kiss against the door.

Isabelle chalked that up in the win column. Breaking up wasn't going to be easy for him either. She knew he cared about her, of course, but the proof was very, very nice.

"How'd you get it back?" she asked, picking her purse up off the floor where she'd dropped it to climb all over him.

"He dropped it," Shane said. "I found it about a block away."

"He got away with the pendant?" she asked, knowing the answer. Dammit. Now what? Was she supposed to try to find him and get it back or did Big Time have a contingency plan for if she screwed up?

"I guess. I stopped chasing him once I saw your purse. I rummaged in your bag and didn't find it, so I assume he took it. But I don't really care. I'd rather not be mixed up in this anyway."

Isabelle felt a twist of disappointment at his words. Shane wasn't having *any* fun?

As they walked back to the car, Isabelle kept replaying all the events as she dug in her purse to be sure nothing had fallen out. Her fingers slipped into the hole in the lining of the purse and she sighed. Dammit, she'd only had this purse for a month.

Her finger connected with something in the bottom of the bag. She frowned. That didn't feel familiar; it was hard, but covered in cloth. She tried to get her fingers around it, but quickly realized that whatever it was had slipped through that hole. "Shane, hang on a second."

She stopped and shook the purse, her fingers probing to find the object.

Sure enough, a moment later she withdrew the pendant.

She held it up to him. "I guess he missed it."

"Dammit," was Shane's response.

"Yeah. Hidden compartment I didn't even know about."

"Well, I guess we're making a stop at the police station after all."

They headed for the car, picking up their pace. Shane pulled his phone out as they jogged, pushing a speed-dial number. A moment later he said, "Michael, it's me. Need you to run a license plate." He rattled off a number, then hung up.

"That was the SUV's plate?" she asked.

"Yeah. Let's see if we can figure out who these guys are."

"Michael runs license plates for you too?"

"I have this gut feeling that there's something going on here. I like to get as much information as I can, however I can."

Of course he had a gut feeling. He was a fantastic cop. "Michael's the guy you go to for gut feelings?"

"Something like that." Shane grinned. "He eats this stuff up. And he's good."

Maybe she could call Michael and bribe him with pizza to keep information from Shane. A great cop and a computer genius could surely figure a game like this out without even breaking a sweat. Looked like Shane was going to find out about the whole thing sooner rather than later.

They made it back to Isabelle's car without incident and found the police station without effort.

They had to park a half block away and they walked hand in hand toward the building. Suddenly, a woman dressed in a business suit and carrying a briefcase, with a phone to her ear, came around the corner of the building, running directly into Shane. Running into Shane Kelley affected most people—football players and businesswomen alike—by setting them back a few feet. At least. The woman stumbled on her heels, her phone flying. Shane caught her by her elbows, keeping her rump from hitting the sidewalk. Her phone was not as fortunate. The outer case and the battery flew in two different directions.

"Dammit, I'm sorry," Shane apologized, making sure she was balanced.

"It's okay, you just startled me," the woman said, a little breathless, splaying her hand over her generous cleavage. "I should have been paying more attention."

"Me too," Shane said, squatting to the ground to gather the phone pieces.

Someone grabbed her arm as Shane was trying to fit the battery back into the phone.

She spun to face Bradley.

"Give me the pendant," he whispered. "You can't take it in to the cops. It's a ton of paperwork to get it back."

She nodded and handed it over. "Now what?"

"You'll see." He winked again and slipped behind a tree and out of sight.

Isabelle turned back to find the woman's hand on Shane's arm, standing way too close and smiling up at him like he was Superman rather than the guy who'd about knocked her on her ass.

Seriously?

"Thank you so much," the woman said. "The phone is working better now than it was before."

Isabelle rolled her eyes.

"Sure thing. I'm sorry again about plowing into you."

Isabelle knew that he didn't mean it sexually, but damned if her brain didn't go there. She stomped forward and hooked her arm through his—the one the other woman wasn't draped all over. "Shane, sweetie, don't we need to be going?"

He looked at her. "Yep, that's right. We've got some business. Nice to have met you."

"Oh, you too," the woman purred as she stepped aside so they could pass.

They got a few feet away and Isabelle asked, "What color was her suit?"

"Uh, blue."

"Red. Bright red. Very hard to miss."

He chuckled. "Right, red."

"Uh-huh. Well, while you were being so helpful, I got rid of the pendant."

Shane stopped. "What?"

"Bradley showed up. Said we couldn't take it to the cops."

Shane crossed his arms. "And you just let him take it?"

"He's the one who gave it to me. As far as I know, it's his. And you said you didn't want to be involved anyway."

Shane sighed. "How did he know we were going to the cops?"

Right. Good question. "Uh, maybe he's been following us. Making sure we're following his instructions. Which we weren't," she reminded him.

"If he's going to be following us all the way to the drop site, why not just take it himself?"

Uh, huh. It didn't make any sense. She got that. But most people playing the game *knew* it was a game and were willing to let a few details slide here and there.

Her mind spun with ideas. "Maybe there are other people following him too. We're the...mules." She thought that was the right term.

One corner of Shane's mouth twitched. Was that an almost-smile?

"What's so important about this pendant anyway?" he asked.

The twinkle in his eye allowed her to let her imagination run. "Maybe it's got magical healing powers. Or maybe it's the key to finding a lost civilization."

"And a city of gold?" he asked, the frown he'd been wearing since the Corn Palace completely gone. "You've watched *National Treasure* too many times."

She nodded. "Love those movies." She stepped in closer to

him, her hand on his arm. "Or maybe it brings true and lasting love to anyone who owns it." She paused. "That's worth fighting for, I think."

He stared into her eyes. "Yeah, I'd drive across the great state of South Dakota for that."

Her heart thumped and she knew that the shot of adrenaline coursing through her now had nothing to do with the pendant.

Someone else came around the corner and nearly bumped into them. This time the guy just sidestepped and glared at them. He was clearly not part of the game.

"Bradley's going to take it from here?" Shane asked, obviously snapped out of the moment they'd had going. "He'll leave you alone now?"

She doubted it. "He didn't say."

Shane toward the front doors of the police station. "We should still report Harris trying to steal your purse."

"But I have it back," she said quickly. "Nothing was taken. They have more important things to worry about, don't they?"

Ten minutes later, they were sitting in the police station across from an officer anyway.

"You're reporting that your purse was stolen, but you have it back and nothing's missing?" Officer Timmins asked.

"Right."

"We'll keep a look out for him," the cop said simply. They'd given a description of Harris. Shane had even given them the license plate number on the SUV.

Isabelle assumed that Big Time could easily clear anything up if Harris and his handler were pulled over.

But Shane frowned and leaned in. They'd already established that he was a fellow officer of the law in Omaha, but that didn't mean that the guys in Mitchell were any more helpful. Or maybe it did. Maybe they would have been less helpful with an average Joe. Though it was hard to believe that was possible. The guy had stopped even taking notes about three minutes into their story.

"Look, Greg," Shane said, using the man's first name. "Two strange men have approached Isabelle in this town in the past couple of hours. One gave her a pendant that could be stolen property for all we know. The other stole her purse."

"And she got it back."

"You don't care about these men harassing female tourists?"

"Have they hurt you, ma'am?" the cop asked Isabelle.

"No."

"Did any of them threaten to hurt you?"

She frowned. "No."

"And you have all of your belongings?"

"Yes."

He looked back at Shane. "I'm not sure what else you want me to do here. We'll keep a look out for this guy and we'll pick him up if we see him or the SUV."

"What about this mysterious pendant?" Shane asked. "What if it's stolen?"

Shane had shared the photo on his phone with the cops when they'd first told them about it.

Greg turned his computer monitor so they could see it. "It hasn't been stolen."

The screen showed a photo of a pendant that looked identical to the one Bradley had given her. The owner was a Mr. Henry Licthberg in Philadelphia. Clearly Big Time had made a replica of a real pendant. There was no way she was going to be able to keep Shane believing this was all real.

"If it belongs in Philadelphia, what are all these guys in South Dakota doing with it?" Shane asked.

"Maybe they bought it. Maybe he gave it to them. Maybe the one you saw was a knock-off," Greg said. "Whatever the case, there's nothing going on here that I can do much about. No one's reported the pendant stolen. If the guys bother you again, give me a call."

As they walked down the hallway of the station to the front doors, Isabelle could feel the frustration coming off of Shane. "I can't believe Bradley came up to you again and I was *right there*," Shane said. He ran a hand over the back of his neck, his telltale sign of agitation. "This guy either has a death-wish or the IQ of a rock."

Isabelle felt a flicker of guilt. He was truly worried—she felt a little bad about deceiving him. But dang, part of her really wanted to bask in his protectiveness. Maybe she could play up the damsel in distress thing even more next time.

"I'll bet he and the woman were working together," Isabelle said. "She ran right into you and then did the whole 'oh, you're so big and strong' number. She didn't even squeak when he came up to me and she *had* to have seen it."

Shane gave her a little grin. "I *am* so big and strong," he said.

She elbowed him. "But they could have set it up."

"Yep, that would make some sense. And it would be about the only thing about *any* of this to make sense. How the hell did you get involved in this?"

She simply shrugged. She agreed that some of the dots weren't easy to connect—especially from Shane's perspective—and her made-up story about the pendant's healing powers or ties to a long-forgotten society clearly hadn't intrigued Shane enough.

What they needed to sell this was a great backstory on the pendant. Yes, she'd put that on her comment card to Big Time when this was over. Maybe it could be tied to an old poker game in the twenties. Maybe a mobster's girlfriend had put it in to cover his bet but when he lost she'd—

"I guess we can head out of town now," Shane said, pulling her out of her daydreaming. "We did what we could by reporting it. We don't have anything those guys want anymore so we can assume they'll leave us alone."

Isabelle focused on the now rather than the images she'd had going of a girl in a flapper dress, holding one of those long cigarettes between her fingers and exclaiming that if the guy really loved her, he'd do anything to get the pendant back...

"Iz?" Shane interrupted the mini-movie in her head again.

"Yeah?"

"Let's get out of town before Bradley finds you again."

Right. The leaving-them-alone-thing probably wasn't going to happen. Unless Emma had paid for the economy package and that one "mission" was all they were going to get. When she'd asked Bradley what was next he'd said *you'll see*. That didn't sound like it was over. But she had to go along with Shane. Unless she could figure out a way to stay in Mitchell just a little longer…

"We'll keep a look out," Shane reassured her, clearly mistaking her frown of concentration for one of worry. "And I'm still waiting to hear from Michael on that pendant. Maybe there's more to the story than what Greg got, but I don't know what it would be."

Reluctantly, she drove him back to the Corn Palace to claim his motorcycle, but as he started to open the door, she touched his arm. He turned back.

"Let's leave your bike here. Conner and Ryan can come and pick it up." Her sister's boyfriend would love a chance to ride Shane's bike, she was sure. "You can ride with me." She wanted him with her. That was the point of the game, the point of the *trip* since he'd tagged along. All of his protectiveness, his worry, his attention was like a warm blanket around her and now that he was getting out of the car, she felt a definite chill. It wasn't fear of being alone or fear of Bradley. But the little bit of the game they'd played had pulled her and Shane closer somehow. They'd teamed up and worked toward a common mission. With the threat of the fibro pulling them apart, she didn't want to lose that.

Shane didn't respond for several seconds. Then he said, "I better take it."

Her heart dropped and the chill flooded in. The reason for riding separately was in case of a bad outcome once they got to the cabin. Clearly that was still a risk in his mind.

And it should be in hers too. Nothing had truly changed with him knowing about her fibro. The issues between them had just become clearer.

She pulled her hand back. "Yeah. Sure. You're right."

"I'll be right behind you."

She gave him a smile she hoped was convincing. "Okay."

If it wasn't convincing, he gave no indication. He nodded and climbed out.

Biting her bottom lip, she checked her phone. She had a message. Her heart tripped. Maybe it was further instructions. She was surprised by how much she wanted that to be true. She typed in her code and listened as she waited for Shane to start his bike. Once it revved to life, she put the car into drive and pulled out onto the street. The message was a reminder about a dental appointment the next week and she could admit that she was disappointed. She tucked her phone into the tray between the bucket seats and the package lying on the floor of the passenger side caught her eye.

The book about fibromyalgia Shane had bought.

Well, that had to mean something. He was trying to learn. He wasn't running away screaming.

Yet.

CHAPTER
SIX

SHANE FOLLOWED Isabelle as she drove through Mitchell on her way back to the highway.

This was good. Riding by himself, with time and space to think, was good.

They had a lot of talking to do and he was eager in some ways to get the conversation started. He wanted to know that they could work this out, and to be sure about that, he needed to understand a lot more about what was going on with her.

But he felt like an asshole thinking like that because it also meant that there was a chance they wouldn't work it out.

So he needed some space.

He felt his phone vibrate in his pocket and was glad they were pulling up to a red light. He stopped right behind Isabelle and pulled the phone out, finding a message from Michael.

Michael confirmed all of the information that Greg had given them at the police station, but there was something more. He could always count on the kid to dig. He knew Michael was interested in becoming a cop and working his way up to detective. He also knew he hadn't told his dad.

Michael came from a long line of prominent and highly successful physicians. There was a lot of money in his background along with prestige and high expectations. Shane liked Nate. He was a good guy with a great sense of humor and he'd clearly done a great job raising his son alone. But he definitely pushed Michael, and Shane knew that he'd mentioned medical school, more than once, as part of Michael's future.

But he'd make a hell of a detective.

Shane read the message quickly. There was, indeed, a similar pendant owned by a guy in Philadelphia that had not been reported stolen. In fact, it was on display as part of an antique jewelry collection at an art museum in Boston. Notably, that pendant had emeralds for eyes. The photo Shane had sent Michael showed blue gems for eyes. And the kid had found six of them with the blue eyes for sale on eBay.

The one Isabelle had been given wasn't real.

That was good.

But even more confusing. Why did these guys want to get some knock-off pendant to a drop-off site in western South Dakota? The thing was too tiny to have any kind of hidden compartment. It was worth, according to the current high bid on eBay, thirty-two dollars and sixty five cents. It didn't have any historical significance. If it had any sentimental value to the guys involved, they could get a replacement on eBay tonight.

The whole thing made absolutely no sense.

The light turned green and Shane followed Isabelle for two blocks, but then she turned down a side street three blocks before she was supposed to.

Shane frowned and followed. And realized that there was someone in the car with her. Someone had jumped in the car at the red light while he had been distracted by Michael's text?

What the *hell* was going on?

He sped up, staying right behind her now. Close enough that if she touched the brakes, his nose was going to be up close and personal with her back window.

Yes, there was a man sitting in the passenger seat, gesturing with his hands as he talked. They turned the next corner, then the next. Finally they came to a stop sign at the intersection of a quiet residential area. The passenger door opened and Bradley jumped out. He glanced at Shane then took off running in the opposite direction.

Yeah, he'd better fucking run.

Shane jumped off his bike before the engine had even quieted. He sprinted to Isabelle's car. "Are you okay?"

She nodded.

"You sure?"

She looked…like she was fighting a smile.

"I'm fine," she told him. She lifted her hand. The dragon pendant swung from her fingers. "But we're not done with this yet."

Shane smacked the top of the car with his hand and looked in the direction Bradley had run. Chase him or not? Who the hell knew what might happen with Isabelle if he left her alone here. No doubt Harris was still somewhere in Mitchell And he'd be looking for the pendant.

Probably.

Fuck. He didn't know. His phone vibrated again and he yanked it from his pocket. It was Michael.

"What?" he barked.

"Found something on the SUV you might want," Michael said.

Shane felt his heart clench. "Yeah?"

Shane paced away from the car. He didn't want to rile Isabelle up. At least until he knew what was going on. He motioned for her to pull the car around the corner and park at the curb.

"Well, it's weird."

"Jesus, Michael, *what*?"

"The SUV is registered to a company called Big Time."

"What's Big Time?"

"Well…it's weird."

Shane stomped back to his bike, shifted it into neutral and began pushing it toward where Isabelle was now parked. "I'm losing patience here."

"Okay, okay. They stage…like elaborate parties and stuff."

Shane stopped. "Parties? What are you talking about?"

"They make their money putting together these weekend parties for grownups. For instance, there's one here where you get to use this big old house they have. You invite a bunch of people over for the weekend, they cater a big dinner and then at some point, there's a dead body in the middle of everything and the rest of the weekend people have to try to figure out who did it. Stuff like that."

Shane ran a hand over the back of his neck. "What the hell does that have to do with all of this?"

"I'm thinking…it's very possible that you're in the middle of one of their games."

Michael's words made Shane freeze. That actually made all kinds of sense.

Shane looked to where Isabelle had climbed out of the car, clearly trying to figure out what *he* was doing.

She could have easily set all of this up. She had to have known he was going to show up and accompany her to the Black Hills whether she told him what time she was leaving or not. She had already been concerned about it being boring for Shane so she could have come up with this as a way of making this a fun, memorable week.

So they were in the middle of a big game. Did that make sense?

More than anything else. Any other explanation was…there wasn't really another explanation.

"Is there any way of finding out if Big Time was hired for something in South Dakota this week?"

He heard clicking on Michael's end. "Not easily. It's a very secure site. Do you have any reason to maybe serve a warrant and see what's going on?"

Shane sighed again. "No."

"Well, let me know what I can do."

"Will do. Thanks."

"And Shane?"

"Yeah?"

"Have fun."

Shane could hear the grin in Michael's voice. The kid thought a bunch of adults running around playing an elaborate game of keep away sounded fun?

Shane thought about that.

Okay, maybe it did.

He hung up and finished pushing his bike up to Isabelle's car.

She was certainly looking excited and happy. She didn't look scared or nervous about the men chasing after them. That alone should have tipped him off. And she was clearly enjoying herself. Maybe it was a game where the company set it up but didn't give even the host or hostess hints or clues. That way they could play along with a little intrigue too.

Or maybe she knew everything that was going to happen and she was enjoying this for him.

Either way, it was sweet of her to do this.

It didn't give them the quiet, relaxing experience she'd said she needed. Now that he knew about the fibromyalgia it seemed clear that what they needed was a chance to talk and figure out what life was going to look like with that consideration.

But that didn't mean they couldn't have some fun too.

He wasn't going to ruin this by telling her he knew what was going on. He'd go along, enjoy it, have some fun and they'd still figure everything else out. Later. Probably.

"Here's the deal," he said to her. "I don't know what's going on, but as long as you have that necklace, I'm right by your side." He could so play this game. Using it as a reason to stay close and get as many of those jump-into-his-arms-legs-around-his-waist kisses as possible was a good enough reason by itself.

Her smile was bright. "You're riding with me then?"

She'd wanted him to before. Then he'd said no. The next thing he knew Bradley was in her car and she had the pendant again. Yeah, that wasn't suspicious at all.

He shook his head. She really was a lot of work. But this was…kind of cool.

Crazy as it sounded, *this* felt more comfortable, more normal, than the serious conversations they were facing. Being chased by fake bad guys and protecting a not-so-precious-or-mysterious pendant was more his comfort zone than reading about a disease he'd barely heard of and that was going to change his life—one way or another.

He'd always been good at taking care of people, but he did it by making them laugh, giving them a good time, helping them forget about the bad stuff. With Iz, he was going to need to focus on the bad stuff. He was going to have to take it all in, learn what he could, and try to make things work.

He'd do the hard stuff, but dammit, he'd enjoy this reprieve along the way.

"What did Bradley say when he gave that back to you?" he asked.

"That we have to get it to this drop site in the Black Hills." She handed him a piece of paper with driving directions on it.

Shane looked up at her. "Why?"

"Because…" She clearly didn't know how to answer that. She didn't want to say *Because it's a big game and that's how we win.*

He fought his smile. "Maybe we'll figure it out when we get there."

She smiled, obviously relieved he was dropping it. "Okay, so let's go before Harris finds us."

He looked at the woman before him. He was in love with her. And she was apparently having a great time. Oh, yeah. He could play the game.

"Yep, we better get going," he said, pushing off from the car and clapping his hands.

"You're riding with me now, right?"

He remembered the feeling of fear when he'd seen Bradley in the car with her. Even knowing that this was all fake, it still made him a little sick to think that she'd been right there in front of him, but out of reach for him to protect. "Damn, right," he told her sincerely.

He felt a stirring in his gut as he slid into the passenger seat. That familiar, this-is-gonna-be-a-good-time instinct.

It took half an hour to find a place to store Shane's motorcycle for the week, but he seemed happy about the arrangement as they got into Isabelle's car, finally ready to leave Mitchell.

"You sure you don't want to drive?" she asked, buckling her seatbelt.

He held up the book about fibromyalgia. "I have some important reading to do."

As it had at the bookstore, his interest and willingness to learn choked her up. "Okay."

"Unless you need me to drive for a while?" he asked. "I mean, it's been a pretty stressful day so far."

He was sincere, so she didn't snap at him that she was fine. She gave him a smile. "No, I'm good." In fact, she felt great. She'd had a lot of fun so far. Which was probably strange, but it had been like a rollercoaster ride and she was still feeling the effects of the adrenaline.

"But you'll tell me if you need a break?" he asked.

She glanced at him. She loved him like crazy. But if he was going to start hounding her about stuff now that he knew she had a few challenges, she was going to *go* crazy. "Shane, this isn't going to work if you're constantly worrying and bugging me."

He sat back in his seat and nodded. "Okay, you're right."

"I promise to tell you if I need a break." She would try anyway. She wasn't good at asking for help. She pushed. She knew that. Especially with him. But she also knew that she was going to have to get better about taking care of herself.

"Okay." He settled further into the seat and opened the book without another word.

Surprised, but grateful, she pulled onto the main highway out of town and headed west.

CHAPTER
SEVEN

HE READ and she drove for about fifteen minutes before he said, "Emma doesn't know?"

She glanced over. "What?"

"That you climbed into bed for two days in a hotel after that music festival?"

Oh, that. Isabelle was close to her sisters. There were no secrets. Until a few months ago. When she'd started feeling bad, she started with small lies, the ones about needing to work late, for instance. And even now, with it all out on the table, she still kept things from them sometimes. Especially Emma. Emma knew that she got sore and tired and that she needed a night off here and there. She knew about the knitting. She knew about the medications. But she didn't know that Isabelle occasionally hid away. It would have hurt her sister and worried her even more that Isabelle felt the need to get away from her sometimes.

"I haven't told anyone about that stuff but you," she finally confessed to Shane. "I'm trying to figure it all out myself."

"Does Conner know about any of it?"

She glanced at him sharply. "No. And I've told the girls that they're not allowed to tell him. Or my mom."

She wanted to have a better handle on things before she told them. She wanted to know exactly what worked for her and what didn't so she could tell them how it was going to affect… everything. She didn't want them asking a bunch of questions she couldn't answer. That would do nothing to reassure them and would frustrate her.

He flipped a page. "How many books have you read?"

"Books?"

He held up the one in his lap. "Books. About fibromyalgia."

She pretended to be interested in the rearview mirror and changing lanes. "I have five books that my doctor recommended."

"Five. Wow."

She shifted uncomfortably in her seat. Okay, things were supposed to be changing. She needed to start being honest with the people around her as well as with herself.

"But I haven't read more than a chapter or two," she confessed.

"That's it?"

"I've read the brochures the doctor gave me and I've been on a few websites," she said. "And I went to the support group meeting a couple of times."

She didn't really want to read any books about it. She would. Eventually. This week, once she got to the cabin, if things went according to plan. But she'd rather read books about how to excite her man in the bedroom, how to excite her man outside of the bedroom, and how to knit gloves. Reading a book about fibromyalgia would make it way more official and way harder to ignore the things she *should* be doing that she didn't want to do.

She glanced at the book Shane held.

And overwhelming.

The thing was a good two inches thick. That was a lot of information to absorb.

She thought maybe she'd be better with little bits and pieces.

"Support group?" he asked. "You're going to a support group?"

She nodded. "It's a group that my doctor recommended. It's led by a psychologist who specializes in helping people with chronic conditions."

"So you've been sitting around telling strangers all about your condition and issues for the past few months but haven't bothered to mention it to your brother?"

That was his cop voice. He used it with her from time to time, but it rarely worked.

"Or you," she filled in, looking over at him. "That's what you're really upset about—that I didn't tell *you.*"

"Damn right I am," he said.

"Why?" she wanted to know. "Why would you want to hear all this depressing and frustrating crap? I can't do all the things I want to, Shane. I can't load up on sugar and caffeine—two of my favorite food groups—I can't wear four-inch stiletto boots, and I can't stay up until three a.m. rocking your world in every position I can imagine without feeling the effects for days after. And not in a good way," she snapped. "Why would you want to hear all of that?"

He sat glowering at the road in front of the car.

"Yeah. You don't want to. You don't want to hear 'I can't' or 'I hurt' or 'I'm pissed' or 'I'm going crazy'," she said, her tone—and chest—still tight. She didn't want to lay all of this on him. She really didn't. This was exactly why they probably shouldn't come home from this trip as a couple.

They didn't speak for nearly two minutes.

But just when she thought he was going to drop it, he said, "I did yoga at Emma's place last night."

That wasn't what she'd been expecting at all. She waited to see if he was going to add to that.

"And there's a chapter in here about acupressure and massage for at home."

She glanced over. He was still staring out the windshield.

"And Ryan knows a lot about herbs and vitamins and other stuff for improving your diet and getting off sugar. Your brother's been trying it and has been nagging the rest of us on the team about it."

As the quarterback for the Hawks, Conner had more or less fallen into the role of team captain. He was always nagging them about something.

Shane didn't say anything more so she said, "And?"

He looked over at her. "I'm just saying that yoga isn't so bad, I'm willing to try it again. And I can use these massage techniques on you if you want. And I need to eat better too. I could definitely cut back on the beer. And whiskey."

She had to glance back at the road but she wanted to stare at him. She didn't know what to say exactly. The idea of trying to cut down on the caffeine and alcohol had seemed impossible if she was going to keep trying to hang with Emma and Shane. But if he was willing to cut back too, it would be so much easier. And what woman would say no to Shane Kelley offering a personal massage?

"You want to try some of this? With me?" she asked.

He shrugged. "Why not? It's not like yoga and eating well are a *bad* idea for anyone."

"That's...sweet." He may not be quite as willing once he was trying to survive on green tea in the morning instead of coffee, but at the moment it was very nice.

"You can't keep doing things you've always done," he said.

She nodded. "Right."

"And I can't keep doing them if you're not doing them."

She breathed a heavy sigh. "Well, there's the problem. And why I haven't told you before this. I don't want you to change your life for me, Shane. That isn't fair."

He shifted on the seat. "But isn't that what you do? I mean, you've already changed my life. I'm sleeping with one woman now. I'm not asking anybody else to dance. I'm hanging out with your brother in spite of the fact that he wants to kick my ass more often than not. Those are all things I wouldn't be doing if I didn't love you."

She couldn't help but smile at all of that. It was all true, she supposed.

"But you still get to be out and dance and drink and have fun," she pointed out. She wanted it to be as easy as him going to yoga and eating more salads with her, but those were small things. Shane was still Shane. He'd always be Shane. Even if he drank green tea in the mornings, he'd still need the big party, the fun, the noise. "When I cut back on that stuff, suddenly you'll be at the bar at midnight without me. Then you *will* be asking other girls to dance."

Which she also hated. It wasn't just the idea of being without him. It was him being without her. She didn't think he would cheat, but if he broke up with her and *then* slept with someone else, it wouldn't be cheating. And it would still hurt like hell.

She could say that he could go out without her and have fun while she stayed home and knitted and went to bed early. Of course. They weren't joined at the hip. They didn't have to be together twenty-four-seven.

But Shane would always be jetting off to another big party somewhere and there would always be another woman willing and ready to go with him. Eventually, it would hit him that he didn't want to sleep in that Vegas hotel room by himself...and he'd find someone who loved Vegas hotel rooms.

"I don't want to dance with anyone else," he finally said softly.

"I don't want you to, either," she said honestly. "But I don't want you to give up dancing." She meant both things equally, which was what was making her nuts.

They didn't say anything else. Shane read several pages. Isabelle tried to concentrate on the song on the radio.

"We should probably have sex in a hot tub," he said in the middle of a Nickelback song.

She looked over at him. "Okay."

He actually grinned. "You're supposed to ask why."

She shrugged. "Hot tub. Sex with you. Why would I question that?"

He chuckled and she felt some of the tension that had been building ease from her shoulders.

"It says here that moist heat can help with your muscle pain and that some sexual positions can be difficult because of stiffness. Having you on top is supposed to help because you can control the motion and the depth of penetration."

Isabelle felt a little moist heat already at his words. She wiggled in the seat and cleared her throat.

"I figure we can combine all of that to make things better," Shane concluded.

"Well, I think that's a hell of an idea," she said.

He closed the book and turned slightly in his seat. "This is bugging the shit out of me."

She looked over at him. "What is?"

"The sex and you being in pain."

She looked back to the road, then back to him. "Do I act like I'm in pain?"

He frowned. "No. But you also act like Dr. Fitzerman tells hilarious jokes."

Okay, he had her there. Herb Fitzerman, the gastroenterologist Shane had met at her company's Christmas party, was definitely *not* funny. But when he chatted with Isabelle he always left thinking he was clever and witty. And she always left with new sales.

"But we've been together so much," she said. "We've been so close and so…everything. Don't you think you would know if something was painful or hard for me?"

She'd been sore after sex with him once in a while. The wilder they got, the more she felt it. Certainly some of the stuff they tried required her muscles to stretch in ways they didn't like to stretch. But it was worth it. He was worth it.

"Do your feet or legs hurt when you dance in your heels?" he asked.

Oh, boy. She knew where this was going, but she had to be honest. It had been so hard keeping this from him. It was a relief to have him know. "Yes," she admitted.

"Does your head hurt after we've been at the country bar until midnight?"

She sighed. "Yes."

"Do you feel like you were hit by a truck after about five hours out on the river, tubing and playing volleyball and drinking beer?"

He'd gotten a lot of reading done. "Definitely."

"And I never noticed. I never knew." He sounded pissed again. "So saying that you must not have been hurting during sex because I didn't see it doesn't mean a damned thing."

God, this was such a mess.

A sign caught her eye and Isabelle signaled to exit. She pulled onto the ramp, took a right at the stop sign and a minute later pulled up to a car wash.

"Give me six bucks," she told Shane.

He shifted to reach his wallet even as he said, "Suddenly your car is too dirty?"

She fed the bills into the machine, pushed the button for the super deluxe package—the one that would take the longest—and stripped off her shirt as she waited for the lights to prompt her forward.

"Iz?"

She looked over at him, but didn't answer. Instead she unhooked her bra and tossed it into his lap, then took her foot off the brake and eased into the car wash.

Once they were inside the stall, the doors shut and the spray started, she lifted her butt, unzipped her capris and slid them and her panties off, leaving them on the floor.

"Iz, what—?"

She climbed into his lap, straddling his legs. "I have had to push myself having sex with you, Shane, but it's because I've never wanted a guy—I never knew I *could* want a guy—like I want you. The only reason it's a challenge is because I want it to be as amazing for you every time the way it is for me. Because I want to experience everything there is to experience. Because I want to be the best you've ever had."

She wrapped her arms around his neck and pressed close, sealing her mouth over his.

Shane's hands gripped her butt, squeezing, then slid up to her waist, pressing her against his cock as he lifted his hips. The rough denim against her bare clit caused sparks of pleasure and she moved against him again.

The car rocked gently from the car wash spray.

She lifted her head and grinned at him. "I don't know how long this wash cycle is. You ready?"

He lifted his hips again, his arousal more than evident. "What do you think?" He slipped his hands down to her ass again. "How about you?" He kept his hands moving until the pads of both middle fingers met, then slid into her.

She gasped then groaned as his fingers filled her. "Yes. God, yes."

It amazed her how fast it could happen. They could be laughing and talking with their friends about football one minute and the next Shane would say something in her ear or touch her leg just right and she was hot and ready and willing.

It was definitely addictive. She loved the rush he gave her. The way he made her feel like he couldn't get enough of her. The way he looked at her and talked to her and touched her. She never knew sex could be like this. But she loved every second of it. That addiction was what had pushed her to try new things, to constantly make things new and exciting, to work to shock him once in a while. Because she wanted him to feel everything she felt—the need, the heat, the I-could-go-all-night-and-still-want-more.

Bubbles coated the windows, running down the glass in rivulets.

"Unzip me, babe," he said gruffly, stroking in and out.

Pleasure shivered through her. She also loved that he was going with this. He wasn't trying to talk her out of it, he wasn't trying to slow her down or tell her it was crazy to pull over and go at it in a car wash. He was as willing and ready for it as she was.

She complied, unbuttoning and unzipping his fly, then parting the denim to stroke her hand up and down the hot length of his shaft.

"Fuck," he muttered. "Nothing gets to me like the way you touch me, Iz."

Her heart expanded at that. She loved that she could do that to him, that she could make him feel good, that she knew how to touch him. They were in the midst of hot, spontaneous sex, he was praising how she turned him on and she was, stupidly, feeling sentimental. She almost laughed at how silly that seemed, but just then he leaned forward and took one of her nipples in his mouth.

She moaned, squeezing him in her hand.

He knew her, knew her body. He knew that sucking on her nipple while stroking over her g-spot like that would get her going and that if he wanted her to come all he had to do was swirl his thumb over her...

"Shane!" she cried as his thumb swirled over her clit.

Then he swirled and pressed again while sucking hard and she came apart.

It was that easy for him. Every time.

Panting, his fingers still inside her, she scrambled to move his underwear out of the way as the windows were washed clean by the spray nozzles on all sides of the car.

He moved his fingers only when his cock was free and she shifted closer to sink down on him.

He groaned as she took him, sinking to the base of his shaft without pause, his fingers digging into her hips.

Isabelle paused, absorbing the feel of him. Shane was a big guy. When he was inside her she felt every inch. It was why he always made sure she came first. He stretched her to the point that if she wasn't completely primed and slick, it could have been painful. But she loved it. She loved that when he moved she felt it clear to her toes. She loved that each stroke rubbed along every nerve ending she had and made her feel more alive, more aware, more connected than she ever was without him inside her. She loved that when he came she felt the pulses dance up her entire spine.

"We're on the spot-free rinse, babe. Better get a move on."

She glanced out the little windows in the car wash door that separated them from the outside world. "No one's waiting."

He leaned in and flicked his tongue over her nipple. "Maybe that's not the only reason I want you to move."

She smiled and flexed her inner muscles. "Like that?"

He groaned. "Fuck, that's good."

She grinned. "If you like that, check this out." She tightened her muscles, then lifted herself slightly, sliding along his cock.

His head fell back against the headrest. "Heaven. That's heaven."

She lifted and lowered herself, her limbs getting heavier and warmer as pleasure washed over her with each stroke.

Shane reached up, his hand at the back of her neck, while the other rested on her hip. He flexed his butt and pressed her down even harder and deeper with each downward stroke.

"I love when you're on top," he said roughly. "I love watching your breasts bounce and seeing you take me, feeling all that wet heat suck me in. But I wish I could flip you over right now and pound into you."

She sucked in a sharp breath. She loved that too. She had to really relax to take him that way. When Shane got riled up and took over, she sometimes just had to take a deep breath and hold on tight, but she loved when he spread her out or bent her over. She loved making him lose his mind. However, when she was on top, she was more in control. She could set the pace and control the depth and pace of the penetration.

Okay, so her muscles did get in the way sometimes of full-out, any-way-you-want-it sex. But it always worked. It was always amazing.

"Sorry," she said breathlessly, moving up and down on him a little faster. "The front seat of a car is kind of made for me on top."

"Yeah...unless..."

Shane reached down beside the seat and pulled the lever that allowed him to shove the seat as far back as it would go. "Lean your elbows up on the dash, babe," he told her, lifting her up and off of him, then turning her before she even realized what he was doing.

She put her forearms on the dash but looked back over her shoulder. Her forehead was going to hit the windshield. "I don't think..."

But he put a big hand on the back of her head and pressed until she was resting her cheek on her arms. "Shane..."

"This will do," he said, then he gripped her hips and brought her back down on his cock.

Holding on tight, he was able to thrust hard and deep and fast, pistoning in and out.

And just like that the show was all Shane's.

She gasped, then dug her fingers into her arms. God, it was good. She always bounced between intense pleasure and anxiety when Shane took control. She trusted him completely. All she had to do was say no or stop or wait and he would. But she didn't want that. He always made sure it was good for her. Her body craved his and she knew from her reading and studying that the orgasms she achieved with him were something to be cherished. She didn't want to slow him down or make any adjustments. But her body instinctively tightened at having someone stretch and stimulate her to the extent Shane did.

He continued driving into her, his ability to get leverage even in the bucket seat of her small car a testament to how strong he was—and how much he wanted it.

He needed to hold on to her though, pulling her against him with each thrust, to get as deep as he wanted to go, so through gritted teeth he said, "Your clit, Iz. Do it. Come again."

She wasn't sure she could even move but she managed to reach down and circle her clit. Intense pleasure shot through her, her nipples tightened, her toes curled and, amazingly, she felt her body soften and open to take even more of him.

"Yes. *Dammit. Yes,*" he praised.

She kept rubbing, otherwise completely at Shane's mercy.

And he kept thrusting.

Until she felt his cock grow even harder inside her and she detected the change in his breathing that signaled he was on the verge of climax.

"Isabelle," he panted. "Damn. Yes. God."

She came again, clamping down on him, heat streaking through her body.

Then he shouted out and came as well, pulsing into her, holding her tight against him.

She was already slumped forward on the dash, so she let her body sag, trying to catch her breath.

After a moment, she felt his hand run up and down her back.

"Damn, girl."

She looked over her shoulder. "And the car is shiny clean now too. Multi-tasking at its finest."

He chuckled and she felt warmth spread through her chest. That right there was exactly why she kept doing this. Okay, she had to work to relax a little when things got wild and her muscles would be feeling this in a few hours. But sex with Shane, and making him happy, was worth it.

"Someone is going to eventually come along and want to get

in here," he said, swatting her butt and shifting to move out of her.

She crawled into her own seat and they both worked on cleaning up and getting fully back into their clothes.

They pulled out of the car wash a few minutes later and got back on the highway.

Shane waited until they were again traveling west at sixty-five miles per hour to say, "It seems to me that we have a disproportionate amount of oral sex."

She swerved slightly. "Excuse me?"

"I've never analyzed it before because, well, I *love* oral sex—giving and receiving—but it does seem that we do more of that than anything else."

Oh, boy. Shane was a smart guy. A really smart guy. And he was in tune with her, that was for sure. She should have been expecting him to take the fibro information and figure a lot of other stuff out.

"I'm sorry but I left my complaint box back in Omaha," she said with a frown. "I'll make a note, though, about you wanting fewer blow jobs."

"Not complaining. Love the blow jobs." He stretched his legs, then propped one ankle on the opposite knee and balanced the book about fibromyalgia on his lap. "Just noticing."

"Well, notice things quietly," she told him. Did they have to talk about every single tiny detail of how the fibro affected their relationship? Especially the parts that were Shane's favorites—the partying and the sex? It was like rubbing salt in a wound. It already hurt but the more he delved into it, the more obvious it would become that this was going to be hard to work through. Of course, that was part of the point of the trip.

"I think you've done a lot of sex research so that you're always in charge."

Yeah, she'd already known that keeping Shane quiet wasn't going to happen.

Where was that maroon SUV? Couldn't they have a high-speed car chase over the pendant or something?

"I think that you keep coming up with this hot, spontaneous sex stuff because you like to be in charge. And I think it's because it feels better when you're controlling things."

She snorted. "It feels good every time, Shane. Trust me."

"Sure, it feels good." He gave her a cocky grin. "But it feels *better* when you're in charge. You get all the sexy stuff going—like the Nutella blow job or the finger vibrator while on the Ferris wheel—because then I'm overcome and distracted and you can do it however you want."

She shifted on her seat and swallowed. Dammit. She didn't know he was quite this insightful. "I do it because it's fun and sexy and I want you to go crazy for me."

"But you know very well that all you have to do to make it fun and sexy and crazy is say, 'Shane, spread me out and make me scream'."

She sucked in a quick breath and had to wiggle again. Damn. She'd just had two orgasms and she was aroused and hot all over again.

"See, that's all I need," Shane went on, conversationally, as if they were discussing his last football game. "But you keep it more...interesting than that."

"You don't like it interesting?" she asked, her tone sharper than she'd intended.

"I like it. Every time, every way. But I think there's more to it."

She bit the inside of her lip and worked on not saying anything at all. It didn't matter. He could theorize all he wanted.

"I think we need to review how this vanilla sex is going to work," he said.

"What do you mean?" she asked, blowing the not-saying-anything rule immediately.

"Vanilla sex, by definition, primarily refers to the missionary position." He looked over. "That's you on your back and me on top."

"Yes. I know. Thank you," she said tightly. She didn't want to get into this. He was going to think he had to take it easy with her. He was going to change how he did things. She *loved* how he did things now. She didn't want him to be worried, or careful.

"But it seems to me, as I mentally review our positions and routines—"

"You've mentally reviewed every time we've had sex?" she asked.

He nodded. "Yes. It wasn't that hard. After all, I've been mentally reviewing them periodically for the past six months."

"Our *routines* are fine."

"But there are some patterns. For instance, you like standing-up positions best. You also like being on top, specifically in a sitting position, even more specifically facing me. You are okay with all fours, but you prefer bent over a table."

She was getting hot just hearing him talk about it, even as he was annoying the crap out of her.

"Your least favorite is missionary."

She gritted her teeth.

"And I'm guessing it's because in missionary, especially when you're spread out on the bed and I'm standing, I can get especially deep. And can go fast and hard."

Now she had to clear her throat. Wow. Shane was potent.

"Stop it."

He looked over at her. "Stop what? We need to talk about this stuff."

"Don't make me pull this car over, Shane. Because I will. I'll pull over at the next rest area and climb up on that hood and beg you to do what you just said. Deep. Fast. And hard."

A pained sound rumbled from him and she smiled smugly. She wasn't the only one affected by their chemistry and the dirty talk.

"You don't have to prove anything to me, Iz," he finally said.

"That's the point. You've been doing all of this stuff—partying, road trips, crazy sex, to prove that you're fine."

"There's nothing to prove. I'm not dying, Shane. I haven't lost a body part. I can walk and talk and think and dance and have sex in any position and as hard as I want to!"

He didn't say anything for a moment, then he took a deep breath. "Isabelle. We have to think about how what you're doing affects us and make some adjustments—"

"No." She was making some changes. She didn't want to. She'd fought it. But now she was realizing that the everything-in-moderation rule wasn't a bad one. She just wanted to feel good. "I don't want *us* to make any adjustments. I don't want *you* to change anything."

"It says in here that—"

Irritated, she reached over and grabbed the book and threw it into the backseat. It was irrational. Not reading the book didn't make the information inside of it any less true. "You need to hear about *my* condition from *me*," she told him.

That was also irrational. She didn't know everything there was to know and it was sweet that he was trying. In the bookstore, the idea of him reading up on fibromyalgia had made her heart melt a little. And now she wanted to hit him over the head with the book.

"Are mood swings part of the fibro? Or is that just you?" he asked smoothly.

Yeah, if she could reach the book now she'd definitely whack him with it.

"Shut up."

"So a little of both?"

"Shane, seriously—"

"Isabelle," he said firmly. "We're going to talk about this. If you were managing it well and figuring out how to live your life with it, I'd listen. But you're not. I've spent a lot of time with you, girl, and when I'm not *with* you, I'm watching you or listening to you. You haven't made any adjustments that make sense."

He was judging her now?

"Hey—"

"You go to a hotel and crash for two days? You miss work? You lie to the people who care about you most but you unload to a bunch of strangers in a support group? How is this handling it?"

Shane was calling her on her shit. Great.

"You're pissed that I can be honest with people who aren't *you*?"

"No." He shook his head and took a deep breath. "Okay, maybe a little. Support groups are great, I'm sure. I'm glad it's helping you. But that can't be the only thing you do. Just because you went and finally confessed to someone doesn't mean that you're fine."

"What do you want me to do? Break down in tears? Pop a bunch of pills so I can keep doing what I've always done? Stay home and knit *every* night? What?"

"I want you to..." He trailed off, clearly frustrated. "I want you to do what you can do, but make adjustments so you're healthy and happy."

"Well, why do you think I've been trying to break up with you for the past two months?" she shot at him.

The words seemed to hang between them. Isabelle gripped the steering wheel and worked on calming breaths. Her heart was pounding, her whole body felt tense and tears were threatening. Dammit. They'd just had hot sex in a car wash and now they were fighting.

This was going so well.

Several minutes passed without a sound other than the noise of the interstate. Finally, she said, "I'm learning. I'm trying. But I'm struggling. I don't want to change my life. I've been fighting that idea for a while now. But I've realized that my body will always win that battle—it will shut down on me and then I'm done whether I like it or not. No, I don't like crashing, missing work and lying. I'm trying to get to a point where I can manage and not have to do those things. But," she said when he started to respond. "I don't want anyone else to have to change. Not because I'm a martyr but because I love you. I want *you* to be happy too and changing your life around for me won't do it. You need to go and find someone who can keep up with you. Like Candy."

"I don't want Candy!" he shouted.

She turned wide eyes to him. "I know. I said *like* Candy. Or Tracie or Lila," she added. "A girl who can party and who, apparently, doesn't give as many blow jobs as I do."

The idea of another woman even looking at Shane's body made her sick to her stomach, but she was trying to lighten things up here. And it was true. It might kill her, but Shane deserved to be with someone more like him...and less like her.

"I like the fucking blow jobs," he muttered.

Of course he did. She was damned good to start with and then he'd taught her exactly what he liked. Plus she'd read some books that gave her even more things to try. Was she less sore the next day after oral sex? Yeah. But honestly, it completely turned her on and she was very happy to do it too.

"You're purposefully missing my point," she said.

"No, I get your point. I don't like it, but I understand it."

"Well...good." That should make her happy, she knew. It did, actually, on one level. But it also made her heart hurt. He was starting to see her side of things. The side that said they were probably better off apart.

"I need some water or something," he said, gesturing at the sign for the next exit.

"Oh, I have water in the cooler in back..." She trailed off when she glanced at him and saw the look he was giving her. Right. Okay. That was an excuse to stop and get some space. Great.

He was probably already regretting leaving his motorcycle in Mitchell.

She signaled and took the exit.

Shane got out and stalked into the store, while Isabelle took her time following him. Space was a good thing, time to think, get some perspective, all of that.

She stepped into the store and looked around. Not seeing Shane immediately, she wandered down one of the snack aisles. She wasn't hungry, but gummy bears were always a good idea.

She grabbed a package and again looked around for Shane. It probably seemed like she was casing the joint or something, she realized, so she strolled to the closest cooler with drinks and pulled out a bottled Frappuccino.

"You're not even trying."

She jumped and spun. "What the hell are you doing sneaking up on me?" she demanded.

Shane frowned down at her. "I didn't sneak up." He took the bottled coffee from her and returned it to the cooler.

"Seriously?" she asked him. "You're going to monitor my diet now?"

"Clearly someone has to," he said, gesturing to the candy in her hand. "Sugar *and* caffeine are two things they recommend you cut back on."

She reached back into the cooler and grabbed the bottle again. "It's a work in progress."

"If I'm going to be in bed watching *Friends* re-runs with you every night, then you're going to drink more water and lay off the lattes."

She was again speechless for a moment. How did he know there were *Friends* re-runs on at night? How did he know what *Friends* was? "This isn't a latte," she finally said.

"It's caffeine and sugar." He took it from her hand and put a bottle of water in its place. "At least cut the crap in half."

"Can you even name one of the characters on *Friends*?" she asked.

"Rachel."

Her eyebrows shot up. "How do you know that?"

"Jennifer Aniston's hot."

Isabelle stared at him. Then snorted. "You've watched *Friends*?"

"No. I've seen interviews and shit," he told her. "And they advertise the re-runs during the early news."

"You watch the early news?" See, she didn't even know that about him. When they were together they were…definitely not watching the news.

"I take pride in being an educated and informed American citizen," he said dryly, taking the gummy bears away and giving her a package of cashews instead. "Nuts have good fat in them, and protein."

She must have looked surprised again because he gave her an exasperated look. "I read too."

"I'm just trying to reconcile in my head that the man who invented an alcoholic drink at Trudy's and named it after me because it includes maraschino cherries in memory of one very sexy night where we used up an entire jar, is now lecturing me about my water and sugar intake."

He narrowed his eyes. "You're right. That's probably one more of the routines we should take off of our list. Nothing vanilla about maraschino cherries."

"Yeah, but it's oral sex and we've already discussed, at length, how that's okay." She turned to stomp away from him and came up short when she realized a young dad and his two little kids stood behind her waiting for them to move so they could reach the bottles of juice.

The conversation had, thankfully, gone over the kids' heads. They were busy arguing over apple or grape juice. But the dad had definitely heard and understood every word.

He swallowed hard.

"Cherry brandy is better in it than cherry vodka," she said, then flounced around him without waiting for a response.

She rounded the corner at the end of the aisle determined to find some chocolate-covered pretzels. And Shane better watch out if he thought he was going to take *those* away from her.

She'd just grabbed the biggest bag she could find when she felt a hand on her upper arm.

"I'm getting these and I'm eating every last one of them and you're not going to say a damned thing," she said.

"I prefer the ones with white chocolate on them."

That wasn't Shane's voice. She turned. Harris.

"Oh, hey," she greeted with a smile. She dropped her voice as she glanced around for Shane. "Listen, this isn't a great time. Can we do this later?"

Shane was annoyed, and keeping up the charade would be harder if he was in a bad mood. But dammit. Her heart still began to gallop with excitement. She definitely felt like diving back into the game. That was way more fun that talking about Shane's opinion of her snack choices.

He scowled at her. "What? No. What are you talking about?"

"I'll pull over at the next rest area," she said, her plan forming. "Right now, my boyfriend is a little on edge. It would be better if we do it later."

"Sure, okay, you bet. I'll just let you leave with it and *trust* that you'll pull over later," Harris scoffed.

"No, really, I will," she said. "Here—" She pulled her brand new, expensive workout watch from her purse and thrust it at him. "This will ensure that I'll pull over."

He looked bewildered. "I don't want your watch."

"I know—it's collateral," she said. "I'll want it back, so I'll pull over at the next—"

"No. The pendant. Here. Now."

"But...I don't have it," she lied. The rules to this game were really quite simple—get the pendant to the drop site by midnight and don't let Harris take it.

She'd already almost screwed that second one up. If the little dragon hadn't slid into the hole in her purse lining, he'd have succeeded in taking it from her in Mitchell. At least he'd had to chase her there. She wasn't going to just turn it over to him during a random roadside pit stop. It was a game and she didn't even know what the prize was, but they were competitors, dammit.

"Well, a quick search will confirm that," he said, grabbing her purse again.

She gripped the strap. "Hey!"

He tugged harder. "Seriously, I'm not losing this game to some little girl who argues with her boyfriend about gummy bears."

She yanked the purse toward her. "Hey, don't judge. There's more going on here than you know."

He pulled the purse closer to him. "Oh, I'm sure. I'm sure the gummy bears are symbolic of some bigger, more important issue between you."

She narrowed her eyes. "As a matter of fact we're kind of going through something."

"And it's life-altering, right?" he asked with an eye roll.

She frowned. "Have you ever been in love?" She managed to make his grip on the purse strap slip a little.

He scowled and jerked on it harder again. "Of course. My wife and I have been married for eleven years."

"Yeah?" She tipped her head. "Any advice?"

He put a second hand on the purse strap and pulled. "Yeah. Don't make gummy bears more important than his feelings."

Isabelle gaped at him, the leather strap slipping from her fingers. "I don't… They're not… That's not what…"

But Harris was digging through her purse and no longer paying attention to her.

"Hey!" He could try to get the pendant from her. That was part of the game. But that was a new purse.

She grabbed the purse, and when he tried to yank it back, she lifted her foot, then brought it down hard on his instep like she'd learned in the self-defense class she'd taken. He released the bag, pulling his foot off the floor instinctively—and swearing. Then she turned and ran.

Right into Shane's chest.

"Are you okay?" he asked, his words sharp and his frown deep.

She nodded. "Yeah. Of course. No problem."

Shane pushed her to the side as he stalked toward Harris. The man started to back up, limping slightly, his hands up in front of him.

"You need to quit harassing my girlfriend."

Dammit. Shane looked like he might hit Harris for real.

She reached into her front pocket and pulled the pendant out, thrusting it toward Harris. "Here, just take it."

The dragon on the end of the chain seemed to wink at her as the light caught the jewel in his eye.

This was so crazy.

Harris looked from Shane to Isabelle. "Um. What?"

She looked at Shane. "Just take it." Bradley could get it back for her again. Or not. She needed to not make the gummy bears more important than Shane's feelings. Reassuring him and letting him support her was more important than her getting her way. And she needed to put him and his feelings—his concern and frustration about her fibromyalgia—before the pendant and this game.

Harris didn't say another word. He tucked the necklace in his pocket and headed for the doors.

Shane moved in beside her.

"Nice move. I didn't know you knew self-defense."

"Amanda."

He nodded. He knew her sister well enough to know that forcing a self-defense class on her sisters was exactly something the oldest Dixon girl would do. "I've always liked your sister."

Isabelle smiled. "Me too."

Shane's expression—and voice—gentled. "You didn't have to give it to him."

"It's okay. It's been…a distraction." It had been a good one in many ways, but she couldn't keep just distracting him. Eventually they were going to have to face all of this relationship stuff.

Shane looked like he was going to say more, but finally he simply ran the pads of his fingers over her cheek and said simply, "Let's go."

They paid for their food and drinks. Shane didn't say anything about the chocolate-covered pretzels and she gave him a few mental brownie points for that.

They were at the car when Shane suddenly turned her, pressed her back against the car and kissed her.

The kiss wasn't sweet and tender, but neither was it hot and seductive. It was—possessive, maybe, and definitely a little desperate.

"Damn," he said, when he'd lifted his head and sucked in some oxygen. "I know it's not real, but when I saw that he had you back there alone, I thought my chest was going to explode."

She cupped his face. "Not real?" Did he know about the game?

He seemed to hesitate for a second, then said, "I mean, he wasn't really going to hurt you. He didn't have a weapon and he…doesn't seem like that kind of guy."

That made sense. Sizing up bad guys was what Shane did every day. Maybe he didn't know about the game.

She also liked his reaction. Clearly it was purely based on emotion if he knew that Harris wasn't a danger. In that moment when she was with Harris, Shane was reacting as a boyfriend, not a cop. "I'm fine." She stretched up and kissed him. "Totally fine."

"Okay." He breathed in and out, then kissed her once more. "Let's get going. We don't have to worry about that damned pendant anymore."

Yeah. No more distractions. Great.

CHAPTER
EIGHT

SHANE KNEW HE WAS AN IDIOT. Driving across the state of South Dakota to break up with the only woman he'd ever loved was stupid enough. Insisting she eat well and drink more water as they did it was ridiculous.

Being pissed off at the guys who were pretending to be bad guys so that he and Isabelle could have some excitement on their trip was unreasonable.

As was calling a halt to the game back at the gas station. No one was getting hurt and Isabelle was clearly enjoying it. But damn. Seeing that guy with her... Shane gritted his teeth. Isabelle was a pain in the ass but she was *his* pain in the ass.

At least until they got to the cabin.

He shifted on his seat again and turned another page. They'd been driving and not talking for about an hour. She was listening to her satellite radio and he was making his way through *Living and Loving with Fibromyalgia*. But the more he read, the more restless he got.

She probably got migraines on a regular basis. She probably felt exhausted more often than not. She was probably supersensitive to the loud music he liked and the spicy food he liked and…yeah…many of the sex positions he liked.

He, of course, didn't *mind* that she liked oral sex. A lot. That was…awesome. But he hated that she hadn't told him *why*. She was really good at it. But he'd also thought she loved it. Knowing that it was just the lesser of two evils made him feel a little cheated, frankly.

But she *acted* like she liked it.

She was a good actress. He'd seen her in action at her company's Christmas party and at a going-away party for a co-worker. He knew for a fact that one of the guys at the Christmas thing drove her crazy, but she sat next to him at dinner and if Shane hadn't known better, it would have been easy to believe that the guy was charming and brilliant. He knew that she loathed the woman who was leaving and was glad to see her go, but watching at the party, Shane found it hard to believe that they weren't best friends.

She was very good.

And she'd been faking it with him all along.

He turned the page, rolling his neck to loosen the muscles.

She'd said no the first few times he asked her out. Then he and Ryan and Cody had sung David Lee Roth's "Just a Gigolo" during karaoke. She'd come up to him after the performance—which had gotten a standing ovation, incidentally—and asked him to dance.

They'd danced, her hands had wandered, she'd flirted and teased, and they'd ended up outside, in the rain, having sex on the hood of his car.

He sat up straighter in his seat. She'd initiated all of that.

He hadn't been quite ready to give up on her, of course. He'd planned to ask her another dozen times or so before he took no for an answer. But he certainly hadn't planned to take things that far the first night they hung out.

Not that he'd complained. Not that night or any of the nights that followed.

He frowned and studied the yellow dashed line flashing past the car.

Come to think of it, she'd initiated the second date too. He'd wanted to see her immediately the next day, but had figured he should play it cool.

She'd called him at ten a.m. the next morning. And talked him into meeting at her place for lunch. And a quickie.

It wasn't always sex she was initiating either. Sometimes it was just the date. And sometimes it was the craziness *on* the date.

They'd gone to an airshow one day—his idea—but she'd flirted with some of the security people and had gotten behind the scenes. Then some additional flirting with a pilot had gotten her and Shane on a private flight over Omaha.

At the casino, she'd been the one that kept encouraging him to play. Even when he lost all but twenty bucks. Of course, in the end, he'd walked out with two grand.

When they'd gone to the carnival, she'd not only used the finger vibrator on the Ferris wheel—she'd paid the guy ten dollars to stop it at the top. *And* she'd been the one with the naughty cotton-candy-all-over-her-body idea.

None of that had been fake. He knew it. Her cheeks had flushed, her eyes had sparkled, she'd been excited and having fun and…had looked a lot like she did with this whole pendant mystery thing.

He looked over at her, eyes narrowed. Maybe she thought she had set all of this up because of him, to entertain him, to make sure he had a good time. But she wasn't *that* good of an actress. Not for someone who knew her like he did.

Her orgasms were real. Her addiction to gummy bears was real. And that she was as much fun and enjoyed a good party as much as he did was real.

This pendant game was as much for her as it was for him.

"If we break up, who are you going to use as an excuse to get into the demo derbies?" he asked.

She looked over, clearly surprised. "What do you mean?"

"I mean, I get that you didn't know you liked them before I came along, but now that you do, who's going to 'force' you to go?"

She looked back at the road. "I don't know what you're talking about."

He chuckled at that. "Right. You know, I was going along with this whole thing about me running you ragged and being too much to keep up with. God knows I like to go hard and all night once in a while. But when I was thinking about how much you seem to be enjoying this whole stolen-pendant thing, I remembered that you were the one who got us on that yacht for that weekend party last fall and you were the one who bought me the tickets to the hockey games and then made friends with one of the player's wives and got us into their post-game party and *you* were the one who snuck us into the last demo derby."

She still stared at the interstate. "I did that because I knew how much you'd like that stuff."

"And I did. And I'll admit, I was the one who wanted to go skiing at the last minute in November and I was the one who wanted to go hot air ballooning."

"Hot air ballooning in *Arizona*," Isabelle added. "With three hours' notice before our flight left."

"It was gorgeous."

"And then being in Arizona led to driving four more hours to the one-night-only Toby Keith concert at that dive country bar and then driving back just in time to get on the plane to get home."

"It was a hell of a good time."

She didn't answer. Because he knew she'd have to agree with him.

"I'm not saying that I *never* initiate the stuff we do, but I also don't *always* come up with the plans," he said. "And," he went on, his next point a very important one, "when I called to ask you to come to Vegas to hang out with me and Candy, it was the first time you've ever said no."

That sunk in for him as he said it to her. She'd never asked to go home early, she'd never said, "How about another night instead?", she'd never invited him to hang out quietly with her at home. She didn't *know* that he didn't want to do that because she'd never asked.

Shane felt a twist of frustration. She was assuming a lot without input from him. She'd suddenly decided that he was bad for her and her health and the best thing was to end their relationship without talking to him about it. He hadn't even known there was a health problem.

His frustration grew to irritation.

"I didn't want to say no," she told him.

"Exactly. You liked all of it as much as I did. A lot of it was your idea. In fact, you claim that you've been researching new sex ideas to keep things interesting for *me*, but I think you're just as into all of that for yourself."

And again, the whole spy game with the pendant came to mind. Maybe *she'd* been worried about getting bored during this trip too.

She huffed out a breath. "I never said that it wasn't fun with you. But I need to be smart and cut back now. Eating cream-filled donuts for breakfast every day is also fun, but not good for me, so I don't do it. Drinking margaritas and going skinny-dipping is fun...and dangerous, so I don't do it. Staying up all night to read a novel from start to finish is fun, but makes for a bad day at work, so I don't do it."

Dammit, he wished they weren't driving. He wanted to pace and gesture and maybe yell a little bit. He didn't have a temper problem but when he argued, it was like everything else—he gave it all he had.

"But you're not even trying."

She looked over at him. "What are you talking about?"

"You're blaming how you feel on me...and Emma. On having

too much fun, on staying out too late, but you're eating like shit." He gestured to the half-empty bag of chocolate-covered pretzels. "You stay up late watching *House* re-runs some nights. You get up at the crack of dawn to work out before you go to the office. And don't deny you love your mojitos."

She gripped the steering wheel so that her knuckles went white. "What's your point?"

"That it's easy to say 'Shane's the problem' instead of facing all the things that *you* need to change."

"I'm not saying that it's your *fault*, Shane. Just maybe that you're not…good for me. Or we're not good together."

"That's bullshit, Iz," he said sharply. "And quitting me isn't going to be enough. Then what are you going to do? At some point you have to take some of this responsibility."

"I *am*. You think the idea of changing the lifestyle I have with you is easy on me?"

Maybe getting her riled up while they were driving down the road at seventy-two miles an hour wasn't a great idea, but he couldn't hold back. "But why is that the only answer you're focused on? Are you taking vitamins? Trying anything new in your workout program? Maybe it's the kick-boxing that you do twice a week that makes you sore. Maybe you need to wear flats instead of four-inch heels. Maybe you need to chill out at your job a little bit and not constantly push yourself to be the number-one seller every single fucking month."

Isabelle didn't answer or look at him. Her jaw was so tight, he wondered if she was going to crack a tooth.

Finally, she said, "We've known each other for eight months, Shane. Eight *months*. It's not like you promised 'in sickness and in health' and "til death do us part', you know? I'm trying to let you out before it gets hard."

"Maybe I wouldn't mind it being hard." He gripped one hand into a fist, then rolled his neck again.

Maybe he wouldn't.

But maybe he would.

Shit, how the hell did he know? Things hadn't been hard for him for a very, very long time. He avoided hard. He purposefully went for fun and frivolous.

He'd had hard when he was a kid. He'd seen hard in the other kids in their home. But about the time his biological grandmother had come looking for him, he'd decided that someone else could do hard. He was going to do fun.

He'd chosen to stay in the foster home. He'd made the place as fun and happy as he could for the other kids and made sure that his adoptive parents were glad every single day they'd taken him in. His mom had made things hard for him and he was over it.

At age seven, he chose his path and hadn't deviated from it since. He was going to be the guy that everyone wanted around, that no one wanted to leave, the life of the party, the one that people noticed and couldn't get enough of.

Sure, the job was sometimes what people might call hard, but he didn't see it that way. He was on the good side, the side that mattered, the side that made a difference. He did what he could to make things better for the people counting on him. He was the cop who always had teddy bears in his car for the kids he came across on domestic abuse calls. He was the guy who played Elvis in his car even when he was taking a drug dealer downtown. He was the one that could make even the lady he'd busted for texting while driving smile at a stupid joke. And he went to sleep every night content that he'd done his best.

He slept like a baby.

"You make me seem like an ass," he told her. "Like it has to all be about me. Like I couldn't be expected to give up a couple of late nights if it was better for you. You haven't ever told me to chill out. You haven't ever pointed out that I act like a college frat boy who has just discovered life with beer bongs and no curfews."

She cracked a tiny smile at that, then shook her head. "You're you, Shane. You're happy. You make other people happy being who you are. Why would I want you to change that?"

"Because you should want to be with me, dammit."

She pressed her lips together. Finally she blew out a long breath. "I'm sorry. I don't mean to make you feel bad. I'm screwing this all up."

He sighed. "No you're not. Maybe giving up caffeine is harder than giving me up."

His stomach and heart and brain all rejected that idea, but maybe that was it. Maybe he was the most expendable thing in her life. Like she'd said, it had only been eight months.

"That's not it," she said.

Of course she said that. Because what was she going say? *Yes, Shane, if I have to choose, I will* always *choose gummy bears over you.*

"I'm trying to figure this out for *me*. I'm trying to get used to giving stuff up. I don't want to figure it out for you, too," she said, with clear frustration.

"I'll figure it out *with* you."

"I guess...it's too much. The figuring out what exercise I can and can't do. What helps my sleep and what screws it up. How to drink less coffee and not want to kill someone. That's all *enough*. Moving in together, being in each other's lives twenty-four-seven would have been a big adjustment even without all of this. But I can't deal with balancing out how to meld our lives together when I don't have control of my own life. And I can't keep feeling guilty about you too."

"So you're taking the easy way out. Just cutting this part out instead of trying to work it through?"

She blew out a breath. "Yes. Okay? I can't stop eating or sleeping or working so...yeah. You're one thing I can stop doing."

Her voice wobbled as she said it, but she still said it. And Shane's heart stopped for a moment, before restarting with a painful thud.

"And being without me is easy?"

"Being without you *now* is easier than it will be in six more months when I know how it feels to come home to you, when I know how much I love seeing your dirty socks mixed in with mine, when I know that if I forget to buy orange juice, you'll remember. When you decide to leave after all of that, it will be the worst thing I've ever been through."

Shane had no fucking idea what to say to that.

She had a point.

She definitely had a point.

Cutting their losses now would hurt, but it would be less painful that if they realized it wasn't going to work down the road.

"You don't know that it won't work," he said.

"I can't make any promises of any kind," she said quietly. "I don't even know how to live with me right now, so how can I promise you anything about what it will be like?"

He tried to take a deep breath, but his chest wouldn't loosen enough to let his lungs expand.

"And," she said, her words almost inaudible. "You think you'll still want to be with me when I'm different, when I'm not going out as much, or having as much fun. But you might not. And…" She stopped and blew out a breath. "Maybe I won't still want to be with you."

He couldn't stay cooped up in this car for another minute. "We need to stop."

He could tell she was holding back tears as she nodded. "Okay."

She took the exit for the tiny town of Wall, South Dakota, the home of Wall Drug Store, which had been advertised on billboards along the entire stretch of I-90 as they'd been traveling. Shane knew it was a lot more than a drug store. It was a huge tourist trap. But it was huge. It would give him some space and time from Isabelle, and give him a chance to figure out how in the hell he was going to finish this trip. And how he wanted it to turn out.

They parked and got out. Isabelle started for the main building in the sprawling shopping-mall-esque arrangement of shops and restaurants.

"I'm going to make a call," he told her. "I'll meet you inside."

She looked back at him and clearly started to say something before pressing her lips together and nodding.

Shane watched her enter the store, then paced to the end of the sidewalk, pivoted and paced back. Fuck. He needed to run. Or hit the gym. Or hit *something*.

She was completely right.

He knew she loved him. She loved how he made her feel. But she'd fallen for the life-of-the-party guy. She didn't want him to change. Because there was a chance—probably a decent one— that if he changed, so would *her* feelings. It wasn't just that she'd feel guilty if he changed his lifestyle for her and then didn't like it. It was also the risk of him changing his lifestyle, not minding it, and then *her* being the dissatisfied one.

Fuck.

He pulled his phone out and punched in Ryan's number.

"Hey, Shane," his friend greeted.

"Are all the Dixon girls a lot of work, or just Isabelle?"

"Oh, I think it's all of them," Ryan said sincerely. "But Iz might be more work than Amanda."

Shane rubbed the back of his neck. "Yeah. Well, I hope so. For your sake."

Ryan chuckled. "Thanks. So what's going on? You guys to the cabin and bored already?"

Shane snorted. "No. And no. We're still driving."

"But you left this morning early, didn't you?"

"Yeah, we've had some pit stops."

"So things are…"

He'd love to fill in that blank. He had no idea how things were. "A mess," he finally said.

"Sorry, man."

"I don't know if I can fix this."

"What's going on?"

"Do you ever worry about what will happen with you and Amanda if you…change?"

"If I change?"

"Yeah, you know. If you stop doing something you've always done."

"Like what?"

Shane scowled at the tourists passing him. This place was packed. "Like…stuff that makes you who you are. Like…"

"Being a paramedic?" Ryan offered.

Shane felt like banging his head against the wall. That wasn't exactly it, no. But he couldn't come up with another example. "Like playing football."

Ryan laughed. "You're asking if I worry that things won't work between Amanda and me if I stop playing football?"

Shane frowned. "Yeah."

"No. I don't worry about that at all," Ryan said. Shane could hear the grin in his voice. "In fact, I figure someday I *will* stop playing football. And I expect that things with Amanda and me to be fine when that happens."

Okay, it wasn't a perfect analogy. Football didn't make up a huge part of Ryan's personality. It was something he did.

"Well, what if you start doing something you didn't do when you met her?" he asked instead. "Like what if you suddenly decided to…" he needed something that was similar to changing his social habits and personality entirely, "…go into politics."

There was a long pause on the other end of the phone.

Yeah, that sounded stupid.

"What the hell are you talking about?" Ryan asked.

"Isabelle's trying to dump me."

"I thought she already had."

"Ha-ha," Shane said. "She means it. She thinks I'm bad for her. Or she's bad for me. Or something. Both I guess."

"Why?"

"She wants me to…change. She wants me to…" It all

sounded so stupid. It *was* so stupid. The woman he loved wanted to stay home more. So he needed to stay home more.

Except that she didn't want *him* to change.

What bothered him the most was that she wasn't even going to let him try.

"What would you do if Amanda was trying to break up with you?"

"Fight her tooth and nail."

"And what if she was…right?"

There was a long pause on Ryan's end of the phone. "You mean, if it was the right thing for us to break up?"

Shane closed his eyes. "Yeah."

"Then I think I'd work on making it *not* the right thing to do."

"Ryan, I—"

"Shit. Shane, here, talk to Conner."

"No!" Shane barked. "I don't want to talk to Conner."

Hell, Isabelle's brother was the *last* person he ever wanted to talk to about any of this.

"Fine. Talk to Sara."

"Sara who?"

"Sara Gordon. She brought cookies down here and Mac's changing into his uniform and Conner's flirting her up and Mac's gonna kill him if he walk in and finds this."

"I don't want to talk to Sar—"

But a sweet voice said, "Uh, hello? Shane?"

Dammit. "Hey, Sara."

"Hey. Ryan says you're having some woman problems and could use some female advice." She laughed lightly. "I guess I'm nominated since I'm the only girl here right now."

Shane wondered where Gabby and Sierra—the two female paramedics on Conner and Ryan's team—were. He liked Gabby. She was gorgeous and no-nonsense. Not a bad combination at all. She'd tell him straight up what she thought. Sierra was quieter. Shane always had the impression that he intimidated her. He was loud and rowdy so that happened sometimes. He grinned. But not with Gabby.

Or Sara Gordon for that matter. She lived with Mac. And hung out with Dooley and Sam. A little loud and rowdy wouldn't faze her.

Well, what the hell? A little objective female perspective might not hurt.

"I'm fighting with my girlfriend."

"Isabelle, right?"

He should have known Sara would know who he was talking about. The women often sat together in the stands for their games.

"Yeah. I'm mad at her," he confessed, surprising himself. He was mad at her. He just wasn't sure he should be. She was dealing with a lot of stuff, she was trying to figure stuff out with her health.

Except that she wasn't.

He felt his jaw tighten again. She wasn't trying all that hard. In fact, it seemed to him that she was pretty deep in denial, as a matter of fact.

Sara chuckled. "Well, that happens in relationships. What are you fighting about?"

Shane found a spot at the end of the sidewalk to lean against the building where he could avoid a majority of the crowd coming and going and have a few inches to breathe.

Which he did, before saying, "She didn't trust me with some things I think she should have told me about."

"Ah."

That was it. Just *ah*.

"What's that mean?" he asked with a frown.

"Well, trust is important. But you have to earn trust. Is there some reason she thought she couldn't be honest with you?"

Yeah, this was making him feel great. Good phone call. Shane sighed. "Yes, Sara, there was probably some reason she thought she couldn't be honest with me." Like her thinking that he wouldn't love her anymore. Or that she wouldn't love him anymore.

"That's on both of you," Sara said matter-of-factly. "But it's okay for you to be mad at her about it."

"Yeah?" He didn't feel okay about it. He felt like he was being as ass.

"Couples fight," Sara said simply. "It's how you figure how what's important."

"And what if you can't solve the problem? What if fighting is all there is?"

That was his real fear here. That he simply couldn't be the guy Isabelle wanted. And that was assuming Isabelle figured out what that guy looked like eventually.

Sara's tone softened. "I don't know everything about relationships, Shane. But I do know that no matter what happens, no matter what drives you crazy, no matter what sacrifices you have to make, you have to be happy together. Being with her has to be the thing that matters most. If she makes you happy and you make her happy, the rest will be okay. Not necessarily easy, but okay."

Shane didn't notice all the people milling around or the noise or the smell of car exhaust or the feel of the rough wood at his back.

Sara's words hit him hard.

He needed Isabelle to be happy. That he knew down deep in his bones. And he really, really wanted to be the one to make Isabelle happy.

That was pretty simple.

It was the walking away from her that was going to be hard.

"Thanks, Sara."

"Well, sure. I mean, I hope I helped."

She had. Kind of. She hadn't exactly filled him with hope and joy, but she had given him good advice.

He loved Isabelle. He wanted her to be happy. Even if *he* wasn't the one to make her that way.

"Can I talk to Ryan again?"

"Yeah, sure. Hang on."

"Oh, and Sara? Do me a favor and *don't* mention to Conner that I'm fighting with his sister."

Conner didn't like Shane and Isabelle being together and as far as Shane knew, everyone was keeping the news that Shane was on this trip with Iz a secret from her big brother. And Conner also didn't like when Shane upset Isabelle. As he had been doing for a good portion of this trip.

Sara laughed. "I've got your back."

Ryan came back on the line as Shane moved to a vacated seat on a wooden bench in front of the drug store. He was feeling heavy and tired and not like dealing with other people at all. Especially tourists.

And there were a lot of them here.

"Why is this place overrun with tourists?" he asked Ryan when his friend returned to the line. "It's freaking March."

"Spring break, man," Ryan said.

Ah. Shit.

"Hey, I thought you should know…" he said to his friend, hesitant to even say it out loud. "I'm going to grab a rental car here in the morning and head back to pick my bike up in Mitchell. Do you think you can get Amanda out here to be with Isabelle for the week at the cabin?"

"You're leaving?" Ryan asked. "No way."

"I have to." Shane rubbed his hand over the back of his neck. Fuck. He definitely had to. He felt like his insides were a jumbled mess of raw nerve endings. He was jumpy and pissed and confused and he was…never any of those things. "We need some space. We need to figure some things out."

"You're breaking up with her? Or should I say, you're letting her break up with you?" Ryan asked.

"I don't know. I think we need some time. Maybe just a break."

"Fuck," Ryan muttered. "This is bad."

"Tell me about it."

"Amanda is going to be *pissed* at you," Ryan told him.

"Yeah." Like she was the only one. Or even the meanest one.

Conner would be happy that Shane and Isabelle were no longer a couple. Happier than he had been when Isabelle had broken up with Shane after Vegas. After that, Shane had still pursued her, still hung around, still looked out for her.

But that didn't mean that Conner wouldn't be pissed at Shane for leaving her in the Black Hills. Or for making her cry. Or for dating her in the first place.

Conner was the quarterback for a very successful, very *fit* football team. He was well liked by his teammates. He was their leader, their captain, their friend. If he told the defensive linemen to make sure Shane was sore after practice a time or two—or seventeen—they would, no questions asked.

"Okay, well, sit tight," Ryan said. "I'll be sure Amanda gets out there, but don't even think about leaving until she's there."

"No problem." He wouldn't leave Isabelle alone. But he would leave her. If that was really what would make her happy.

They disconnected and Shane sat staring at the row of cars parked at an angle to the curb. Three backed out and three more pulled in right after them. The car doors slammed. A mom shouted for her kids to remember their backpacks. Another family unloaded a stroller and a wheelchair—one for the baby and one for grandma. A pickup honked at a car that pulled out without looking. A dog, left in the backseat with the windows open enough for fresh air, barked at the teenage girls who passed his SUV. A guy walked by, hitting Shane's knee with his plastic bag of purchases.

Fuck, there were people and noise *everywhere*.

He needed to *think*. He needed to figure out how to tell Isabelle he was spooked.

Because he was.

She was right. Six more months and they'd be in deep. Even now it felt impossible to think about not being with her. But every time he started to think that it was no big deal, he felt his gut twist. It was a big deal and they owed it to themselves and each other to be honest about that.

"Do you know how to tie shoes?"

Shane was pulled from his thoughts by the little voice next to him. He looked to his right. A little boy, probably about six years old, sat licking an ice cream cone. His legs were short enough that they stuck straight out, the blue, orange and green logo on his pristine white tennis shoes glinting in the sun. Sure enough, one lace hung untied.

"Uh, yeah," he told him.

He'd helped easily a hundred kids over the years with everything from chasing down a renegade puppy to escaping an abusive adult, but he wasn't in the mood right now. Further proof that he was an asshole.

He glanced around. A woman in her early thirties stood two feet away, talking on her phone, her eyes glued to the little boy. She certainly didn't look concerned about her son making a new friend with the strange adult next to him. But she wasn't ignoring the kid either.

"You need some help there?" Shane asked the kid, watching the vanilla ice cream run down the back of his hand and drip onto his denim shorts.

"Well, *I* don't know how to tie," the boy told him.

Right. He reached over, tied the shoe, then went back to staring at the front bumper of the black Chevy Silverado, trying to get his thoughts together.

"Can you hold my ice cream cone?"

Shane glanced at the little boy again, then over to his mom. She was still on the phone.

"I probably shouldn't," he told the kid.

"Why not?"

"Because I'm a stranger. You should have your mom help you."

"She's on the phone. She doesn't like it if I talk to her while she's on the phone."

Shane sighed. Of course she didn't. He shot her an irritated look—which she missed because she was digging in her purse.

"How long do you need me to hold it?" he asked the boy.

"Twenty minutes."

Yeah, a six-year-old probably didn't have a great sense of time. "Fine." He held out his hand. As long as the kid was quiet while he held the cone, what could it hurt?

The boy handed the ice cream over and Shane winced. The cone had been filled with melting ice cream long enough to get a little mushy and sticky. Great.

The kid scrambled off the bench and knelt in the tiny patch of dirt near the edge of the curb where minuscule weeds sprouted. He poked a finger into the dirt and started swirling it around.

Fine. The kid was preoccupied. Shane tried to focus again on him and Isabelle.

He thought Isabelle was who and what he wanted. But he had to be completely honest—could he and Isabelle be what the other truly needed? They wouldn't know for sure until they tried. But he was beginning to think that they needed to try back home, rather than at the cabin. This was a lifestyle change for both of them. And that would be best tested in their regular environment.

It had nothing to do with him still being a little leery of the week-long knitting-marathon idea.

"Can you hold my spider?"

With a heavy sigh—that a six-year-old would never understand or appreciate anyway—Shane looked down. Sure enough, the kid held a spider in his hand. The hand that had previously been sticky with ice cream and was now coated with dirt.

"I don't like spiders."

"But I can't eat ice cream and hold my daddy long legs."

"You should let the spider go. He lives here and needs to stay here with his family."

"But he's my pet."

"Well, dude, you're gonna have to pick between the bug and the ice cream." He held the cone up to remind the kid of what he might be giving up.

He had much bigger stuff to be contemplating here, couldn't the kid see that?

Shane gritted his teeth as ice cream dripped and ran over his knuckles.

"'Kay, I'm done with that," the kid told him, pointing to the ice cream.

Of course he was.

Shane stretched to his feet and tossed the cone into the trashcan. "Tell you what, I'll give you a dollar for the spider." Shane pulled his wallet out.

"Okay!"

Yeah, that's what he thought. He handed the kid the money, took the spider and waited for the kid to run to his mom. The woman looked very confused about how her son's ice cream had turned into a dollar, but Shane figured that served her right for not taking care of the untied shoe and the melting ice cream herself. She was going to have to now deal with the dirty handprint on her light blue shorts. She should be grateful she didn't have a new creepy-crawly friend too.

When the kid looked away, he let the spider go, then faced the front of Wall Drug.

He wasn't getting any real thinking done out here. There was too much going on, too many people, too damned much noise.

Fricking spring break anyway.

He knew that would sound crazy out loud. He never wanted quiet and was absolutely the spring break kind of guy. Sure, his idea of a great spring break involved more beaches, bikinis and Mike's Hard Lemonade than Wall, South Dakota had to offer, but in general he was behind the idea of taking a break from the real world and kicking back.

Until now. Now he was contemplating *leaving* a vacation to go back to the real world.

Perfect.

Fricking spring break.

💋

"Hey."

He was finally back. Isabelle turned from the display of sunglasses to face Shane. He'd been outside on the phone for a long time. "Hey, look what I got for you."

She held out the tiny flashlight that he could clip to his keychain. She clicked the button to turn it on and off for him.

"I don't need a flashlight. I kind of get issued a really big one from the precinct."

"Oh, I was—" She broke off as she looked at him. "Are you okay?"

"Can we go? Somewhere quiet? This place is driving me nuts."

Isabelle nodded slowly. "Of course. Sure." There was something up with Shane. He looked stressed out. Shane never looked stressed out. "Let me pay for this and we can go." She had her little shopping basket full of souvenirs. She'd been collecting things as they went along the trip for their friends and her family. She loved souvenir shops.

He stood behind her in line, his hands tucked into his front pockets, jaw tight. Typically, Shane was the kind of guy to strike up a conversation with the strangers in line around them, to tease the sales clerk, to try on fifteen hats he'd never actually wear and ask the people around for their opinions and then buy souvenir shot glasses for all his buddies.

He wasn't even making eye contact with anyone.

She didn't know who he'd talked to, but something was not right.

"Shane?"

"Not now, Iz."

"Everything okay at home?"

"Yes."

Shane also wasn't the one-word-answer guy.

"You sure?"

He looked down at her. "Can we not do this right here and right now?"

"Do what?"

He put his hands on her shoulders, turned her to face the cash registers and nudged her forward. "Not. Now."

She stood shifting her weight from side to side, itching to turn around again, but not at all brave enough for that. He was worked up. Fine, she'd wait. But if he thought she was going to let it go completely, he was crazy.

Finally it was her turn. The clerk rang up her purchases and Isabelle reached into her purse for her wallet. She pulled it out… along with something else.

"Uh, Shane?"

"Isabelle," he said firmly. "Seriously. Let's go somewhere else."

"I need your help with something."

She turned and held the pendant up.

He stared at the chain swinging from her fingers.

"How the hell—"

"I don't know how I got it back," she said. "I didn't see anyone, I didn't talk to anyone." She assumed Bradley had something to do with it, but why wouldn't he talk to her if he was here? Had they hired someone to drop it in her purse? That was strange. Of course, that wasn't the first or only thing about all of this she'd label that way.

His jaw firmed. "Fuck no."

"No?" That wasn't exactly the reaction she'd been expecting…or one that even made sense really.

"No. I'm done. I'm not doing this anymore."

"But…"

He tossed two twenty dollar bills on the counter, grabbed her stuff and her hand and started for the front of the huge store.

"Shane."

But he kept going, dodging people and displays.

He ran into a man who stepped back suddenly from a rack of T-shirts. The guy apologized, but Shane barely looked at him and kept moving. A kid stepped on his toe, he banged his knee against a stroller, he nearly got hit in the face with a paper fan a woman held up to show her daughter, but he kept going.

Until he found a corner out of the way, near the restrooms. Then he pulled Isabelle in, turned her so her back was in the corner, braced his hands on either side of her head and said, "I think you're right."

Completely confused by his actions and attitude, she said carefully, "Love those words."

"We need to take a break."

Her heart plummeted. "Oh. That." Never mind then.

But it was what she'd been saying. So why did it suck so much to hear it from him?

"We need to both think things through, think about what we want."

She nodded. They did. It made total sense to do that.

"I'm going to rent a car and drive back home tomorrow. Amanda's coming up to be with you."

"You told my sister that you're leaving?"

"I told Ryan."

Isabelle crossed her arms over her stomach and pressed. It made it seem even more real knowing that someone else knew about it. "Ryan thinks it's a good idea?" she asked.

Shane shook his head. "No, but he understands."

She took a deep breath. "How much did you tell him?" She couldn't explain it, but she didn't want anyone else to find out about her fibro yet. Or ever.

"I told him that we're working on things. And that I thought we needed space. But he and I agreed that you shouldn't be up here alone. It's up to you if and when and what you tell anyone else," he said.

"Thanks." She wet her lips before asking, "Does knowing all of this help you?"

Shane knew more than she'd intended to tell him at this point too. She'd known about her condition for ten months and okay, she knew she wasn't embracing it and learning everything she could, but it was overwhelming. She needed more time. Some trial and error. Some…space. Like Shane was suggesting. Having him there reminding her to drink water and give up her gummy bears wasn't helping.

"Yeah," he finally said. "It helps knowing that there was a good reason for the breakup."

She sucked in a quick breath, surprised that his answer stung. *A good reason.* So he agreed that it was a good reason. A good reason for them to be apart.

"But no," he added. "In some ways it's just frustrating as hell. There's only so much I—*we*—can do for you, so it's…hard."

Right.

"Then you're leaving in the morning?"

"Yeah. It's about an hour and a half to the cabin from here. I thought we might as well go the rest of the way to the cabin for the night and then you can take me back to Rapid City in the morning. The car rental options are probably better there."

Made sense. Made her stomach hurt too.

But it was what she wanted. Kind of. Space. Time. A chance to be *sure* they could make this work. Though having him five hundred miles away wasn't exactly conducive to seeing how they each adjusted to the lifestyle changes they needed to consider.

She dropped her hands, ready to move, then remembered that she held the dragon pendant.

"What about this?" she asked, holding it up. They could still take it to the place Bradley had asked her to drop it off.

"This," Shane said with clear disgust. He took it from her. "This is one more example of things I can't fix."

She froze. "What's that mean?"

He was focused on the pendant as he said, "It seemed like something I could handle at first. I even thought it could be a good thing that would bring us closer. But every time I think you or I have taken care of it, it pops back up. It's never completely gone." He shifted his gaze to her. "I guess I have to accept that no matter how determined I am, no matter how tough I am, I can't change everything I want to."

Isabelle couldn't swallow past the sudden swell of emotions in her throat. The metaphor was pretty clear.

After a moment of simply looking at one another, as if waiting for the other to say something magical to make it all okay, he turned and stalked back into the gift shop. Isabelle followed. "Shane, what are you—" He hung the pendant on a hook with some other necklaces, peeled a price tag off a set of earrings hanging nearby, stuck it on the dragon and grabbed her hand. "Let's go."

Isabelle let him tug her toward the door again, but she reached out and snagged the pendant. "You can't just hang it up in a gift shop," she said. "We can't leave it behind."

"It's not my problem."

Leaving it behind was easier than continuing to deal with it. A lot like getting in his car in the morning and leaving *her* behind. Yeah, she got the metaphor loud and clear.

They stepped out of the store. "It's our responsibility," she said, wondering if he'd get *her* metaphor. "We kind of made a promise to take care of it."

"Drop it, Iz. It was a sweet idea at first, but I'm done."

She stopped and looked up at him. *I'm done* were not words she wanted to hear from Shane. Ever. In spite of her attempts to break up with him, she loved knowing he'd keep trying. In that moment, she realized that she'd been counting on it. Yes, part of her mind believed that he would be happier without her and her issues, but her heart needed to know that even if it didn't make sense, he'd be there for her. "What are you talking about?" She needed to know *exactly* what he was done with.

"The game."

So he *had* figured it out. She'd known it was only a matter of time.

"Sha—"

"Ma'am, I'm going to need you to come with me."

She turned to face the security guard that was standing behind her, hands on his hips. Dammit, she and Shane were having a moment here. "Excuse me?"

"You left the store without paying for merchandise. I'm going to need you to come with me."

She held the basket of souvenirs up. "Sorry, you can have the basket back. We paid for these. We—" Shit. They hadn't gotten a receipt. Shane had just tossed money at the cashier. "We gave her forty dollars," Isabelle said. "The sunglasses are only twelve bucks." The rest of the silly trinkets she'd collected couldn't possibly add up to twenty eight dollars.

The guard ignored the basket, but took the pendant from her fingers.

Oh.

He looked at the price tag. "That doesn't cover the price of the necklace," he said. "And I assume you don't have a receipt."

Well, no. She shook her head.

"Dammit, Iz," Shane muttered, just realizing she'd grabbed the pendant on the way out.

"This is ours," she told the security officer. This doesn't belong to the store. We brought it in with us."

"You took it off the display," the man said.

Dammit. Yes, she had. "I promise you it's ours."

"Oh, well, as long as you *promise* I'll have to believe you" he said dryly.

"The price sticker is ours." He stepped back, indicating that he wanted them to head down the sidewalk. "Let's go."

Shane did nothing but take her elbow and steer her past the man.

"You're not going to tell him you're a cop?" she said, loud enough for the guard to hear her.

"Won't matter," Shane said. "Cops don't get to shoplift either."

"We didn't shoplift it!"

"But we're not going to prove that by standing on the sidewalk and insisting," Shane said.

This wasn't part of the game. The security guard was serious. The game had made *some* sense in her kitchen that morning when Emma had told her about it. It had seemed simple, entertaining, harmless. But it had gotten unexpectedly complicated.

Like her whole relationship with Shane.

She glanced at him as they followed the sidewalk in the direction the guard indicated.

The game had been intended as a break from the somber subject of her condition and its effect on their relationship. But it had turned into a frustration for Shane. Much as her symptoms would over time. The guard stopped them at the door labeled *Security*. Shane leaving made sense. Being apart had been *her* idea initially. She'd broken things off with him months ago. But she was more than happy to think that his leaving might get postponed. Even if it was by an accidental shoplifting.

She was a mess.

"Take a seat," the guard said, pointing toward two chairs in front of his desk. It was clearly not a request.

They sat. Shane crossed one ankle over his knee and linked his hands together on his stomach. Isabelle crossed her legs too, her foot bouncing up and down as the guard typed a few things into his computer.

No one spoke.

Strangely, the relative quiet grated on Isabelle's nerves.

"This is crazy," she said. "We didn't do anything wrong."

Shane gave her a long look that clearly said *don't*. She frowned at him.

"If you didn't do anything wrong, then there's nothing to worry about," the security officer said. "Let me check on a few things."

He resumed typing. Shane sat quietly. And Isabelle started nibbling on her thumbnail.

It wasn't nerves about the necklace. That would get cleared up. It was the jumble of emotions swirling through her in general that made her feel so restless. Shane was leaving and he seemed so *calm* about it. Yes, that's what it was.

She shot him an annoyed glance. He didn't look her way.

For months she'd tried the break-up thing and instead of agreeing to give her time and space, he'd sung to her and started a petition and brought a carnival to Trudy's for her.

Now though, now that he knew everything, he was on his way home before even getting to the cabin.

And while that did make the most sense, it also annoyed the crap out of her.

Where was the big talker now?

"The necklace is not a part of the store's inventory," the guard finally said.

Yeah, they knew that. Obviously.

"So we can go." Isabelle started to stand.

"Just a minute."

She sighed and sank back onto her seat.

"Does this necklace belong to you?"

Isabelle glanced at Shane. Finally he made a move. He shifted to put both feet on the floor. "It was given to us."

"Uh-huh. It was a gift?"

"It's a favor," Shane said smoothly.

"For the owner of the necklace?"

"Sort of."

The guard gave him a *yeah, right* look and reached for his phone. Ten minutes later, the local cop strolled in.

"Hey, Larry," he greeted the security guard.

"Hi, Kyle."

"What's up?"

"Stolen necklace." Larry held the necklace up.

Kyle's eyebrows rose. "You guys sell those here?"

"Nope." He pointed at Shane and Isabelle.

Kyle looked at Shane and Isabelle. "Hi, folks."

Shane gave him a nod. "Officer."

"I'm Kyle Henson. Want to tell me what's going on?" Kyle asked Shane.

Isabelle sat back in her chair, crossed her legs, crossed her arms and waited for Shane to explain the situation in a way a cop would understand. At least, that's what she hoped he was going to do.

Shane leaned forward to prop his forearms on his thighs. "It's a game. The necklace is a knock-off of an expensive piece owned by a guy named Henry Licthberg. The game is a way to make our vacation a little more fun."

How long had he known? Isabelle wondered. And had he enjoyed it at all?

Officer Henson leaned back against the edge of Larry's desk. "Tell me about this game."

"Big Time is a company that stages murder mysteries, extreme adventures, treasure hunts, that kind of stuff," Shane said. "That's all this is. We're in the middle of one of their games.

The cop just looked at him for several seconds. Then he pushed up off the desk. "We're going to have to check that out."

"Of course."

"We're going to keep the necklace," he added.

"Please do. I'd rather not see it again, to be honest," Shane said.

"We'll run it and see if your story is legit, if the necklace is missing, if we can get a hold of Big Time. We have some work to do."

"And you'd like us to stick around," Shane said.

Officer Henson nodded. "I can hold you in a cell for the time it'll take to track all this down. But I ran your name and badge number on my way over. I'm willing to give you the benefit of the doubt if you promise to stay in town."

Shane sighed and pushed to his feet. "We can do that."

It was already after seven anyway. They'd been traveling for twelve hours. A motel was sounding damned good right then, actually.

"Great" Isabelle said, getting quickly to her feet.

"I'd recommend the motel down on Third Street," Henson said. "And keep your phone on."

"Got it." Shane turned and opened the office door, gesturing for Isabelle to go ahead of him.

When the door shut behind them Shane said, "Can we just not talk until we're at least in the car?"

Isabelle pressed her lips together. Damn.

CHAPTER
NINE

IT LOOKED like Shane's plan to leave their vacation early was not going to work out.

Isabelle tried not to smile too big about that.

Smiling didn't make sense. She should be relieved he was going to leave. That's what she'd been going for since Vegas. Where had this big give-her-space gesture been a few months ago?

But as she settled into the car next to him and took a deep breath, she admitted that this whole I'd-better-leave-you-alone thing kind of sucked.

"How long have you known it was a game?" she asked, finally breaking the weird silence that had been going on since he'd come back into the gift shop from his phone call.

Shane glanced at her as they pulled up to a stop sign. "Since Michael called me about the necklace in Mitchell."

"And you went along with it. Why?" she asked.

"I thought it was sweet."

"Sweet?" she repeated. "How is this sweet?"

"You set it up to make this trip more fun for me."

"I didn't set it up. Emma did."

"Oh."

Yeah, oh. The gesture that was so sweet wasn't even from her.

She felt a heaviness in her chest. "But I guess that doesn't matter. It's still not enough."

"Enough?"

She looked at him. "To get you to stay."

He huffed out a breath, his expression pained. "I thought you didn't want me to stay."

"I thought we were going to figure out if we can make this work."

"I don't think a cabin far from home is the way to do that after all."

The heaviness grew. The guy who had rented a cotton candy machine for her only a few days ago was leaving her in the morning. She was losing him.

"So you'll go home and…what?"

"Give you space. To figure out how you're going to deal with everything, the adjustments, what you want and need help with, and what you don't."

"And then I'm going to let you know and…then what?"

"We'll see if there's a place for me in your plan and adjustments."

It sounded good, but the heaviness in her chest wouldn't go away. "You'll be there? When I'm ready?"

He took a deep breath. "I want to say yes. But that's probably not fair. I *want* to be there when you're ready but…what if it takes three years? Or you meet someone who gets this and is happy to stay home on Saturday night?"

She actually felt a little sick at the idea.

Shane pulled up in front of the motel and they got out and headed in to register. The clerk didn't ask if they wanted more than one room and Shane didn't ask for two.

That was fine with Isabelle, of course. They might not be

sleeping here anyway. They might be allowed to leave town yet tonight.

Which would mean they could still get to the cabin. Which would mean that Shane would still be on schedule for leaving.

"You've been quiet," she finally commented as Shane tossed their bags in the corner of the room and she slumped down on the end of one of the beds.

"I've been thinking," he said without looking at her.

"Is that a good thing?"

"Maybe. I've been thinking about how mad I am that you didn't tell me about everything that was going on with you. That you were content to give up rather than work on it. And then I realized, trust has to be earned. You didn't trust me enough to be honest and that's on both of us."

"Oh, Shane, I—"

"It occurred to me that there's one very important way I need to earn your trust. We both need to know that I can do this."

"Do what?"

He turned to look at her. "Make love to you."

Her breath caught at the look in his eyes. It was that determined look she'd seen a lot lately but it was also hot and… almost mischievous. Her heart rate picked up and she wet her lips.

"I think we're in triple digits there, big guy."

He shook his head. "We've had hot, amazing, better-than-I-ever-had sex in the triple digits. But you've been too distracted by making it wild to make it really about love."

She swallowed and crossed her arms. "And what about you? What were you feeling all those times?" Did she want the answer to that question?

"I thought love," he said, moving closer. "But how could it be love when I didn't know everything I needed to know, when I wasn't meeting every need you had, physically and emotionally?"

He moved even closer, stopping right in front of her, toe to toe.

Her breathing hitched a little. It was nuts. She'd been as close to him as two people could possibly get. She'd been this close to him hundreds of times, but this felt different somehow. Almost like it was new.

"It's always been so good, Shane," she said, putting as much feeling into the words as she could. She loved him. She loved sex with him.

"It is good," he agreed. "Very good. Amazing, even. But I think it can be better."

His words made a shiver of heat sizzle through her, but she tried to put some attitude into her response. She hesitated to give him too much power here—like being able to turn her on with just a few words. She raised an eyebrow. "Better than the time with the ice cream sandwiches?"

He narrowed his eyes. "That was damned good."

"But you think it can be better?"

He took her chin between his thumb and first finger and looked into her eyes in a way he never had before. Like he knew exactly what he was searching for, but wanted to see it. He held her face, and her gaze, in a way that kept her from hiding anything.

"We've had your sex. And it's been awesome. Ice cream sandwiches, strawberry pie, banana pudding—all awesome. But we haven't had *my* sex."

She thought about smiling but there was something about the way he said it that made her tingle down deep.

"We haven't?"

"You've been in control."

"You've been there. You've—"

"Been thinking that I'm the luckiest son of a bitch in the world. Having a woman like you want me so much that she's constantly working on ways to give me the ultimate pleasure is addicting."

She swallowed hard again. "That's what I've been doing," she said sincerely. "I do want you."

"I know. And I've been selfishly going along, enjoying the ride. But I want you so much that I want to work on giving *you* the ultimate pleasure too."

Her mouth went dry. Wow. If the tone in his voice and the look in his eyes was any indication, this was going to be good. Really good. Maybe too good.

"You do," she told him.

"Oh, babe," he said, his voice dropping to a delicious huskiness. "You ain't seen nothin' yet."

He dragged his finger from the center of her chin, down her throat, then leaned in and captured her lips with his.

The kiss was different too.

Usually Shane was enthusiastic, passionate, hot, but yeah, he followed her lead.

Now he was in control. She could feel it. And it made her shiver with desire. And trepidation. She needed some control. She didn't know how to let go completely.

When he pulled back, he studied her for a moment, then said, "Take your clothes off."

Well, there was nothing to protest there. She stood and stripped quickly, her body responding to the way he watched her. She loved how it was so obvious even on his face how much he wanted her. His breathing changed, the way he stood changed, the way he curled and uncurled his fist like his hand was aching to touch her changed.

She started forward. The countertop next to the TV looked pretty steady. She could just shimmy up there and—

"No."

She looked at him. "What?"

"No. Bed." He pointed to the mattress.

She lifted an eyebrow.

"Isabelle." He pointed at the bed again.

Damn, she hadn't brought any edible body lotion or toys.

She'd told him this would be a vanilla-sex trip and she'd meant it. At the time. He'd reminded her, though, that missionary was considered pretty vanilla and he was right when he said that wasn't her favorite position. Not enough control for her.

She was going to have to get creative now.

Dirty talk had never let her down.

"I want your mouth on me, Shane," she said, stepping toward him, her hand going to her breast. "I want you to lick—"

"Bed. Now." He even snapped his fingers before pointing this time.

And damn if that didn't give her a little thrill.

She took a deep breath. Okay, she'd play. Shane could hardly help being commanding, and it did something to her. Even when she was in charge, he was right there with her, heightening things, encouraging her, his words and hands and even the way he let her have complete free reign over his body making her hotter and bolder and feeling as possessed by him, as filled by him, as marked by him as if he'd had her tied up and at his mercy.

In fact, she sometimes regretted that she couldn't give it all up to him like that. The constant drive to be exciting and to keep things spicy was exhausting sometimes. And though she knew it might hurt a little, the idea of being at *his* mercy was tempting.

"Fine." She walked to the bed and sat on the edge again.

"Lie back." He hadn't moved yet.

She did.

"Move up to the pillows."

She did.

"Now close your eyes."

Okay, this sounded promising. It wasn't like she was *never* on her back during sex. He was quite good with his fingers and tongue in this position. She just always made a point to move into more comfortable positions for the main show.

She closed her eyes and sighed happily.

The next thing she knew, he'd handcuffed her to the headboard.

She had no idea how he'd done it.

The element of surprise was a big part of it. That he was pretty good with handcuffs didn't hurt either.

"Hey." She tugged on the metal rings. "What are you doing?"

"Showing that you can trust me...with everything."

She frowned. Her heart was pounding and it wasn't entirely in the good I'm-so-hot way. She tugged again, but she wasn't getting out of the things until he let her out. "Shane, come on."

"I think we both need to know what would happen if I was in charge in bed once in a while."

"It's not like you just lie there."

He shook his head and pulled his T-shirt off. "Nope, I don't just lie there. I do exactly what you want me to do. And now I'm going to do a few things *I* want to do."

She'd never get tired of looking at his chest and abs. She paused, drinking in the sight. Then she remembered that she was annoyed. "What about what I want?"

"You want this." His hands went to his jeans.

"When did I say that?"

He looked her up and down. "You don't have to say it."

Isabelle moved her legs restlessly on the bed. It was annoyance, she was sure. She felt flushed because she was angry. Probably.

Shane unzipped and pushed the denim to the floor, stepping out of the jeans and kicking them away. The bulge behind the black cotton made Isabelle swallow hard.

He was big. And passionate. And totally in control of what was about to happen.

Okay, so how to handle this? Compliment him on how huge he was while gently reminding him that it could be a bit of a problem? Talk dirty—specifically about blow jobs—and try to get him worked up to the point that he'd have to unhook her to get the blow job that she was going to tempt him with? Beg? Yell? Threaten?

"It's hard for me to relax like this," she said, settling on guilt. "You were right that this position might be painful."

"It's hard for you to relax because I've never proven that I can take care of you like this."

He climbed onto the bed, on his knees at her feet.

"There are lots of other ways you've taken care of me," she told him, meaning it completely.

"And now that I know all the reasons to be extra careful, I'm going to show you that you can relax in *any* position with me." He reached to take one of her feet in both hands, rubbing then pressing a thumb into her arch and making her moan. "And I'm going to show myself that I can take care of you like this."

Ah, the guilt had worked. He was feeling bad about not being more careful in the past. But that wasn't his fault.

"You didn't know. You can't feel bad about it," she said.

"And now I do know," he said, meeting her gaze. "Which means I finally get a chance to use my cuffs on you."

"You've thought of that before?"

He gave her a wicked grin. "Of course."

She wiggled in the cuffs again and his attention dropped to her breasts. "Fuck," he said, his voice suddenly husky. "I love what that does to your breasts. The way they're on display for me, thrusting into the air, begging for my tongue."

Another flush of heat rushed over her and she acknowledged that she felt decidedly less angry now.

"I'm nervous," she confessed. "I always worry that if it hurts, I'll flinch or clench or gasp and make you feel bad."

He narrowed his eyes and looked at her again. "Don't fake *anything* with me, Iz. Don't protect me or do something just because I like it. If it hurts, you tell me." He said it firmly, his thumb pressing hard into her arch.

She bit her lip and pulled on her foot.

He looked down, then let go of it. "Right. Okay, like that."

She smiled at him. One thing she knew, deep, deep down, where she also knew she loved him, was that Shane would never hurt her.

"I'll tell you."

"Great." He moved up, leaned in and kissed her stomach. "Then we can get started."

She took a deep breath. She could do this. For him, she could do this.

On his side facing her, he ran one big hand over her stomach, up between her breasts and down again, stopping with the heel of his hand on her pubic bone. He repeated the path three times, his rougher hands on her skin making goose bumps erupt and spread in all directions, her nipples bead and her nerve endings crackle with awareness and anticipation.

"Shane," she breathed.

He was watching her skin react to his touch. "I've never realized how fast we always go."

She arched into his hand, unable to keep from trying to get closer to his touch. "What?" she asked, only half listening.

"We always go so fast. Like we're on a deadline."

She bit her lip and wiggled her hips, trying to get him to slide his hand lower. They did go fast. She did that on purpose. She pushed, made it hot and spontaneous, which many times meant a surface other than a soft feather-top bed. Bare ass on marble flooring, or metal car hood, or Formica countertop was not something she necessarily wanted to prolong.

Besides, Shane was very good at hard and fast.

"I love touching you," he said, still watching his hand move over her. "I love how silky you are. I love how it affects you. I haven't spent nearly enough time doing this."

"I love you touching me too," she told him. "Some places more than others."

He didn't move his attention from his hand as his slid it down one of her thighs to the knee and back up again. "Don't make me gag you too, Iz."

"You wouldn't."

"I would. You're not going to speed this along with your dirty talk. I'm going to take my time. I've been against and inside your body so many times that I assumed I'd touched and tasted and seen every inch."

Her body reacted to his words, growing warmer and wetter. She parted her legs slightly, willing him to slide up and over a few inches.

"But turns out that there are some gorgeous, and probably delicious, spots I haven't gotten to know."

Shane stroked the pads of his fingers over the back of her knee, causing a tingle to shoot straight to her clit.

Wow. That was…nice.

He did it again, then bent her knee and placed a kiss on her knee cap.

Her knee cap. And it totally made her hot.

"Do you have all the classic tender points?" he asked.

He swiped his tongue over her knee cap this time and she gasped.

"Isabelle?"

"What?" she said, breathless. From him touching her frickin' knee cap. Geez.

"Do you have all the tender points they talk about in the book?"

Tender points? She was feeling achy right now but not really tender…oh. She stopped wiggling. He was talking about her fibro. "Um, yeah. Most of them." That damned book.

"So, this is one of them." He pressed a kiss to the inside of her knee.

She caught her breath again. The sensation was tingly like when he'd kissed her knee cap, but now there was something else. There was a sweetness in how he did it.

She cleared her throat. "Yeah. But that sure doesn't hurt."

He smiled up at her. He ran his hand up and down her calf, over her ankle and across the bottom of her foot. "I know about the tender points. What else is sore?" he asked, stroking his hand back up the length of her leg to her stomach.

"You memorized the trigger points?" she asked, referring to the tender points spread through her body the way the doctor had.

"Yep. There are a few in your neck and shoulders, a couple in the low back and hips."

Wow. She didn't know what to do with him. All of the things she'd been hiding from him were now the things he was most focused on and the things that were making her wonder how she'd make it even forty-eight hours without him.

"Sometimes if my hips get stretched too far, they hurt."

He grinned, moving up to lie beside her again. "And I definitely stretch things out, huh?"

She gave a surprised little laugh. Instead of feeling bad about it, he was almost bragging. "Yeah, you do, big guy. But I don't usually mind until after."

He nodded, still looking smug. "That makes sense. But I don't want you to hurt after either. Other than in the wow-he-really-did-me-good way."

She chuckled again. "Well, there's always some of that too."

He rubbed back and forth over her lower stomach again. "What else?"

This wasn't so bad. She took a deep breath. "If I'm up on something hard and you're…going fast…" It was so stupid to hesitate over those words. She'd often begged him to go fast in the midst of sex and it wasn't always to get her off the hard surface she was on.

He was the one to chuckle this time. "Yes?"

"It gets sore on my back. But I figure any girl would feel that way."

His hand slid up to her ribcage and he rubbed back and forth. "Yeah. But it probably hurts you more. Or longer."

"Yeah, maybe." She hadn't had wild sex on hard surfaces with anyone else, so she couldn't say.

"Anything else?"

She knew he was going to keep asking and she knew she had to tell him this part, but it was more sensitive. Again, that was silly considering all the things they'd done together, but she still felt it.

"Yeah, there is."

His hand paused. When she didn't go on, he reached for her chin and turned her to look at him. "Tell me."

Another deep breath and she said all at once, "When you go really deep it hurts. My pelvic muscles get sore and tighten up and it hurts. For about a day after."

He stared at her for several long seconds and she wondered what was going through his head.

"I love it deep, though," she said. "Which I know doesn't make sense, but—"

"How deep?"

She licked her lips. She had to be honest with him. It wasn't fair to tell him only part of this. He wanted to know because he cared about her and he wanted to keep having sex with her and to make it good for her. "Like when I'm on top and you take my hips and thrust up. Or when I'm on my back and you put my leg up on your shoulder."

She could feel the tension in his body, but his hand went back to stroking over her stomach gently.

"I really like both those positions," he said thoughtfully.

She smiled. "I know you do."

"No problem when you're on hands and knees?"

"If you go a little slower, it's fine."

"And if you're on top we're okay as long as I don't take over on the rhythm?"

"Right. If I can control the speed and everything, it's fine."

"And you like it sitting up."

She smiled. She was feeling lighter, freer with him knowing this stuff. "Yes, I do. A lot. In fact—" she arched her back and succeeded in pulling his gaze to her breasts, "if you'd unhook me, I'd show you—"

He shook his head. "No. We're doing this with you cuffed."

Isabelle felt her eyebrows shoot up. "Oh?" After everything she'd told him?

"I'm starting to think that sex is like ice cream."

"Because it's sweet and sticky?" she guessed.

He grinned and moved over her, his hands braced on the mattress on either side of her. "Because of the variety. You might have your favorite flavor, but if that one runs out there are *lots* of others that are good. And, of course, there's always *vanilla,* which let's be honest, actually kind of rocks. You can't have a root beer float without it."

They were talking about ice cream, but Isabelle's body didn't seem to know that. She felt like her skin was sizzling as Shane hovered over her, his heat notching her body temp up a few degrees.

"You're sad about losing your favorite sex positions?" she asked, as he moved a knee between her legs.

"Not sad," he said. "Eager to try something new."

"Like wh—"

He leaned in and took a nipple in his mouth as he slid his hand lower, over her mound, the middle pad of his finger brushing over her clit and the sensitive folds below.

"Oh," she gasped. It wasn't new, but it was very good.

He nudged her knees apart with his and leaned back, releasing her nipple from his lips with a little pop. He trailed his tongue down the center of her stomach as his fingers made another pass over her clit. He wasn't touching with much pressure at all, but she felt the jolts of pleasure clear to her toes.

"I'm thinking," he said, kissing her belly button, then looking up at her. "Maybe we can make things a little more comfortable for you by softening things up and getting things nice and slick."

She worked on breathing normally. "That's called foreplay. And we've done that." Boy had they.

She often orgasmed before he was inside her from their foreplay. And then she often orgasmed again. That wasn't a problem.

"But it's still hard and fast. You're still in uncomfortable positions. You're still tense. Why don't we see what can happen on a nice big bed with lots of pillows and lots of time?" He pressed a kiss to her mound and swirled his tongue over the sensitive skin.

The bed was nice. But it also bugged her. Anyone could have sex on a bed. Where was the fun and excitement in that?

"Stop thinking of arguments," Shane chided.

She looked at him in surprise. "How did you know what I was thinking?"

"You get that little crease between your eyebrows when you're trying to think of how to get your way."

Great. She had a tell. "How long have you known that?"

"I think a while. I never consciously paid attention. You try to get your way with me a lot."

She couldn't deny it. "I *get* my way with you a lot."

"And now it's my turn." He moved farther down and put a hand on each of her thighs. "You trust me, right, Iz?"

He was looking her directly in the eye and she could tell that it mattered to him.

"Yes."

"You're not just telling me that because you know I want you to trust me? You do trust me?"

She nodded. But then said, "I *want* to trust you. I want to be able to fully relax on this bed and know my body will do what we both want it to."

He paused before answering, "Okay. That will work."

"Really?"

"For sure."

He slowly moved her legs apart, until her knees rested over his thighs. His gaze moved from her eyes, over her breasts, down her stomach and finally to the apex of her thighs. She felt vulnerable and exposed and helpless and…hot.

"You are so beautiful," he told her, just looking. "So often I look at you and I can't believe that you let me even buy you a drink not to mention be with you in all the ways we have been. And now," he looked back up at her face, "you've let me know things about you that no one else knows and now you're here, letting me do this."

He couldn't get mushy on her. She couldn't handle that too. She already felt like she was on sensory overload, and if he started getting all emotional she'd end up crying, or swearing, or swearing while she cried. Neither had a place here.

She wiggled her wrists in the handcuffs. "Letting you?"

He grinned. "You want me to unhook you?"

Did she? Lying spread out like this, fully exposed, felt strange. She wasn't leading the dance here. She didn't know what was coming next. She didn't have any tricks or toys.

But the look on his face was worth it. He was incredibly aroused and, if she wasn't mistaken, touched by this moment.

"I'm good for now," she conceded.

"Awesome." He reached out and dragged a fingertip over her clit and down to where she was hot and wet for him. "Awesome," he repeated softly, watching his finger.

He repeated the path a few times until she was wiggling, then slowly he pressed his finger in halfway. "I'm thinking," he said, moving in and out in short strokes, "that these are muscles here. And runners stretch their muscles before they run, right?"

She wasn't *exactly* sure what he was talking about. Or if she cared. "Uh-huh."

"So we should maybe do some warming up."

He stroked in again, then pressed gently, moving his finger in a U-shape, tracing her pelvic muscles from one side to the other. He eased his finger in further, slowly. She arched closer. "More, Shane."

"I'm with ya, babe." He added a second finger, still slowly stroking side to side with slight pressure, working in deeper and deeper.

The pressure was perfect, she felt like everything was getting heavier and softer even as tension built.

Shane eased her thighs farther apart, moving down to settle his shoulders between her legs, his fingers continuing to move in and out slowly, pressing deeper each time until his fingers were knuckle deep.

Isabelle felt her back arching, moving closer to his hand, but as he went deeper she felt the urge to pull back. It was good right now, but what if… She worked on breathing deep.

"Focus on me," Shane said softly. "How is it right now? In this moment?"

How did he know she was starting to hesitate?

She relaxed her stomach and opened her eyes—she hadn't even realized they were squeezed shut. "It's good."

He kept his eyes on hers as he brushed his thumb over her clit. The air in her lungs whooshed out. He smiled and did it again with more pressure while also easing his fingers in.

"We're going to take this one moment at a time, Iz. You with me?"

She nodded and wiggled against his hand. If he kept doing what he was doing she was with him and then some.

He gave her a knowing look and slid his fingers out, added a third and slid back in. The pressure made her moan but she also felt her thighs begin to tighten.

"Oh, no you don't." Shane leaned in and ran his tongue over her clit, circling as he pressed deeper.

The rigidity in her thighs let go, her legs feeling boneless as she gasped from the pleasure of it. Instead, the coiling tension moved into her pelvis—a *good* tension, a climax building.

A moment later, Shane pressed his fingers deep and sucked on her and she came apart as pleasure swept over her. Her whole body seemed to tighten and release at the same time and warmth rushed through her body.

She gave a heavy sigh as her internal muscles unclenched from around Shane's fingers and she let her eyes drift shut.

"Isabelle," Shane said gruffly, running his hand over her stomach.

She looked down at him. "God. You're good."

He grinned. "That's exactly what I wanted to hear."

"And thank you for not asking me if I'm okay," she said sincerely.

"Oh, I know you're okay," he said with a wink. "I could tell."

She appreciated that he was taking her at her word. She was okay. She was better than okay. She felt amazing. "I think this bed is working for me."

He chuckled. "I'm buying a new bed tomorrow."

She hesitated, then quickly covered it. Shane buying a new bed because it would make sex better for her spoke of a man who thought they had a future.

Of course it wasn't the bed. It was the man. He'd taken his time, he hadn't let her issues become a barrier, he'd found a way to make it all work. So far anyway. She felt her belly tighten. They'd done this stuff before. He'd never spent so much time or played with such purpose, but this wasn't wild, crazy, fun sex either.

"What are you thinking about?" he asked, stroking her belly. "I can feel you tensing up."

He'd been amazing. He deserved the truth. "Sex."

"That's good. At least you're not thinking about needing to schedule a manicure or something."

"Well, now that you mention it…"

He pinched her butt. "I'm not done with you yet."

Exactly. She worked on *not* tensing.

"Ready for my next great idea?"

She had to admit his first idea had been pretty good. She was still tingling from it. She nodded. "Sure."

He didn't look totally convinced, but he shifted anyway, lifting her legs and moving to lie horizontally across the bed. He draped her legs over his hip and reached to move her knees apart before he stroked through her wet heat again, pressing one finger deep, then withdrawing to run it up over her clit.

She shivered with renewed desire.

"You're with me, right?" he asked.

She felt his cock against her, big and hard and capable of making her feel so many wonderful things. She was on her back, but in this position her legs weren't stretched and none of his weight was on her. This might just…be great.

"I'm with you," she told him, a little breathless, anticipating his first stroke.

It was a good one. Long and deep but slow. She felt him press forward, filling her inch by inch. She didn't even have to try to relax. This position felt almost decadent. He could reach her clit, he could reach her nipples, he could look into her eyes, he could stroke his big hot hands up and down her thighs. And he did all of those things, over and over, as he eased all the way into her, then pulled out with excruciating slowness.

Her body welcomed him, rejoiced at having him fully inside, stretching her, heating her, igniting every nerve ending from breasts to knees and beyond.

She moved, trying to grind closer, but the handcuffs limited how far she could slide and Shane was all about being in charge here.

"You with me?" he asked again.

That was starting to sound like a disguised "You okay?" but she didn't mind suddenly. She was turned on and climbing toward another orgasmic crest, but he was doing all the work. She was essentially lying there—like a princess with a servant boy whose entire job was to pleasure her.

She could get used to this.

But then she frowned. "Are *you* with *me*?" she asked him, looking down.

"Does it not feel like I'm with you?" he asked, giving her a little extra thrust.

That was very, very nice.

"Yes. And I love this. But is it…enough for you?"

Shane looked at her like she was crazy. "Seriously?"

"Well, it's not as deep as usual or—"

"You're spread out here like a frickin' buffet," he said. "With you like this—I can see every inch of you. I can *reach* most of those inches. I can watch and feel how every stroke affects you. I can feel every time your pussy clenches, I can see when you take a quick breath, I can see your breasts bounce, when you wet your lips, the way your tummy trembles when I hit a certain spot."

He intentionally hit that spot to prove it.

Sure enough, ripples started in her tummy before swirling out like a pebble rippling a pond.

"This is amazing. Do you know how often we've had sex in the dark? I'd guess eighty-six percent of the time. This is awesome. Lights are on, there are no hard surfaces or sharp corners to watch out for, no one's gonna walk in on us or over-hear us… I could do this for hours."

She smiled as he flexed and moved deep again. "Glad to hear it." She wished she could touch him.

His phone rang.

She looked from it to him. He laughed and shook his head. "No, I'm not stopping to answer that."

He thrust again.

"Glad to hear that too," she said, her voice catching as his long stroke filled her. But it wasn't in a bad way. Not at all. She felt all of it clear to her toes.

She flexed her pelvic muscles and Shane groaned. He reached up to tease a nipple. She moaned for him and squirmed, sliding her legs farther apart.

"That's such a pretty sight," he praised, gaze on her clit and where they were joined. He ran his finger over her sweet spot, making her inner muscles clench again.

His strokes picked up speed and Isabelle found herself opening her legs farther and pressing her hands against the headboard to help her meet his thrusts, craving him deeper and faster. There was no instinctive tightening, no hesitation, no holding back.

Shane must have sensed that she was right with him now without asking. He put his bottom hand under ass and wrapped his upper arm around her thigh closest to him, keeping her from sliding away as he drove into her. She felt her body pull and pulse around him, climbing, climbing, until she again went over the peak, crying out his name.

He immediately stroked over her clit with his thumb, then circled, saying random dirty words, keeping her orgasm rolling, as he thrust again and again until she felt his orgasm sweep through him hot and hard, her name on his lips.

He stayed pressed against her for several long seconds. Then flopped to his back. Neither of them moved for several minutes after. When Shane finally did shift, it was to unlock her hands and then lie down beside her and pull her against him to spoon.

She absorbed the feel of him all around her and sank into the pillows and feather-top mattress that she was going to have a hard time leaving behind when it was time to go.

"Holy shit that was good." His voice rumbled from his chest against her back.

She even loved that.

"It really was," she agreed.

"Yeah?"

"Definitely. You? Honestly?"

"Absolutely. I'm not sure why people haven't discovered how great sex can be in a bed."

She giggled at that and cuddled in closer to him. "We've done it in a bed before."

"I seem to remember *two* dildos and some mango motion lotion one time," he said.

She kind of liked the motion lotion and had definitely liked the dildos, but still, *this* bed thing was the favorite.

"And then there were the three or four times when we started on the bed but ended up on the floor," she said.

"And the time we played that sexy board game."

She smiled at the memories. They were hot but, yeah, they'd done fine with just a bed.

And a pair of handcuffs. She turned to her back. "So that was vanilla?"

He grinned. "Let's call it the root beer float."

She laughed. "And what about the handcuffs? That's actually a little kinky, right?"

He thought about that. "Okay, we added a twisty straw to the float this time."

She put her hand against his cheek. "This was…amazing. Thank you."

He captured her wrist and pressed a kiss to her palm. "My pleasure. It was for me too, you know."

She nodded. She did understand that.

She grinned at that thought. Sex with Shane was good for her. Like taking her daily vitamins.

"You're not too sore?" he asked, running his hand over her hip.

"I'm fine," she told him, moving to kiss him.

He kissed her sweetly, then sighed. "I guess I better check the phone call."

"I'm going to shower."

CHAPTER
TEN

SHANE DIDN'T RECOGNIZE the number of the missed call, but he wasn't surprised when the person on the other end answered, "Police department," when he returned the call.

"This is Shane Kelley."

"Hold please."

A moment later he heard, "Officer Kelley."

He recognized the voice of Kyle Henson. "Officer Henson."

"I wanted to let you and Ms. Dixon know that we were able to get a hold of Big Time and they verified everything. Someone is coming to retrieve the pendant. You're free to go. Thank you for staying in town until we could clear things up."

"Thank you. I appreciate the call."

They disconnected and Shane shoved his phone into his pocket and looked around the room. They hadn't gotten as far as unpacking. Isabelle had pulled a few things from her bag for her shower, but otherwise they could just zip up and head out.

He heard the shower stop and thought about going in to help her dry off, but he held back. A month ago—hell a week ago—he would have done exactly that. They would have had hot sex on the bathroom counter or on the floor or back in the shower—or all of the above. But now… He ran a hand over the back of his neck and looked at the bed. Now things were different.

Shane felt a tickle of unease and scowled. His first reaction was that he didn't want to have to hold back and analyze every urge he had for whether or not it was something that would work or be good for Isabelle. And it wasn't just sex—it was how late they stayed out and what they did when they were out, it was where they went to dinner and what they bought grocery shopping. It was everything. His impulses and whims, his habit of doing what felt good in the moment would now need to be examined each time. It was going to be a big shift.

He looked at the door to the bathroom. It was Isabelle. He was a selfish ass if he wasn't willing to give up a few things here and there to be with the woman he claimed to love.

He looked at the bed.

That certainly wasn't all bad. He hated to give up some of his favorite positions, to be sure. It would be hard for him to hold back some of his cravings for hard, fast, do-it-anywhere sex. He would miss being able to flip her over, spread her out and go at it. But he loved that she'd let him handcuff her. Sure she'd complained, but if she hadn't wanted it—*really* hadn't wanted it—she would have let him know and he would have released her.

Instead she'd trusted him.

He felt his chest get a little tight. This was big. He'd needed her to know that he could take care of her, but *he* had needed to know it too.

So he needed to take things down a notch or two.

He could do that.

Isabelle opened the bathroom door, wrapped only in a towel. When she saw him her lips stretched into a huge, bright grin.

His chest got tighter. He had to do this or he was going to lose her.

"We're free to go," he told her, coming up off of the windowsill.

"Yeah?" she asked, bending over to rummage in her bag.

Shane watched, curling his hands into fists. He couldn't go over there, push the towel out of the way and do her from behind. She'd said hands and knees were okay, but she was probably a little sore, considering they hadn't even been apart for twenty minutes, and maybe standing up wasn't the same as hands and knees.

He had a lot to learn.

"Yeah, they apparently got in touch with someone at Big Time and now we're free to leave."

Her towel slipped slightly, exposing the upper curve of one breast, and Shane breathed in through his nose and out through his mouth. Up against the wall would probably be uncomfortable for her and again, it hadn't been very long since he'd stretched her out.

He hadn't ever realized how horny he was around her.

Maybe it was the dieter's dilemma he heard girls talking about—you didn't crave something as intensely as when it was off limits.

Yeah, that's what this was—he was going on a sex-with-Isabelle diet. He wasn't giving it up entirely, just cutting back.

He sighed. Everyone knew diets sucked.

"Should we go on to the cabin tonight then?" she asked, heading back into the bathroom to—hopefully—get dressed.

It was after eight at night, but he was thinking that staying here in the motel room wasn't a great idea. It was an hour yet to the cabin, but he could drag that out. Maybe by the time they actually got there, she'd be too tired and they could go to bed. To sleep. Then they could deal with everything in the morning.

"Yeah, might as well." He paced across the room, determined *not* to think about her dropping that towel and shimmying into her panties and bra again. "Do you want to eat something here before we leave town or do you want to grab something on the road?"

And there was another thing he was going to have to think

through—where should they stop for food? Was any burger joint along the interstate okay? He wished he could ask her, but at this point—six chapters into *Living and Loving with Fibromyalgia*—he knew more about it than she did. Which frustrated the crap out of him, but he understood that she needed to figure this out her own way, in her own time.

He couldn't do it for her. He wanted to. He definitely wanted to. He was a one-hundred-and-ten-percent kind of guy. Once he started, he didn't stop until a project was done. If someone asked him to pick up a case of beer for a party, he brought three. If he thought a bouquet of balloons would cheer someone up, he'd send balloons via singing-telegram clown. It stood to reason then that if he finally knew everything he needed to know about Isabelle and their relationship, then he'd jump in and work on it full-throttle. He'd read six chapters in the book in a few hours. He could take in a few books in a couple of days.

And in that moment, it hit him.

To make this work they had to figure out how to fit what they both needed with what they both wanted.

They *both* needed to figure out how to fit what they both needed with what they both wanted.

Sure, he could read a few books. He could read a thousand books. But Isabelle also needed to read a thousand books. Or even one book. And so far that wasn't happening.

He needed to know that she would make that happen. To be with him.

"Yes, let's eat," she said enthusiastically, buttoning her last button as she came back into the room.

God she was beautiful. She was sexy and funny and sweet and confident and if she chose to take this thing by the throat she'd kick its ass and they could live happily ever after.

If she wanted to.

He sure as hell hoped she wanted to.

He cleared his throat so he didn't sound like he was about to swear or beg or cry. "Sounds good." They'd find a place with salads. Until he could read more, he'd err on the side of healthy. No one shouldn't eat salads. At least, he was pretty sure that was true.

Shane loaded their stuff up and checked them out. Then they headed farther into town to a basic family restaurant after Isabelle said she didn't care where they went or what they ate. That wasn't especially helpful, but Shane resisted pointing that out. They ate without much talking, both hungry and starting to feel the effects of a day-long road trip with the rollercoaster of excitement and emotions.

Finally, Isabelle put her fork down and looked at him across the table. "Are you still leaving tomorrow?"

Ah, the question he'd been avoiding even asking himself.

Lying beside her in the hotel room, he'd thought some things had shifted. He could be a part of this now, knowing everything, helping her adjust and learning right along next to her. But now, away from her naked body and a soft horizontal surface, he admitted that he was still edgy. Because he was afraid the hotel room had maybe made things worse.

He'd had to handcuff her. If he hadn't, she would have taken over with—God knew what. She was always surprising him with the sexy and creative stuff she came up with. But there was no way she would have just laid there and let him pleasure her like that. She wouldn't have answered all his questions, telling him where and when it hurt. He still wouldn't know that it was painful when she was on top and he took over the rhythm.

And she would have kept doing it. She would have kept climbing up and letting him do what he wanted to do.

Sex wasn't everything in a relationship, but in theirs it was turning out to be very representative of nearly everything else.

He didn't want to have to handcuff her—literally or metaphorically—to get her to open up about what was going on with her and how she was feeling and what he could do to help her. He didn't want everything to be about her making him happy. He wanted it to be a two-way street.

Shane leaned in and looked her directly in the eyes. "I want you so bad right now."

Her eyes widened and her lips parted.

"I want you to go into the ladies room and take your panties off. I'll be there in two minutes. I want you up on that counter, legs spread when I get there."

She glanced in the direction of the bathroom. "Um." She looked back at him. He could see that her breathing had changed slightly and her cheeks were flushed. "Okay." She started to slide out of the booth.

He loved that he could turn her on so easily. He loved that she *wanted* to do what he'd suggested. He hated that she shouldn't do it and he hated that she wouldn't tell him that and he *hated* that he had to think twice about everything now.

"Dammit, Isabelle."

She paused on the edge of the booth bench. "What?"

"We can't have sex on the bathroom counter."

She looked around the restaurant. "Why not?"

"Hard, cold, stretching in awkward positions."

Her shoulders slumped and she slid back into the booth. "I guess."

"And *you* need to be the one saying no."

She frowned at him. "But I *want* to have sex on the bathroom counter."

"Me too." He did. The sex-diet-plan was already sucking a little bit.

"I don't like saying no to you."

He nodded. "Yeah, I know."

"Why do you say it like that? You want me to say no?"

"You need to say no to me." He sighed. This was all fucking confusing as hell. "You need to be able to say no to me without worrying that I'll be mad or that it will mess things up."

She tipped her head to the side, watching him. "Are you sure you won't be mad and that it won't mess anything up?"

He wanted honesty from her. He had to give it back. "I don't know. People don't say no to me very often."

She couldn't argue with that. He had a long track record with a lot of people she knew personally. Her brother had a drunk-and-disorderly charge on his record because he hadn't said no to Shane.

"I've noticed," she said. "It's really easy to say yes to you. Fun too. There aren't a lot of reasons to say no."

"Except that I need to calm the hell down sometimes. And think about consequences. And consider other people."

Her eyebrows climbed. "You don't do the things you do because you're selfish, Shane."

"You sure about that?"

"You do most of what you do because it gives the people around you a good time."

Yeah, that's why he thought he did the things he did. But it was a good time for him too. "I still think you need to feel able to say no to me."

"It's your own fault that you're hard to say no to."

He gave her a smile. He worked on that. He wanted to be the life of the party, the one everyone wanted around. Now it was coming back to bite him in the ass.

"I don't want to lose you," she said softly.

"I don't want you to lose me either."

"But you can't promise that I won't."

He felt the heaviness return to his chest. "It might be good for me to hear no once in a while. To pull my head out of my ass and stop acting like I'm twenty-one."

She smiled again, but it was sad this time. "I don't know if I can say no to you, Shane."

"I can't be the only one thinking about what's best for you, Iz."

"I hate that saying no to you might be what's best for me."

They sat looking at each other until the waitress interrupted with their bill.

They walked to the car quietly and got in. When he'd started the engine he said, "I think I'm still leaving tomorrow."

She nodded. "I knew you were going to say that."

He shifted into drive and pulled out onto the street. "I'm going to fill up here before we leave. Then we'll head to Rapid City."

She didn't reply.

Because really, what was there to say?

This vacation officially sucked.

And that was saying a lot, considering how much sex had been involved.

Isabelle couldn't remember feeling so many emotions in the span of one day in her life.

It was exhausting.

The sky was getting darker. In the side rearview mirror, she watched Shane fill the gas tank. Maybe saying no to him was what she should do, but her need to make him happy made that difficult. She wasn't the only one who was weak to resist Shane's charming, fun-loving ways. He made people happy and they responded to his wide come-on-you-know-you-want-to grins, going along with things that no one else could talk them into. Her brother had a tattoo he hadn't planned on getting, Ryan had invested in a brewery he'd never even seen, and Cody had adopted a dog he didn't have room for.

I can't be the only one thinking about what's best for you. Remembering those words made her heart ache. He was trying. He really was.

As he finished with the gas and headed into the store to pay, she sighed deeply. She'd underestimated him.

She'd broken things off because she hadn't believed that there was an option. She'd thought she had to choose to be right beside him as his fun, sexy girlfriend who was up for anything any time, or to be nothing in his life. She hadn't realized that there was the possibility for compromise. Shane was just so…*Shane*. He was a force to be reckoned with, for sure. He lived his life big and loud and he loved it. How could she have believed that he was willing to give any of that up?

There was more to him than she'd expected, more than she'd seen.

Which didn't say much for her. Or their relationship.

Maybe if it had been more than six months, maybe if they'd spent more time talking than they had partying, maybe if they'd kept their clothes on even fifty percent of the time they were alone together, she would have seen that there was a depth there.

And maybe if they'd been more real together, it wouldn't have lasted even six months.

She blew out a breath and swiped the tear from her cheek. Then her eyes focused on the book on the dashboard. *Living and Loving with Fibromyalgia.*

Fuck.

She didn't *want* to live with fibromyalgia. The brochures the rheumatologist had given her had depressed and scared her enough. She sure as hell didn't want a big old book about it.

But that wasn't making it go away.

Fuck.

With a huge knot of dread in her gut, she pulled the book into her lap and opened to the table of contents.

There was an entire chapter on the importance of reducing stress. Which stressed her out. There was also a chapter on diet that she was pretty sure didn't include cupcakes. Which sucked. But there was a long chapter on massage and positive touch. And then there was the one on sex.

There was nothing saying that she couldn't skip ahead. She wasn't quite ready to face the truth about the cupcakes, but the sex chapter might have some good suggestions—and pictures. Her repertoire included several not-fibro-friendly things like having to hold herself up against slippery shower stalls. She could use some new ideas.

She was engrossed in the information—and yes, pictures—on the fifth page of the sex chapter when someone knocked on the window beside her. She jumped and turned, then quickly slammed the book shut as she looked into the smiling face of the eight-year-old girl outside.

Isabelle rolled the window down. "Um, hi."

"Hi. Would you buy a candy bar from me? I'm raising money to go to summer camp. The bars are a dollar apiece, which my grandma says is kinda high for candy, but my sister says they're pretty good and she knows 'cause she eats lots of chocolate."

Isabelle smiled at the unique sales pitch. Not that she needed it. Chocolate sounded like a hell of an idea frankly and she hadn't read the diet chapter yet, so she could still pretend that it was fine.

"You bet. I'll take one." Over the girl's shoulder she saw Shane step out onto the sidewalk and her heart thumped. She loved him so much and he was leaving tomorrow. "You know what? Make that two." She handed two dollar bills over. Then she pulled one back. She had to *try* to do the right thing. "No, just one."

The girl dug out a chocolate bar from the sack she carried and traded Isabelle for the money.

"Thank you, ma'am," the girl said.

"Thank *you*."

Shane was chatting with another guy on the sidewalk. The guy was laughing at whatever Shane had said—because of course he was—and Shane's grin made something deep in Isabelle's belly clench.

She tore off the wrapper of one of the bars as the girl headed for the red pickup that was parked in front of the convenience store. She needed some chocolate before Shane got back into the car.

She took a huge bite. The girl's sister was right—it was good chocolate. Chewing, she tore more of the wrapper back, but as she lifted the bar for another bite something fell onto her lap and she looked down. The silver glinted in the sunlight as Isabelle tried to swallow.

It was the dragon pendant.

How the hell had that happened?

Her phone chimed with a text. She opened it with a frown. *Open the candy bar. Finish the game. The drop-off site is close.*

She looked down at the candy bar. They had thought she might not eat the chocolate right away? Ha.

Her phone chimed again. *The pendant has to be at the site by midnight.*

Yeah, yeah, she was Cinderella. She got it.

The next text included directions to the drop-off site and instructions to find a man in a bowler hat.

Seriously? A bowler hat? She grinned and looked up as the red pickup backed out of the parking spot, made a huge turn and then came back toward where she was parked. The little girl was sitting in the passenger side and she gave Isabelle a thumb's up as they rolled past.

Isabelle didn't know if the little girl belonged to someone with Big Time or if they'd just recruited her and her parent to help with the game. It had been creative either way.

Yeah. She'd take the pendant to the drop-off and finish the game. Why not? She didn't want to abandon the whole thing just because it had gotten a little confusing. Something from this trip needed to turn out the way she'd intended it.

Emma had set this up to prove to Isabelle and Shane—and Emma herself—that Isabelle could still be adventurous. Maybe it was time for her to be adventurous by herself. Lord knew that she couldn't be a sidekick when it came to facing the fibro. She was front and center for that.

She nodded at the little girl. The girl grinned and waved. As the pickup passed her window, Isabelle saw that Shane was headed her way.

She swallowed the chocolate and started to put the rest of the bar away, then thought better of it and shoved the rest of the candy into her mouth as she tucked the pendant into the glove compartment. She didn't want Shane to see any of the above. He'd disapproved of the gummy bears, so she knew he would frown about the chocolate.

He'd *really* frown—or worse—about the pendant.

She swallowed and wiped her mouth as Shane opened the car door and slid in.

He was leaving tomorrow. She'd just wait until he left and take the pendant to the drop-off site. It was a game and it was fun and she would finish it after he was gone.

"Ready to go?" he asked, setting two bottles of water into the cup holders in the middle console.

"Yep."

"You okay?" He started the car, but looked over at her.

"Yep." She stared straight ahead, not wanting to look guilty and not sure she could hide it.

"What are you…"

She glanced at him to see why he'd trailed off.

He was looking at the book in her lap. He cleared his throat. "You're reading it?"

She looked at the book, then back to him. "Yeah."

His gaze found hers. "I was under the impression that you didn't want to know the info in there."

"I don't." She took a deep breath. "It's denial, Shane. Pure and simple. The longer I *don't* learn about fibro, the longer I can put off making the changes I don't want to make."

His jaw tightened, but he nodded. "Okay." He shifted into drive and pulled out onto the street.

"I don't need a book to tell me the things I shouldn't do," she said, quietly, determined to let him in. Up until now she'd been reluctant to tell him much, worried it might scare him off. But he was leaving tomorrow anyway. "I know that caffeine bothers my stomach and that I need about nine hours of sleep at night and that the tops of my shoulders and the sides of my hips are the most tender and that I'm sensitive to bright light and that my tolerance for crowds and a lot of noise is about two hours. I've learned all of that through trial and error."

Shane's hands gripped the steering wheel tighter, but he didn't say anything.

"And I hate all of that." She shifted in her seat, staring out the windshield instead of looking at him. "I hate that my body is betraying me. I hate that I have to make adjustments and have special considerations for everything. I want to go and do and have fun and not worry. And I hate that my mind gets foggy sometimes and I have to carry sticky notes with me everywhere I go so I don't forget something someone told me on one of my sales calls or—" She cut her rant off before admitting to Shane that she didn't always remember the details of being with *him*.

"Or?" He looked over at her. "Dammit, Iz, or what?"

She could hear the frustration in his voice and felt the waves of it in the air between them. It matched her own. She felt like she was a dog on a leash. She had some room to move, and she could see the great big wide world out there that she wanted to explore and enjoy, but there was a limit to how far she could go. If she ran at it hard and fast, the leash would pull tight and snap her back. And it would hurt. She knew because that had been her strategy for the last several months—pretend the leash wasn't there, pretend that if she ran hard enough she could break away from it. She couldn't, of course, and the trying was painful, but she'd kept at it. And Shane was just at the edge of her leash. She could reach him now, but if he moved even a foot in a new direction, she wouldn't be able to go with him.

She looked at Shane. It was going to hurt no matter what. "My bedside table drawer is full of notes. About us."

He glanced over, clearly surprised. "It is?"

Fortunately he had to focus on the road again instead of staring at her.

"Not big stuff. I remember that. But little details get lost sometimes. So I write down things I want to remember. Like if you say something amazing to me, or the way something you did made me feel, things I want to be sure to tell you or do with you."

He swallowed hard. "That's…nice."

"I do it because my memory is horrible," she said. "The fibro makes me foggy. I get this fuzzy-headed feeling when I'm too tired or been too over-stimulated or…I don't know. For lots of reasons probably. But anyway, when that happens, it's hard to concentrate, hard to keep track of details. It's a problem with work, of course. And it was keeping me from remembering the little things about being with you."

"Iz—"

His voice was gravelly so she plunged ahead, wanting to say the rest before he said anything too sweet. Or told her that it was creepy that she wrote down the things he said to her.

"But I realize," she continued, "that maybe this book, or other books, or whatever, could help me. It won't take the fibro away —" She had to stop and swallow. God, it was hard to admit that she had a chronic condition. It wasn't going to kill her, but it was going to be with her forever. That idea made her incredibly tired and pissed off. "It won't take it away," she said again, her voice firm. "But there are probably ideas in here about how to make it better, or easier, to live with it. I'm willing to read and try some things."

He didn't say anything to that. He did, however, reach over and take her hand. That was it. He held her hand. And some of the tense knots in her shoulders relaxed.

They drove without talking for nearly twenty minutes. She wondered if they'd ever touched so innocently for so long.

Then Shane said, "I wasn't always loud and fun and rowdy."

She sat up straighter, sensing something big here. "Okay."

"I was quiet when I first went to the Kelleys," he said. His grip tightened on her hand, but otherwise he looked relaxed and calm. "Three of us boys slept in the same room in a twin bed and a set of bunk beds. I hated bedtime because it reminded me of going to sleep when my mom left and the night I spent alone."

Her stomach felt like it suddenly twisted into a hard knot thinking about how that must have been for him. God. It made her want to cry and hug him and assure him nothing bad would ever happen again.

But, of course, she couldn't tell him that.

"It was okay, though, because Pam would read or sing to us after she turned off the light," he said.

Isabelle knew that he referred to his foster mother as Pam. She'd heard him talk about her a lot. He'd never mentioned his biological mother until he'd told her his story that morning.

Was it really just that morning? Isabelle shivered a little at the realization. So much had happened.

"We would lie there with only the nightlight on and I could feel my whole body was tense and tight, but then she'd start singing or reading and I could feel it relax, feel the bad stuff leaving. I never had a hard time sleeping there. I knew there were people around, lots of people, and I knew—somehow— that I would never have to be alone again."

Isabelle swallowed. She had nothing to say. But it didn't seem that Shane needed her to speak.

"I remember soaking up that feeling. That feeling of having people around. Being surrounded. I loved sharing a bathroom. I loved fighting over bacon at breakfast. I loved squeezing in tight in the backseat of the car. It meant there were people around me, everywhere I went."

He stopped and breathed while Isabelle felt like she was holding her breath.

"But then a little boy came to us. Pam put him in our room because he was about the age of one of my brothers."

She loved how he thought of and referred to these people as his family. She squeezed his hand.

"His name was—is—Josh. He was scared to death of the dark. That first night he laid there and cried. He tried to keep it quiet and the other boys fell asleep right away, but I heard him. And I hated it. I hated that anyone should be scared like that. I knew how he felt and I knew how great it felt to let it go, to be able to sleep and not be scared. So I started talking to him. I told him funny stories—I made some of it up—I told him jokes, whatever it took to make him feel better."

Isabelle felt herself smiling, imagining Shane hanging over the edge of the top bunk and talking the kid through his fears. She didn't know if he'd had the top bunk, but that's what she pictured. "Did it help?"

"Kind of. But not enough. Over the next few nights I got the other guys involved. We'd wait until Pam went to bed, then we'd get up and turn on flashlights and play games, or get our comic books out, or we'd sneak out to the kitchen for cookies—whatever it took to get Josh through those first few dark hours."

She wanted to hug him again. "That's awesome."

He shot her a little smile. "I loved it. That feeling of making someone happy, of helping them forget their problems and fears. Things grew. Every time a new kid came, I took it upon myself to do whatever I could to make them feel better. I came up with all kinds of stuff and things got bigger and louder. I got into trouble for some of it, but it was always worth it. And, looking back, I know Pam knew what I was doing. That's why I never got into any serious trouble. She'd make me take extra dish duty or clean out the garage, stuff like that, but it was never anything bad."

"What kinds of things did you do?"

"Accidentally breaking lamps when acting out action movie sequences with homemade swords, sneaking out to have midnight snowball fights, bringing guinea pigs home without permission, using the good sheets to make tents in the trees in the backyard. Stuff like that."

She shook her head. He really was a lot like Emma. "So rowdiness is a learned behavior."

But he didn't smile. "You're the first person I care about who I can't fix with my method."

Her smile died instantly. "Shane—"

"I can make people happy after a hard day at work, after they lose a job, after they go through a breakup, after they lose the big game. But I can't fix you."

"It's sweet that you want to," she said quietly.

"In fact," he went on, almost like he hadn't heard her, "the stuff I usually do—the rowdiness—is the last thing you need. So I'm pissed. Pissed because I've never had anyone I've wanted to fix this bad, and I'm completely lost about how to do it."

"It's not your fault."

In fact, it was very much *her* fault.

The realization hit her hard.

She wanted to give him something to do that would help her. She could see clearly how much that mattered to him. Helping her would make him happy and she needed to make him happy.

She needed to figure out what worked for her and what didn't and now she had a *really* good reason. Maybe it was sad that she wanted to do it for Shane more than she wanted to do it for herself. Then again maybe that's how love worked—the other person made you better than you could be on your own.

"Maybe not," he admitted. "That doesn't make it easier."

He was leaving tomorrow so she could figure things out, figure out where he fit into her new lifestyle. She could do this. She would do this. And Shane would have a big part. She would be able to give that to him.

She pulled in a long breath. "I think you going home tomorrow is good. It will give us time to figure things out."

She felt his body stiffen beside her and he didn't look at her when she glanced at him.

"Yeah," was all he said, but he shifted in his seat and pulled his hand from hers.

She sighed. Dammit. He was mad. This was his idea too. He had been the first to bring it up.

She took a deep breath. Okay. That was how it was going to

have to be for now. She needed some time to muddle through all of this. But he'd wait. She was pretty sure.

And they had tonight together. Alone in the quiet cabin. The way she'd planned. Suddenly butterflies kicked up in her stomach and she pressed her hand to it. She'd never been nervous about being alone with Shane. Even in the beginning, any butterflies about being with him were excited butterflies.

This was Shane. What was there to be nervous about?

She glanced at him again. Other than him breaking her heart, of course.

They pulled into Rapid City and Isabelle dug out the directions she'd been given to the cabin. They spent the rest of the drive with her giving the instructions and Shane following them.

The house was only about ten minutes outside of town, but it was tucked up into the hills at the end of a climbing, winding road and surrounded by trees. It was pitch black up here—no streetlights or lights from neighboring houses—and Isabelle wondered if they'd drive right past it without knowing.

A minute later, that fear was completely laid to rest.

The monotonous wall of trees opened suddenly to reveal the cabin. If cabin was the right word. If nothing else, "huge" should be put in front of it.

Like a sparkling jewel in a dark velvet box, the cabin—or more accurately, the *mansion*—rose up out of the dark middle-of-nowhere. It was mostly stone and glass and was lit warmly from within. The front faced them and the gorgeous view of the Black Hills behind them and Isabelle's first thought was…holy shit.

She knew her boss was wealthy, but *holy shit*.

"Um, this is it?" Shane asked, putting the car into park and staring through the windshield.

Somehow the house managed to look rustic and modern at the same time. The stone exterior blended with the surroundings as did the rough wooden railing on the five wide stone steps that led to the double front door. The loose rock pathway from the parking area to the house and the rocking chairs on the porch added some country charm, but the light fixtures on either side of the door were definitely of this century. And expensive. The evergreens that hugged the house on all sides had clearly been there for generations, but the small ones around the porch and steps were well manicured and probably less than two years old judging by their size. And then there was the fact that the place was three stories tall, took up a space equivalent to half a city block and had electricity—lots of it, judging by the number of lights on inside—and running water—as evidenced by the tall, stone fountain to the left of the path.

"Guess so," Isabelle said, still a little stunned.

"Is someone already here?"

Someone must be, Isabelle reasoned, but she hadn't been expecting anyone to be there but her and Shane. "I don't know. Let's go see if this is right." She got out of the car and waited for Shane to join her before starting for the house.

They rang the doorbell. She had a key, of course, but if there had been a mistake in her spending the week here, she hated to just walk in. A moment later, the door swung open and a woman with a bright smile greeted them.

"You must be Ms. Dixon," she said warmly. "Please come in." She stepped back and gestured for them to come in.

Isabelle nodded, still hesitant. "Yes. And this is my friend Shane Kelley."

"Mr. Miles told me you were bringing a friend. I'm Sylvia, the housekeeper. Mr. Miles asked me to get the house ready for you."

Ah, the housekeeper. Of course. Isabelle stepped into the foyer and tried not to gawk at the high ceiling, polished wood and grand staircase. "It's nice to meet you."

Sylvia closed the door behind Shane. "My husband, Dean, takes care of the repairs and the grounds, while I keep things clean and get linens and food ready for guests. Mr. Miles loves to entertain and loves to send friends to use the house when he's not here."

"It's wonderful of him to let us stay," she said brightly to the housekeeper.

Sylvia smiled and motioned them to follow her. "I'll show you your room and help you get settled. Unless you're hungry?" She glanced back as she asked.

"No, we're fine," Isabelle assured her.

"Then we'll get you settled for the night."

"I'll grab the bags," Shane said.

"Oh, don't be silly," Sylvia said. "I'll send Dean out."

Shane started to protest, then seemed to think better of it. "Okay. Everything's in the backseat."

"Wonderful." Sylvia led them up the curved staircase to the second level. "One bedroom or two?" she asked sweetly.

"One," Isabelle said quickly. They were about to embark upon several days apart but all of a sudden, she was not in a hurry for that to happen.

Shane raised an eyebrow, but said nothing.

They followed Sylvia down the hall past three doors before she stopped and opened the fourth on the right with a flourish. "Here you go. Everything you need should be here, but please let me know if I can get you anything. Dean will bring your things up soon."

Isabelle stepped over the threshold and had to bite her tongue to keep from commenting on the room and sounding like an idiot. Because her comment would have been another *holy shit*.

The room was *gigantic*. There was an enormous bed, a huge armoire, an old-fashioned dressing table with a mirror, and a sitting area with two wingback chairs and a table near one of the windows. One wall of the room was covered with bookshelves—full bookshelves.

She could happily stay right here for the entire week she was supposed to be at the cabin.

"The bathroom is right through there," Sylvia said, pointing at the door in the wall opposite the bookshelves. "Linens are in the cabinet."

"Thank you. It's beautiful," Isabelle told her.

Sylvia smiled. "Make yourself at home." She pulled the door shut behind her, leaving Isabelle and Shane alone together.

And the butterflies were back.

She'd never been nervous alone with Shane. She'd certainly never felt strange alone with him in a bedroom. There had been a little anxiety at times—doubt that she would be able to pull off whatever sexy surprise she had for him, worry that she'd let on that something was uncomfortable—but never true nerves.

She wandered to the dressing table and studied the intricate woodwork around the mirror. Or pretended to study it anyway. She didn't actually care about the woodwork.

"Usually we'd be naked by now."

She straightened at Shane's words, but didn't turn. "Yeah, probably."

"I swear I thought I knew your favorite kind of pasta."

That, however, made her turn. "What?"

He was looking at her with a strange, almost puzzled expression. "I swear I thought I knew all about you. But I don't know your favorite kind of pasta. Or your favorite song. Or if you wash your hair first or last when you shower."

Isabelle stared at him. Her heart was pounding, but she wasn't sure why. She wasn't even sure what he was talking about. Except, she kind of was. "We haven't spent a lot of time talking, huh?"

He shook his head. "We've talked. Just not about…real stuff, I guess."

She sighed. "You know my favorite drink."

"And your favorite vibrator."

"And my favorite flavor of lube."

They stood looking at each other across the several feet that separated them.

"I swear, I feel like I know more than that," Shane finally said. "I don't, obviously. But I feel like I do. Is that stupid?"

Her heart gave a little squeeze. She knew what he meant. It was insane that she didn't know if he'd been an A or a C student in high school, or if he followed major league baseball, or if he was allergic to any foods. Because she did feel like she *knew* him.

She approached where he stood, still near the door. "The great thing is, we can fix all of that."

He reached for her as soon as she was close enough and pulled her in against his chest. "I'm sorry, Iz."

She wrapped her arms around him tightly and mumbled against his chest, "For what?"

"For not letting you know I cared about what kind of pasta you like."

She laughed and squeezed him. "I wasn't asking you about macaroni either, big guy. And I was completely okay with finding out which vibrator was my favorite." She felt the rumble of laughter against her cheek and felt her heart squeeze again. In a good way. "Want to stay up all night talking?"

He sighed. "Strangely enough, I do."

She pulled back and looked up at him. "I have three sisters, you know."

He gave her a suspicious look. "Yeah."

"I've done more than my share of up-all-night talking. In fact, I'm kind of a pro."

He smiled. "Then I'll gladly follow your lead."

"Okay, we need pajamas, popcorn and nail polish."

His smile died. "Nail polish?"

She grinned. "If we're not doing nails, we have to work on hair."

He tipped his head, regarding her seriously. "Can you teach me to French braid?"

Surprised, she pulled back even further. "How do you know what a French braid is?"

"I had sisters too. And I knew how to get lost when the pony-tail holders and hairspray came out."

Oh, this was gonna be good.

"You get the popcorn and I'll get the pajamas."

"I don't sleep in pajamas."

She should have seen that coming. Heat coursed through her as she immediately imagined drizzling butter over Shane like he was a piece of popcorn. She licked her lips. "This is probably why you don't know my favorite pasta."

It was clear he felt the chemistry as well. His eyes were hot as he stared at her mouth. "I think this is *exactly* why I don't know your favorite pasta."

"You're going to have to wear sweat pants."

"Yeah. I can do that." He let her go and stepped back, holding his hands up in surrender. "At least, I *think* I can do that."

"Popcorn," she said simply.

"Right. Popcorn." He turned away and headed for the door. Then turned back. "Butter?"

For the popcorn, for the popcorn. She cleared her throat. "Yes. Butter would be good."

He cleared his throat too. "For the popcorn, right?"

She almost said something dirty. Very dirty. But she caught herself. She did want to know his favorite kind of pasta. And if he liked *Sherlock Holmes*. And if so, if he preferred the books, the Robert Downey Jr. movies or the TV show. And if he chose the TV show, which one.

But butter could be fun.

"Yes. For the popcorn. Of course."

"Right. Great." He turned away again. "For the popcorn."

As he pulled the door open, she called out, "Rotini."

He looked back with a smile. "That will save some time."

"Right. Bring extra butter."

CHAPTER
ELEVEN

TWENTY MINUTES later they had popcorn—from the extremely well-stocked pantry—and were in their pajamas. Or sweatpants, in Shane's case. He also had a T-shirt on. He'd started to strip it off—that was how he slept after all—but Isabelle quickly made him put it back on.

They were lying on the bed, propped up on the softest pillows Isabelle had ever felt. The popcorn was almost gone and they'd avoided touching each other or even making any innuendos as they compared their favorite police television dramas. They were both quite proud of the accomplishment.

"There is no way a police department would let a novelist follow their detectives around full time," Shane said.

She laughed. "But the mayor asked them to do it."

"Oh, sure, well then—"

He broke off as a car horn sounded from outside. Though it didn't sound like a simple car horn—for one thing, it was playing "La Cucaracha".

They looked at each other, then quickly scrambled off the bed and to the window. There was a big, hot pink bus in front of the house. The side read *Dolly's Party Bus.*

"What the hell?" Shane started for the door.

Isabelle opened the window and leaned out. "Oh, crap."

"What?"

"It's Emma."

Shane turned back. "What?"

"Emma. She's here."

Shane looked at the party bus again. "Well of course she is." Who else would show up in the middle of the night in a pink bus?

He glanced at the clock. It was just after midnight.

They started for the stairs together.

As they hit the top step, Emma burst through the door, a huge duffle bag over one shoulder. "We're here!" She was followed immediately by another woman about her age that Shane had never met and a younger girl he judged to be about seventeen.

Isabelle stopped on the sixth step from the bottom, Shane one step above her. "Gee, no kidding. I think everyone in the county knows you're here."

"That's the thing!" Emma exclaimed. "There is *no one* here. I mean, holy crap, this is isolated. Why would you build such a gorgeous place up where no one can see it?"

"I think the point is not having people see it," Isabelle said. "It's *private* and *quiet.*"

"Boooorrrring," Emma said with an eye roll. "Right, Shane?"

He frowned at her. "I haven't been bored."

"Yet," Emma said, dropping her duffle with a thump. "You just got here."

"Who's that?" Shane whispered to Isabelle about the woman and girl with Emma.

"Emma's best friend Dena and her daughter Shannon."

"That girl is her friend's *daughter?*"

Isabelle gave him a little grin. "Dena had Shannon when she was sixteen."

"Wow."

Dena was beautiful and did not look old enough to have a teenage daughter. Shannon looked exactly like her mom. Shane sighed. As if the Dixon girls weren't enough for mankind to deal with, they also had gorgeous friends with gorgeous daughters? It wasn't fair.

Then things got *really* unfair. Women began coming through the front door, all talking and laughing and carrying suitcases.

Shane felt his mouth drop open.

There were more blondes, a few brunettes and even two redheads. They were all pretty, dressed in short skirts with high heels and they were *loud*.

There were nine total. In addition to Emma, Dena and Shannon.

"*What* the hell is going on?" Shane asked Isabelle. He didn't even need to whisper. There was so much commotion in the foyer that he could barely hear Isabelle answer in her normal voice.

"I don't know."

He turned her to face him. "You don't know?"

She frowned. "No. I have no idea why Emma's here with a bus full of her friends."

He looked over the top of her head at the gaggle of women. "Doesn't Emma have any *un*attractive friends?" he asked.

Isabelle punched him lightly in the stomach.

He rubbed the spot. "So you had no idea that—"

The front door banged open again.

"For fuck's sake," Shane muttered. But he was pleasantly surprised to see that the new arrival was Amanda.

Olivia also stepped through the door behind Amanda. Both were looking around with shock.

"What is going on?" Amanda asked over the noise.

"What are you doing here?" Emma asked, pushing through the gathering of women and suitcases to get to her oldest sister.

"Ryan told me Isabelle needed me," Amanda said. "What are *you* doing here?"

"I'd planned to come spend a few days with Isabelle while she was here," Emma said. "We got on the bus this afternoon."

"And you thought it would be quality sister-bonding time if you brought ten of your closest friends?" Amanda asked.

Isabelle started down the stairs and Shane followed right on her heels. He didn't want to be left alone in this crowd anyway, and he needed to be closer to hear this exchange.

"It's a gigantic mansion-cabin in the woods. I thought it would be a perfect yoga-spa-girlfriend-weekend spot," Emma said.

"How did you know it's a gigantic mansion-cabin in the woods?" Isabelle asked once she got close to her sisters.

"I Googled it," Emma said. "The architect who built it is very proud of it. There are tons of exterior and interior shots online."

"What do you mean a yoga-spa-girlfriend weekend?" Shane asked.

"I called up my friend who's a masseuse." She pointed to one of the blondes. "And my friend who does facials and mani-pedis." She pointed to one of the redheads. "And asked if they wanted to do a spa getaway. Then we each called a few of our best clients and asked if they wanted to come to this fabulous cabin with the workout room and pool and hot tub for a few days and get away from it all. I'm going to do two yoga classes a day, they'll have massages, a different facial every day…it's going to be so fun."

Shane knew he was staring. Isabelle must have been too—she wasn't making a sound. He nudged her from behind. She coughed.

"Um, how long are you staying?" Isabelle asked.

"Oh, this place is huge," Emma said, obviously noticing

Isabelle's hesitation. "If you need to rest, you won't even know we're here."

Shane was absolutely positive that wasn't true. The din in the foyer was only growing. He assumed there had been refreshments on the bus on the way up here. And it was a solid eight-hour drive without stops. That was a lot of refreshment time.

"You can't just show up on someone's doorstep, Em," Amanda chided. "It isn't like this is *Isabelle's* cabin. And it would still be rude even if it was."

"Yeah, what are you doing here again?" Emma asked, facing Amanda and crossing her arms.

"Ryan said that Shane said I needed to come up here to be with Isabelle," Amanda told her.

"Is that right?" Emma turned to look at Isabelle. "If something's going on, you could have called me."

"It is true that a great mani-pedi can make everything all right," Shane said dryly.

Emma frowned at him. "And why would Isabelle need *any* of her sisters if *you're* here, Shane?"

"You realize that it's possible that you don't *always* know what you're talking about, right?" Shane asked her.

"Then why did you come to me for advice?" Emma asked, taking a step closer to Shane. "I thought I was pretty straightforward with you."

"Sure, I should absolutely take advice from the woman who shows up in a pink *party bus* with eleven people Isabelle doesn't even know," Shane said, feeling his blood pressure rising.

"She knows Dena and Shannon. And Brittany and Chloe," Emma said.

Shane didn't care who Brittany and Chloe were. "Seriously, Emma, if you understand *anything* about what's going on with Isabelle you would see how asinine your little stunt here is. But you clearly don't get it at all."

"Are you kidding me?" she said, taking another step

forward. "This plan is all about Isabelle. It's why we're here. It's exactly what she needs. Exercise, massages, yoga, pampering."

Shane stepped closer too. "With a few tequila shots and some pole dancing thrown in?"

Emma lifted her chin. "Pole dancing is an incredible exercise. It strengthens the core, works on flexibility and balance—"

Unbelievable. Emma Dixon was unbelievable. "You need to get your butt back on that bus and turn it around," he said, pointing at the door.

"What?" Emma stared at him, her mouth open.

"Shane—" Isabelle started.

Amanda stepped up next to Emma and took her arm. "Emma, we need to give Shane and Isabelle a minute."

"How did *you* get here anyway?" Emma asked Amanda. "Why didn't you say anything about coming?"

"It was a little last minute," Amanda said, glancing at Shane. "And I didn't know you would be here."

"The three of you were going to have a nice weekend without me?" Emma asked, looking from Isabelle to Olivia.

"Amanda only told me because she didn't have Nate's new number," Olivia said.

Emma's expression was instantly suspicious. "Nate's number? Why did you need that?"

"To ask if we could borrow his plane," Olivia said with a shrug.

"His *plane*?" Isabelle asked.

"His private plane," Olivia said with a grin. "And he was happy to let us use it."

"It's not Nate's plane," Emma said. "It's his grandfather's."

Shane watched the way Emma rolled her eyes. She seemed inordinately irritated by any mention of Nate. Since Shane was exceedingly irritated by *her*, he found it entertaining to see her get huffy.

"Well, it's Nate's *family's* plane," Olivia admitted. "But he uses it. When we took it to Chicago for that fundraiser—"

"That's how you knew about it?" Emma asked, facing her younger sister squarely. "You've been *on* that plane before?"

"Yes." Olivia tipped her head to the side, watching Emma carefully. "When we went to the fundraiser in Chicago."

"I knew he was asking you to fundraisers since Amanda's with Ryan now, but I didn't know he was taking you out of town. On a private plane." Emma had a hand propped on her hip.

"I didn't realize you needed to know," Olivia said calmly.

Emma stared at Olivia for a long moment. Finally she said, "I don't think you should go out with him."

"I'm not going *out* with him," Olivia said. "I'm going *with* him to fundraisers."

"Why can't he go alone?" Emma wanted to know.

"Because the women won't leave him alone if he's not with a date," Olivia said simply.

Emma's cheeks flushed slightly. "Oh, I'm sure."

Olivia looked a little smug. "We have a good time. He's very charming and a complete gentleman and…well, there's the private-plane thing."

Emma made a little growling noise and Amanda gripped her arm.

"We need to deal with the girls," Amanda said. "They're getting restless."

"Put them back on the bus," Shane said simply.

"No way," Emma protested. "We drove nine hours. And it's late."

"This is smack dab in the middle of party-time for you," Shane said. "It's not even one a.m."

"This is my *business*," Emma said. "Do you understand that? These are clients and Brittany and Chloe's clients are potential clients for me."

He couldn't believe this. "This is your sister's *health*. Do you understand *that*?"

"Isabelle doesn't need complete quiet constantly. And the

girls will hardly be making noise when they're doing yoga and getting massages."

Shane rubbed a hand over the back of his neck. He could use a massage right now himself. "Emma—"

"Let's let Isabelle decide," Emma interrupted. "If she wants us to leave, we will."

Shane dropped his hand to his side. He couldn't see Isabelle's face, but his gut knotted. Emma was essentially asking Isabelle to choose between them.

"The spy game was my idea," Emma went on. "I knew that you both needed to see that Isabelle can be adventurous and fun in spite of everything. And yes, this spa thing with the girls is also a great idea. And—" Emma glanced at Amanda, "—apparently you needed some backup anyway."

Shane gritted his teeth. "Amanda's not backup."

Emma crossed her arms. "Then why's she here?"

Was he going to admit that he was on his way home tomorrow morning?

"Emma, why don't you and the girls go upstairs? There's plenty of room," Isabelle said calmly.

Emma looked like she was going to reply, but she must have seen something in Isabelle's face that made her simply nod. "Okay." She stepped around Isabelle and Shane. "All right, chicks, everybody upstairs! Pick a room. Brittany, Chloe and I will be around in a little bit to fill you in on the agenda for tomorrow."

As the herd of women started up the staircase, Amanda grabbed Olivia's hand. "We'll, um, head upstairs too."

Isabelle didn't say anything but she nodded. Shane could feel the tension in her body and he felt the rigidity in his spine ratchet up. They were about to fight. He could feel it.

When everyone was on the second floor except for them, Isabelle turned. She had her arms crossed over her stomach and he could see the strain in her face.

Yep, they were definitely about to fight.

Isabelle took a deep breath and turned to him. "I know what you're going to say."

Well, he was going to say it anyway. "That having your sister here, yoga or not, especially with eleven *additional* women, isn't exactly the way to relax and get a handle on things?"

Isabelle nodded. "Right."

"So tell them to leave."

"I can't."

He raised both eyebrows. "The hell if you can't. In fact, you *need* to."

"It's not that easy." She looked at him, pleading in her eyes.

"It needs to get that easy, Iz," he said firmly. "*You* have to take care of you. This is exactly like what we talked about. When I want to have sex on the bathroom counter in a restaurant, you have to say no. And when Emma wants to show up and throw a four-day party at your boss's cabin—whether she uses the word *spa* or not—you have to say no."

"But—" She pressed her lips together, then started again. "Emma's having some trouble dealing with all of this too. Maybe this is good. This will help her feel like she's helping me and I can use the time to help her understand things better."

He pulled in a deep breath. "This isn't about Emma, Iz. I know you're used to letting Emma call the shots, but...you can't get caught up in her stuff without thinking anymore."

He remembered something Emma had said to him, that he *couldn't* tone things down, that this was who he was, that if he tried to change he would be miserable. And that he would fail at it and break Isabelle's heart.

"You can't expect Emma to change, okay?" he said, gently, but seriously. "This is who she is. And if she changes she'll be miserable and that will hurt you too. Don't expect her to do the work in understanding this and don't expect..." He sighed. "Don't expect her to stop renting party buses. You have to be the one to say no to getting on the party bus that Emma will definitely keep on renting."

Which meant, he couldn't blame Emma either. He knew that she didn't mean to hurt her sister or make things harder on Isabelle. She did, however, need to become a better listener. And Isabelle absolutely needed to get better at saying what Emma needed to hear.

Laughter drifted to them from upstairs and Shane saw the wistful look on Isabelle's face.

"Tell them to leave," he urged. "Amanda and Olivia will stay and you can go on according to plan."

"If they stay, I can practice relaxing in spite of other things going on and I can start working on saying no."

She wasn't going to make Emma leave. Of course she wasn't going to make Emma leave.

"Bullshit," Shane said, his voice tight. "We both know that with Emma here, there's no way you're going to make it through five books. What you're *actually* going to do is party with your sisters, probably drink too much, stay up too late, and do all the things you *shouldn't* be doing."

A little crease formed between her eyebrows. "Thanks for the vote of confidence."

"I'd love to give you a vote of confidence—if I felt confident in the decisions you were going to make."

She sucked in a quick breath, clearly surprised by his words. "There's only one way to find out what I'll do," she said tightly.

"I guess there is." She could take all the fucking time she needed to figure this out. He wanted to be supportive, but he couldn't take it more seriously than she did. And he couldn't hang out and watch her not take it seriously. "And I guess you don't need me to hang around then."

"I guess not. My sisters are here for me."

Yes, because he'd called them. Well, one of them anyway. Whatever. He could be supportive if she was trying to make changes. He *would be* supportive. But he wasn't going to push her, he wasn't going to do it for her and he wasn't going to watch her mess around.

"So you're leaving?" she asked as he stomped up the stairs.

"Yes."

"Tonight?"

"Yes." He headed into their room and paced to where he'd tossed his clothes when he'd exchanged them for his sweatpants.

"With my car?"

"You have a whole party bus to use to get home."

"You know what? That is a great point." She turned and headed for the door.

"Where are you going?"

"To find my sisters. I'm *definitely* in need of some relaxing now!" She slammed the door behind her.

He slumped onto the bed. He'd handled that *so* well. It was amazing that she hadn't wanted to confide everything in him from the beginning.

Living and Loving with Fibromyalgia lay on the table next to the bed. He picked it up, weighing it in his hand. It was heavy. There was a lot of information to learn in there. Living with fibro was one thing, but loving—yeah, that would definitely add some pages.

He clearly had some homework to do. He tucked the book into his bag, pulled the strap up on his shoulder and headed back downstairs to start his trip home. Without Isabelle.

Isabelle stepped out onto the porch, slamming the door behind her.

She pulled in a deep breath through her nose, letting it out and working on calming her heart rate.

She hadn't asked Shane to come along in the first place. She hadn't *invited* him. In fact, she'd pretty specifically *not* invited him to come with her. She needed to figure some stuff out.

Why was that so hard to comprehend? And was it so hard to believe that this would be *difficult* for her sisters to handle too? Really?

"Argh!"

She stomped down the steps. She had no idea where she was going, only that she couldn't stay and watch Shane pack to leave her and she wasn't quite up to diving into the midst of all the girls in the house.

"Argh!"

Halfway down the front walk, she stopped and looked around. It was really dark out here. She wasn't going to get far... Dammit.

Then her eyes landed on the pink party bus. It was hard to miss, of course, but she focused on it now. And realized that no one would think to look for her there.

While Shane and Emma had been arguing in the foyer, she remembered seeing the driver—an older guy in a chauffeur's hat and jacket—come into the house. Emma's friends and clients had brought him into their fold and Isabelle assumed he now had a room somewhere upstairs too.

She pushed on the door to the bus and was pleased to find it unlocked. She climbed in and looked around. It was dark now, but it was clear where the strips of pink neon lights ran along the ceiling and floor. The walls were silvery and likely reflected the neon nicely—or gaudily depending on who you asked. The two sides of the bus were lined with black leather seats broken up here and there by little tabletops with cup holders. There was a bathroom at the back, two mini fridges and at least ten stereo speakers.

Isabelle had to admit that this seemed like a lot of fun.

Something shiny caught her eye. The keys were still in the ignition. Of course, clear out here, she could understand the driver thinking the bus would be more than safe.

Isabelle slid into the driver's seat and turned the key.

Pink neon lit up the interior and the stereo blasted "You

Shook Me All Night Long". She could imagine her sister belting out those lyrics with her friends.

In fact, Isabelle couldn't help but start singing along herself. She got up and moved farther into the bus, shaking her hips a little as she went.

She sat down in the middle of one of the benches, pleased to discover the seats were extremely comfortable. She pivoted and laid back, folding her hand on her stomach, and worked on breathing.

This was nice. Alone. Closed off from the world where everyone had an opinion on what she should be doing and how she should be doing it. No one insisting she do things differently. No one insisting she do anything at all.

And Shane was leaving. In about ten minutes she'd be free. She could do whatever she wanted. No one would be nagging her about gummy bears or getting enough sleep. That would be great.

Tears pricked at her eyes.

There would also be no one holding her all night or giving her special little smiles or making her laugh.

Dammit.

She swiped at her eyes.

"Do you still have the pendant?"

Isabelle sat bolt upright, a scream lodged in her throat.

Emma stood at the front of the bus.

"Holy crap! You scared me." She glared at her sister.

Emma leaned over and turned the volume on the stereo down. "Did you drop the pendant off or not? I just got a text that said they didn't find it at the drop site."

"I still have it. I'll take it over there tomorrow."

"Dammit. I'm going to have to pay for another day since it wasn't returned by midnight."

Isabelle raised an eyebrow. "You got on the wrong party bus if you're looking for sympathy."

Emma sighed. "Fine. I'm sure I can talk them out of the additional fee." She plopped down on the bench across from Isabelle. "What are you doing out here anyway?"

Isabelle looked around. "I was just wondering if my sister and her friends drank all the liquor on board and if not, where the rest was."

Emma leaned over to open one of the mini fridges. "Peach schnapps and champagne. Which do you want?"

"Either. Both."

Emma pulled out the bottle of schnapps, poured two fingers' worth into a disposable paper cup and handed it over.

Isabelle shot it back and swallowed with a satisfied "aahh".

"You okay?" Emma asked.

Isabelle leveled her with a serious look. "Of course not. Shane's pissed and leaving."

Emma leaned in. "He can't leave."

"Uh, he can and is."

"He can't." Emma shook her head. "Part of the whole plan here was to help him see that you can still have a good time *and* take care of yourself. We'll do yoga and stuff all day. I brought this great recipe for fruit smoothies and everyone brought a different salad recipe to try. Then at night we'll go out and have a good time. Maybe a barbecue. Oh, and there's this great bar in Rapid City. It's got country dancing and…"

"No."

Emma stopped and blinked at Isabelle. "No to which part?"

"No to all of it." Isabelle felt a knot of insecurity tighten her stomach. This was who Emma was. Shane was right about that. Emma couldn't completely change her personality. If Isabelle started saying no, if she distanced herself from the good times with Emma, would she distance herself from Emma in general?

"I don't understand," Emma said. But her expression said that she was afraid she did understand.

"I can't keep up like this, Em."

"I get that you're scared," Emma said quietly. "But I don't get why you want to curl up into a ball now and give up on everything."

Isabelle felt tears prick at her eyes again. "I don't want to do that," she said. "I don't want anything to change. But it has to."

"I look at you and I don't see a sick person, Iz. I see the same girl I've always seen. The one who has always trusted me and wanted to be with me and who's always been there for me."

Isabelle felt fear and frustration shoot through her bloodstream. She got up from the bench. "Is that what this is?" she asked. "You're worried about losing your sidekick? You're worried you're going to end up calling Amanda or Conner for bail money and you won't have anyone to share the blame with?"

Emma stood up too. "No, that's not what I'm saying at all. You seem *fine*. And, believe it or not, I've been reading and learning about it too. There are no x-rays or anything that shows what's going on."

Isabelle stared at her. "I know that."

"It's based on a set of symptoms."

"Yes."

"But there are lots of reasons that someone could have those symptoms."

Isabelle crossed her arms. She knew where this was going. She and her therapist had talked about the fact that a lot of people didn't believe there was such a thing as fibromyalgia because there were no outward signs—no rashes, nothing that would show on an MRI or x-ray. People with fibromyalgia *looked* fine so it was hard for some people, even loved ones, to believe that they weren't fine.

"Yes, there are other things that could cause most of the symptoms," she agreed.

"And," Emma said, her tone changing slightly, becoming almost tender. "I'm not saying that you don't feel bad. But are you sure it's not depression or stress?"

Isabelle was torn between wanting to lash out at Emma for

being one of the doubters and wanting to hug her, and assure her that even though this was all real, Isabelle was going to be okay. She knew that was Emma's true concern. Not that Isabelle was crazy, but that she was…different.

She had to take control here.

Emma had always led their escapades. Their relationship had been built on fun and laughter and sharing secrets and wonderful memories. But now Isabelle had to take charge. This was new territory and Emma didn't know the way.

Isabelle stepped forward and took Emma's hand. "I went through all of that. I promise. I almost *wanted* it to be depression. There are great medications for depression. But it's not. If it was stress, if my job, for instance, was causing me to feel like this, I'd quit in a heartbeat, I swear."

Emma met her gaze and Isabelle saw the tears shimmering there. After a long moment, Emma grabbed Isabelle in a big hug. "I'm sorry," she whispered. "I'm sorry. I just…I want you to be okay. I want you to be happy and to feel good and to be healthy."

Isabelle hugged her back, letting her tears run. "I know you do, Em. I know."

"I screwed this up," Emma said. She took a deep breath and pulled back. "I'll go talk to Shane."

"No." Isabelle took a deep breath as well. "No, he needs to go. He probably already left." He'd seemed in a huge hurry to get away.

"We'll run him down," Emma decided, turning toward the front of the bus. "We'll follow him in this party bus, blowing the horn all the way to Nebraska if we have to."

Isabelle wiped her eyes and laughed. "I'm not sure a pink party bus playing 'La Cucaracha' is the right way to go." She sighed. "I have to get some stuff figured out before I go after him anyway."

Emma turned back. "You sure? Because I'll do whatever I can to help."

Isabelle stepped forward again to hug her sister. "Really?" she asked.

"Really."

"Then…I need you to pack up your girls and your party bus and leave."

Emma pulled back. She looked at Isabelle for several heartbeats. Finally she said, "Yeah, okay. In the morning."

"Sounds good. We can do yoga and have smoothies before you go."

Emma laughed. "Deal."

They shut the bus off and walked back to the house with their arms around each other. Isabelle noticed that her car was gone. Which meant Shane was gone.

She tried to ignore the feeling of loss. It was temporary. She was going home to him in a few days.

Still, it felt…wrong…for Shane to not be here.

Then a thought occurred to her. "Uh, Em, you're going to have to *really* sweet talk the Big Time people."

"Why's that?"

"The pendant is in the glove compartment of my car. Which is now on its way back to Mitchell."

Emma processed that, then groaned. "Dammit."

Isabelle chuckled and squeezed her sister.

At the porch, Emma said, "Shane is going to forgive me for showing up here, right?"

"He's going to have to," Isabelle said. "Once we're living together, he's going to see a lot of you."

"You're moving in with him?"

Isabelle smiled, the rightness of it coursing through her. "Definitely."

"Then, do you think Shane would lend me the money to pay for keeping the pendant until I can send it back?" Emma asked.

Isabelle laughed. "Absolutely not."

"But it's kind of his fault that it didn't get turned in on time."

"Does it help you to know it was totally worth it?" Isabelle asked Emma.

"See? Maybe I should hang around. I can send the girls back on the party bus and you and I can—"

"Emma?"

"Yeah?"

"No."

Emma tipped her head to the side. "It's still weird hearing that from you, but you're getting better at it."

"Thanks." Isabelle opened the front door and nudged Emma inside. "But I have a feeling I'm going to get a lot more practice saying it to you before it sticks."

"HANG ON," Emma said from the Camel Pose the next morning. "You think you're fun *because of* Shane?"

"And you," Isabelle said moving into Heron Pose. "You're the ones who crave the fun and craziness."

Olivia snorted from where she was lying on the yoga mat on her back, eating the rest of Isabelle's gummy bears. She didn't do group exercise, even with her sisters. She ran. By herself. In the quiet park or along the river. In total silence. She said she needed the run less for exercise and more for the release. In any case, she considered yoga a spectator sport.

"Bullshit," Emma said.

Isabelle frowned at them as she transitioned to a Garland Pose. "What? You and Share are the fun ones—ask anyone."

"Emma and Shane are the loud ones, the ones who like to be the center of attention—that's what distracts everyone from the fact that you're a total instigator," Olivia said, biting the head off a bear.

"I am?" Isabelle thought about that. "Well, I guess I have ideas sometimes."

"A lot of the time," Emma said, stretching an arm overhead. "I come up with stuff that gets attention, but your stuff is the creative stuff. And you bring the ideas to me because you know I'll love them and go for it. But they come from you."

"Like all the sex stuff with Shane," Olivia said. "I know you said it was to keep his interest, but I don't believe you were *un*interested for one second."

"And he's like me. He'll go along for the good time any day," Emma said.

"Shane instigates plenty of stuff," Isabelle said.

"Sure. Conner got that tattoo he didn't really want," Emma said.

"And Cody got that dog he didn't really want," Olivia commented.

"Exactly," Isabelle exclaimed.

"Sure," Emma agreed. "Shane's..."

"Shane," Olivia and Isabelle said together.

"Right. He's Shane. You can't change that. You wouldn't want to. But you can't go around thinking that it's all him. Or me. *You're* a part of all the fun."

Isabelle had to admit that the pendant caper had been fun. She'd been the one disappointed when it was over. She'd been the one to keep it going given the tiniest chance.

And okay, Shane's sexual appetite had been a great reason to look up and try some stuff she'd been curious about—and *really* liked once she did try it.

"I'm an instigator."

"Yeah, a big one," Olivia said.

"So the idea of cutting Shane out like the other stuff you think you have to avoid wouldn't have worked anyway," Em said. "You would have gone looking for some fun and excitement within a week."

Emma was right. She didn't want Shane in her life just because he was fun. She also wanted him because he shared in whatever fun she already had going, he made things *more* fun and, when things weren't fun at all, he made her feel better. Not having Shane around would be awful.

Like how she'd felt this morning after waking up *alone*.

"But I do need to cut stuff out," Isabelle said.

"Or maybe you need to be a grownup," Emma said.

Isabelle felt her eyebrows rise. "Excuse me?"

"Instead of partying 'til two, you go home at eleven. Instead of four tequila shots, you take one and drink club soda after. You sleep in once in a while. And maybe you tell me no once in a while."

Isabelle lost her balance, tipping over onto her mat. "*You* are lecturing me about being responsible and saying no?"

And sounding a lot like Shane as she did it, Isabelle thought to herself.

"I read a few chapters in that book last night. The *Living and Loving* book. You just have to take care of yourself."

"You read part of that book last night?" Isabelle was touched that Emma had picked the book up. Not to mention impressed with her reading speed. They'd finally gotten to bed well after one a.m. and then had risen for yoga at eight.

Isabelle noticed that none of the girls Emma had brought along for the "spa weekend" were up and at 'em this morning, though.

"Yeah." Emma rolled her eyes. "And hell, I should take some of the advice too. The fracture and surgery and rehab have shown me that sometimes you just have to slow down. And it's not all bad."

Isabelle was beyond moved by the way her sister was reacting after their talk last night. "I could teach you to knit," she said lightly.

Emma groaned. "I said slow down, not never have sex again."

"Hey, I've been having plenty of sex."

"Yeah with *Shane*. You can only knit around people who love you unconditionally."

Suddenly Isabelle had a hard time swallowing.

Shane loved her unconditionally. No matter what happened or how she felt or if she was fun or sick or wanted sex on his bar covered in Kahlua or to just cuddle all night, he loved her.

Wow.

"You're right. That's amazing," she said, sitting up and crossing her legs, her entire body feeling warm and light. And not yoga warm and light. "I could knit *every day* for the rest of my life and he'd still be there."

Emma reached over and patted her hand. "I know he loves you, honey, but let's not push it, okay?"

"Uh, Shane?"

Shane looked up from the teeny tiny pieces of paper scattered all over the tabletop in front of him.

Conner stood in the doorway to the dining room of the bed-and-breakfast where Shane had been camped out for the past three hours. His eyes hurt from squinting at the tiny scraps, his fingers were sticky from the glue and his heart hurt from not seeing Isabelle for seven days.

"Hey, Conner," Danika Bradford greeted as she came through the swinging door from the kitchen with two glasses of iced tea.

"Hey, Dani, what's up?" Conner asked, watching Shane suspiciously.

Yeah, there was reason for him to be suspicious. Shane was in love with Conner's sister and about to ask her to move in with him. Again. He had a whole new approach this time though. Well, mostly new.

"I'm here helping Morgan put some new faucets in the bath-rooms in the guest rooms."

It was widely known that Danika had been thrilled when Dooley's wife, Morgan, had bought a bed-and-breakfast. Doing fix-it jobs and renovations for Morgan was Dani's idea of heaven, while playing with Dani and Sam's twin girls was Morgan's favorite way to spend the afternoon. It was a perfect set-up.

Shane hadn't been surprised when Dani suggested he meet her at the B & B when he'd asked for her help.

"Shane's helping with the faucets?" Conner asked.

Shane itched to brush the scraps of paper and paint brushes into his lap and play along with Conner's assumption. It wasn't completely unlikely that he could be helping with the sink project. He could twist some screws.

Before Dani could tell Conner the truth, the kitchen door swung open again.

"Well, hi, Conner."

Conner straightened fully and his mouth stretched into the grin that no one but Sara Bradford Gordon ever got from him.

"Hey there, Sara."

"Did you come to help with the fixtures or the decoupage?" She set a plate of brownies on the table beside the box Shane was working on.

Shane wondered if Conner had ever tasted her brownies. If he had, it was no wonder the man thought he was in love with her.

"Whatever needs done," Conner said smoothly. "I want you to always think of me first when you need a guy who's good with his hands."

Sara's eyes widened and her cheeks got a little pink.

Shane had to admit that Sara handled Conner's flirting well. She acted appropriately flattered and slightly amused, while never leading Conner on or making anyone question her love or commitment to her husband.

"Well, everyone knows that women go crazy for a guy who

does crafts." Sara reclaimed her seat at the table and reached for the jewelry box she was doing.

"Is that right?" Conner moved closer.

Fuck.

Conner was thirty minutes early picking Shane up for their game. He'd asked Conner for a ride to the game so that he'd have a chance to tell Isabelle's brother his intentions. He knew he should have considered his friend's opinions and feelings more in the past and now meant to show both Conner and Isabelle how serious he was by asking for Conner's approval before he asked her to move in this time.

Of course, if Conner said no, Shane was doing it anyway. Still, he thought it would be a nice gesture.

He didn't, however, intend for Conner—or any of the other guys for that matter—to find out about the box.

Dani Bradford was the only one besides Isabelle that he knew would know how to decoupage and today was the only day she was free. And he needed to talk to Conner before he talked to Isabelle—or so his hazy concept of etiquette led him to believe. And he was going to see Isabelle today—the minute she set foot back in Omaha. And there was no way he was going to keep from asking her to move in with him the moment he had the chance.

So he had to have this box done before their game.

He rubbed his finger and thumb together, feeling the glue residue he may never fully get rid of and the glitter that Sara had talked him into using. He was stuck with Conner finding out. Literally.

"Have you ever decoupaged before?" Sara asked Conner.

He raised an eyebrow. "Not unless that's a fancy term for something I have been doing without knowing it."

She raised an eyebrow right back at him. "You glue little pictures and stuff onto something."

Conner looked at Shane, then at the box in front of Shane that was eighty-percent covered with little bits of paper with handwritten words on them, then back at Shane.

Shane braced himself. Conner wouldn't be too hard on him with Sara here. He wanted Sara to think he was a nice, charming guy.

But instead of commenting on Shane's new hobby or his masculinity, Conner said, "I assume that's for Isabelle?"

Sara grinned. "Isn't it sweet? He knows she likes to decoupage so he asked Dani to teach him. And all those little notes he's putting on there are things about him he wants Isabelle to know."

Shane grimaced. He'd told the girls because they, of course, had noticed what he was covering his box with. But he didn't need Conner to know that he'd handwritten the words, or that they were things like his favorite book from childhood, his favorite Christmas treat, and the name of his grandmother. They were the things they hadn't gotten to yet. With the box, they could sit together on the couch and talk about all of those words and what they meant to him and all the things he wanted to know about her.

"What are you putting in that box?" Conner asked him.

Shane took a deep breath, then met his friend's gaze. "A key. To my new house. Where I want her to live with me."

"House?" Conner tucked his hands in the front pockets of his jeans. "That's pretty mature and stable and stuff."

Shane picked up a little scrap of paper that said *Charlie*. His first dog.

"I'm settling down. With Isabelle. I hope—" He stopped and cleared his throat. He wasn't good at asking for permission. "I hope that's okay with you. I'm in love with her. I want to be there with her every day. And night."

Conner closed his eyes and groaned. "See, you were doing okay, until that last part."

Since Conner wasn't looking, Shane grinned. "So I shouldn't mention the new king-sized bed."

Conner covered his face with one hand. "No, definitely not."

"Or the hot tub."

Conner's other hand flew up as he groaned louder. "No."

"Or the Tantra Chair."

Conner dropped both hands and stared at Shane. "You did not order a Tantra Chair."

"Oh, I did. In burgundy."

"But you won't put it in your living room. I don't care what the website shows…that isn't right."

"Front and center," Shane said, fighting the urge to laugh. "It goes perfectly with my new couch."

"I won't ever be able to come to your place," Conner said.

"Huh. I hadn't even thought of that," Shane said casually.

"You're a bastard."

"Who loves your sister."

"I know."

"Who's going to live with your sister."

"On one condition."

Shane rolled his eyes. Of course there was a condition. Like separate bedrooms.

"You put a ring in that box with the key."

Shane frowned. "Any old ring?"

"Any old ring that costs you an arm and a leg and means you're going to marry her," Conner clarified.

Shane felt his heart stutter, then flip, then expand. Conner was telling him to *propose*.

Conner was telling him to propose.

To Isabelle. His sister.

Shane figured he had two choices here. He could point out all the reasons that proposing was crazy. Or he could go for it. Hell, Conner might even be willing to drive him to the jewelry store.

It wasn't that tough of a decision.

He always went for it.

"Okay, let's go." Shane shoved his chair back.

"But you haven't finished the box," Sara protested.

Shane reached for a picture lying in Sara's stack of materials, grabbed a glue bottle and glued it on the box over the remaining blank spot.

Dani came back into the room. "How's everything—" She zeroed in on Shane's box. "Isabelle has a thing for frogs?" she asked.

"She and Ava have that in common," Sara said dryly. She had been decorating a jewelry box for her niece.

"It won't matter," Shane assured them. "She'll be impressed anyway."

"You don't have even one layer of varnish on," Dani pointed out.

"I'll do it later."

"If you get the paper wet or dirty before you varnish it—"

"I know," Shane interrupted. "But I have to go."

"Leave the box and I'll finish it for you. Then you can give it to her this weekend or something," Dani offered.

Sara nudged her sister-in-law. "He needs it today."

"But she doesn't even know about it or the key, right?" Clearly it was bugging Dani immensely to leave a project unfinished.

"Now it's going to have a ring in it too," Sara said.

"Well, great, but…" Dani trailed off as the words sunk in. "A ring?"

Sara grinned. "Yeah. A *ring*."

Dani looked from Shane to Conner and back. "Well, what are you still standing *here* for?"

As he jogged to the car with Conner, Shane couldn't help but grin. He'd had no idea how involved decoupage could be. But he was definitely walking away from it feeling better than he had walked away from the yoga class. Things were getting better.

"So it's fine?" Isabelle asked Trudy. "No problem at all with bringing in a model of Mount Rushmore and making the place up to look like the Corn Palace?"

"Nope. It's fine. You and Shane have pulled in the best crowds I've had in a long time," Trudy said with a grin. "Decorate however you want."

"This Mount Rushmore thing is pretty big," Isabelle said. "I mean, it's going to take up some space. If there's anything else going on here, it might be in the way." She and her sisters had created the paper mache model during the past week at the cabin.

She wondered if Shane had any idea what paper mache was.

Trudy turned away from stacking glasses on the back counter behind the bar. "Isabelle, nothing else is going on here tonight. No one has told me they're bringing in a mechanical bull or a petting zoo or setting up a bowling alley or anything. Isn't that a good thing?"

Sure it was. Of course it was. She wanted the place for *her* plan for tonight.

But she wouldn't have been upset if Shane had planned some big thing for her first night back in town.

They hadn't seen each other or even talked in seven days. And this was *Shane*.

He didn't have any big welcome-home-I'm-so-glad-to-see-you thing planned?

Of course, she wanted it to be something they could sneak out on within an hour or so, but some over-the-top gesture wouldn't have been out of line.

Which was why she'd come up with a plan of her own. Shane was a unique guy. When a girl wanted to tell him that she was madly in love with him and wanted to wake up next to him every morning for the rest of her life, she needed a unique gesture to show it.

She didn't have the experience with over-the-top public displays of affection that Shane did, of course. Her gesture involved decorating with a few dead presidents and a bunch of corn and setting up a mini treasure hunt for a dragon pendant—that had cost her thirty-two sixty-five on eBay and matched the one she had hanging around her neck. The pendant might not have been magical or had a romantic backstory, but it had sure contributed to some of the healing between her and Shane. Hanging onto a copy as a reminder that she could be and have everything she wanted to be seemed like a good idea.

But they could easily get out of here and naked within sixty minutes. Seventy-five tops.

She grinned as she rolled up the treasure maps she and Olivia had created of Trudy's. She *did* have experience with over-the-top-not-as-public displays of affection. Especially ones that involved chocolate body pens and naughty dice.

"We never actually made it to Mount Rushmore," a deep voice said in her ear.

She sighed, pulling in the feel of him behind her.

"I know, but it reminds you of our trip, right?"

"I don't need anything to remind me of our trip. I remember every minute."

She turned, bracing herself for wanting to jump on him. She tried to look huffy instead. "Including leaving me in the Black Hills for a week?"

"You know I had to leave." Her huffy attitude—fake as it was—didn't seem to even register with him. He looked at her with heat—and something a lot stronger and deeper—in his gaze.

She took a deep breath. "I didn't want you to. Even though we argued, I wanted you to stay. You knew that."

"We both needed to come down off the adrenaline and process all the new stuff we learned," he said.

She almost couldn't make herself ask the next question. In her gut, she knew the answer. In her head she knew he wouldn't be here even now if the answer wasn't yes. But she really needed to hear it. "So now that you've processed it, are you still…?"

"You're going to have to keep letting me in. You have to tell me things, Iz, and then you have to deal with me having an opinion on those things and sometimes worrying and making adjustments."

She still kind of hated the idea that he had to change things to live with her. But at the same time, it made her feel like the most loved woman in the world. She nodded. "Okay. And you have to sometimes just listen and *not* give me an opinion and sometimes let me figure it out myself."

He nodded. "Okay."

Suddenly a pounding erupted on the front door of Trudy's. "Come on already!" someone hollered from the other side.

Then she heard a familiar voice say, "Just shut the fuck up for a minute."

She turned wide eyes on Shane. "What was that?"

"I told them I needed a minute without a crowd."

She smiled. "Shane Kelley *without* a crowd."

He shrugged. "Sometimes it's nice to keep things quiet and private."

Isabelle definitely recognized the sentiment behind his words. "You locked the door?"

"Yep. With Trudy's blessing, I might add."

"Who's out there?"

"Everyone."

"So that was Conner's voice I heard telling them to shut up?"

"Yep."

"He's not wondering what's going on in here?"

"The only thing he's wondering is why this is taking me so long."

"Why what is taking you so long?"

Shane pulled something out of the duffle bag she just now noticed sitting on top of one of the tables. He pulled out a strange-looking little wooden box. "This."

"What is—" She gaped at the box. Bits of paper—tiny bits of paper—were glued all over it with the exception of the area covered by a much bigger picture of a frog. The smaller pieces all had words on them, but they were smudged and curling at the edges. "Did you have a niece or nephew decoupage for you?"

He looked completely offended. "*I* did decoupage." Then he looked at the box sheepishly. "I just haven't finished it yet."

"With these tiny pieces it would take forever."

"Yeah. Knowledge that would have been helpful to me *this morning*," he said dryly.

She grinned and took it from him. A scrap of paper came loose and fluttered to the floor. She bent to pick it up and read, *April 4th*. She looked up at him. "What's that mean?"

Someone banged on the door again. "Open this damn thing up, we're dying of thirst."

"Settle down, dammit!" Conner shouted.

"I'll tell you the whole story later," Shane said. "They're getting restless outside."

Isabelle racked her brain trying to figure out the significance of the frog. There had to be a reason for it. Shane always had a great, creative reason behind everything. Dammit.

"Come here," he said, pulling her forward and sitting her in a chair.

He knelt in front of her and took her hand and Isabelle's heart began to pound. Then he started speaking and she felt stupid. It was way too soon for him to propose. They'd only been dating a few months and they'd found out a bunch of stuff they needed to work on. Still, she liked the picture he made down on one knee.

"Making other people happy makes me feel good," he started.

The pounding on the door was louder this time, as if two or three people were putting their fists behind it.

Shane grimaced, but went on. "But making *you* happy, makes me feel…right. Complete. Whole. I didn't even know I felt incomplete or empty. I mean, I always have people around me, noise, lights, laughter. But this past week, I sat in my house, on my couch, alone. For the first time ever. And it felt great. Because

I have you. Even when you're not with me, I have you here—" He thumped his fist against his chest over his heart. "And I realized—I was constantly trying to fill the silence and the emptiness around me with people but deep down, I always knew they would leave, that being alone was always right around the corner. But now, with you, I don't need all that craziness. I have you and there are no more gaps, no more corners to be afraid of, no more loneliness."

"Get the fuck away from that door or I'll make sure Trudy never serves you another drink in your life!" Conner yelled from outside.

Isabelle tried not to, but she snorted.

Shane grinned too. "I guess I can keep going with this stuff at home. I want you to open the box and know that your brother helped me pick out what's inside."

Suddenly her hands were shaking. She lifted the box and two more pieces of paper floated to the floor. But she barely noticed. She was staring at the ring with a key stuck through the middle.

Her thoughts swirled. She'd been expecting the key. At the same time, she'd made a copy of hers and had brought it to give to him if he didn't bring the subject up tonight. Conner knew about this? The key or the ring? Both?

"What do you think?" Shane asked after several seconds of silence.

She looked from the box to him. "I think that if you say something smart ass about this being a key ring, I'm never bringing Kahlua to your house ever again."

His grin was wide and warm. "I plan to keep plenty of Kahlua stocked in *our* house from now on. And I wish I'd thought of the key ring thing…that's pretty funny."

She shook her head and set the box on the table. "You have to ask me, you know."

"I am asking you."

"You handed me a box. And that's sweet. I love the box. But you still have to ask."

"If you two are having sex in there while we're out here hungry and thirsty, I'll never forgive either of you!" Conner shouted through the door.

Ah, now he was getting anxious to get inside too.

Isabelle raised an eyebrow at Shane. "That beer crowd could totally break a door down. You better do this quick. Unless you're waiting for an audience? Maybe you'd like to do this on stage with the mic?"

She wouldn't mind. She didn't care where he did it as long as he did it soon so she could say yes.

Shane looked at the stage. "I can't deny that doing it up in front of everyone is tempting."

She laughed. Of course it was. "Then let's let them in." She stood and started for the door, but before she could grab the handle, Shane caught her hand and pulled her around and up against him.

"Isabelle, let me take you to cheesy tourist traps and monitor your gummy bear consumption and buy you an equal number of health books and sex books. Let me always be the one you get naked in car washes with and the one sitting next to you when you're being questioned by security guards. Let me help you find trouble and let me help you get out of it. For as long as we both shall live." He slipped the ring on her finger, then put the key in her palm. "And please, please knit me a scarf, teach me to varnish my decoupage boxes, and show me how the hell you made that model of Mount Rushmore."

She held his face between her hands, absorbing the fact that this was the face of the man she would call her husband, and the father of her children, and the love of her life. "I'll do even better… Have you ever heard of macramé?"

He gave her a mischievous grin. "Is that from one of the sex books?"

She patted his cheek. "I think it's something you have to experience to really understand."

Shane looked at the still-locked front door, then glanced

toward the back of the bar. "I think I'm in the mood for some macramé."

"Oh, you have no idea."

And so on the biggest night of his life, Shane Kelley slipped out the back door of Trudy's bar without a bit of fanfare to go home and spend a quiet night in with his girl…and a giant ball of string.

Thank you for reading Why You Should Never Kiss Your Ex! I hope you loved Shane and Isabelle!

Why You Should Never Kiss Your Enemy, Nate and Emma's story, is next!

The last thing single dad and surgeon Nate Sullivan needs is more stress and distraction in his life.

That makes his best friend's gorgeous, mouthy, doesn't-respect-schedules, hates-authority, has-no-boundaries sister a huge threat to his carefully balanced life.

Nate is the kind of guy Emma Dixon hates: buttoned-up, rigid, his-way-or-the-highway. So why is he the guy she can't quit thinking about and who she most loves sparring with?

They're like oil and water. But when they're thrown together on opposites sides of a "project"--Nate trying to keep his son from falling for the wrong girl and Emma playing cupid for the couple– they find they're more like gasoline and a match.

Get *Why You Should Never Kiss Your Enemy* now! Or read on for an excerpt!

ॐ

Find all of my books (including a printable book list) **at ErinNicholas.com**

ॐ

And join in on all the FAN FUN!

Join my **email list!**
bit.ly/Keep-In-Touch-Erin
(be sure you get those dashes and capital letters in there!)

And be the first to hear about my news, sales, freebies, behind-the-scenes, and more!

Or for even more fun, join my **Super Fan page** on Facebook and chat with me and other super fans every day! Just search Facebook for Erin Nicholas Super Fans!

ॐ

Enjoy this excerpt from Why You Should Never Kiss Your Enemy!

"I need you to tell me where they are."

His hand came to rest on her hip and she took a shaky little breath. He was going to *seduce* the information out of her?

He leaned in, his mouth near her ear. "Please, it's important." He paused, then pulled in a breath. "Dammit, you smell good."

Okay, the seduction thing might work.

Crap.

She closed her eyes. Maybe that would help. She put her hands up on his chest, to hold him back. Because that mouth this close was dangerous.

Not that touching him helped. He was warm and solid and smelled damned good himself.

"Nate—"

His hand slid around to her butt and he pulled her closer. "How about a hint?" he asked. "I want to be sure he's okay."

Emma tried to shake her head, but she wasn't sure she pulled it off. "Shannon trusted me. This night means a lot to her."

"Then you leave me no choice," he said huskily.

Oh, boy. What was he going to try next? She almost couldn't wait to find out. If he kissed her, or pulled her more firmly against him, or slid his hand to her breast...she'd tell him anything. Even that she'd been attracted to him for a good year and a half now.

The next thing she felt, though, was her phone sliding out of her back pocket.

Her eyes flew open as Nate stepped back.

"Seriously?" she groaned. "That was low."

And she'd fallen for it. Completely.

He gave her a smug grin. "And you fell for it. Completely."

Dammit. He now had something far more important than her phone—the knowledge that he could affect her. She had a feeling that was going to be a bad, bad thing.

He held the phone up to her face to get past her lock screen, then started swiping and she knew he was looking for messages from Shannon. Which he would definitely find if he kept going. Emma grabbed for the phone, but he lifted it up out of her reach.

"Nate. You can't go through my phone."

"Afraid I'll call all your lovers and tell them what a pain in the ass you are?"

She made a grab for the phone again. And missed. "No. I'm afraid you're going to ruin the relationship that your son is building with this girl he cares about a lot—and maybe even his relationship with *you*."

She saw the change in his face. He hated that idea.

She could work with that.

Nate sighed heavily. "I will listen to suggestions. As long as they *don't* include the words 'leave them alone'."

That had been her exact suggestion. She frowned. "You can't go barging into wherever they are, and Michael's not answering your calls, so what are you going to do? Spy on them?"

Nate's face brightened immediately.

Emma groaned. "*No*. You can't spy on your son."

"The hell if I can't. That accomplishes all of the objectives," he said. "It helps me know where they are and what they're doing, but it's not barging in or dragging him away from his friends—or whatever."

"Nate, seriously. You can't stalk your son. That's…creepy."

He shrugged. "Don't care. My job is to protect him, whether he likes it or not, by whatever means necessary."

He was serious. Part of her admired how strongly he felt about his role and how protective he was. Part of her thought he was in need of a prescription or two from his friendly neighborhood psychiatrist.

"You're not going to be able to figure out where they are," she said, feigning cockiness.

"Shannon didn't text you about how to get to the Washburn Theater downtown?" he asked.

Dammit.

"That might be for something else."

"*I wish you could come with us tomorrow night. You'd love the band,*" Nate read from her screen. He looked at her. "She sent it yesterday. Which makes tomorrow night tonight."

Emma sighed. "Michael's taking her to see this band she loves. She was amazed they were coming through Omaha. It's a one-night show."

"Thank you." He handed her the phone and started for the front door.

Oh, no. No way. She ran after him, slipping around him and blocking his path. "You're not going down there."

"I am."

"You can't seriously want to hear this band play for two hours. You'll hate it."

"Not as much as I'll hate being a grandfather already."

Emma felt her mouth drop open.

He scowled at her. "What?"

"Overreact much?" she asked.

"Get out of my way."

"No."

He put both hands on her upper arms and started to move her. "There's no way you can physically keep me from going down there."

Emma thought fast. He was going down there. This had disaster written all over it. She shrugged off his grasp. "Fine."

He let her go and stepped around her.

She headed for the kitchen, grabbed her purse, and was out the door, down the steps and beside Nate before he got to the truck.

He looked at her as he reached for the door. "What are you doing?"

"If you think I'm going to let you go after them by yourself, you're nuts."

Nate sighed, that familiar put-upon expression on his face as he regarded her. He didn't seem particularly surprised. He seemed annoyed.

She could live with that. Nate was pretty much perpetually annoyed with her and she'd survived this long.

"Besides," she said, opening the passenger side door. "You're going to make an ass out of yourself and I *must* have a front row seat for that."

Grab *Why You Should Never Kiss Your Enemy* now!

WHY YOU SHOULD NEVER... THE SERIES

Why You Should Never...

Kiss Your Boss (Ben & Jessica)

Kiss Your Blind Date (Sam & Dani)

Kiss A Grump (Mac & Sara)

Kiss Your Fake Boyfriend (Dooley & Morgan)

Kiss Your Ex-Husband (Kevin & Eve)

Kiss Your Brother's Best Friend (Ryan & Amanda)

Kiss Your Ex (Shane & Isabelle)

Kiss Your Enemy (Nate & Emma)

Kiss Your Best Friend (Cody & Olivia)

Kiss Your Roommate (Conner & Gabby)

MORE FROM ERIN

Want more hot protective guys who wear badges? Try my Badges of the Bayou series!

Badges of the Bayou
Gotta Be Bayou (Spencer & Max)
Bayou With Benefits (Michael & Ami)
Rocked Bayou (Colin & Hayden)

*

If you love steamy romance with big groups of family and friends, check out my Boys of the Bayou series!

Boys of the Bayou
My Best Friend's Mardi Gras Wedding (Josh & Tori)
Sweet Home Louisiana (Owen & Maddie)
Beauty and the Bayou (Sawyer & Juliet)
Crazy Rich Cajuns (Bennett & Kennedy)
Must Love Alligators (Chase & Bailey)
Four Weddings and a Swamp Boat Tour (Mitch & Paige)

*

ABOUT ERIN NICHOLAS

Erin Nicholas is the New York Times and USA Today bestselling author of over thirty sexy contemporary romances. Her stories have been described as toe-curling, enchanting, steamy and fun. She loves to write about reluctant heroes, imperfect heroines and happily ever afters. She lives in the Midwest with her husband who only wants to read the sex scenes in her books, her kids who will never read the sex scenes in her books, and family and friends who say they're shocked by the sex scenes in her books (yeah, right!).
Find her here:

facebook.com/ErinNicholasBooks
bookbub.com/authors/erin-nicholas
goodreads.com/author/show/3155383.Erin_Nicholas
tiktok.com/@erinnicholasbooks

www.ingramcontent.com/pod-product-compliance
Lightning Source LLC
Chambersburg PA
CBHW061537210726
48287CB00006B/1997